D0376589

Black Thursday

OTHER WORKS BY LINDA JOFFE HULL

The Big Bang (Tyrus, 2012)
Eternally 21 (Midnight Ink, 2013)

Hull, Linda Joffe.
Black Thursday : a Mrs.
Frugalicious shopping my
[2014]
33305231478656
ca   03/02/15

A Mrs. Frugalicious
Shopping Mystery

Black
Thursday

Linda Joffe Hull

MIDNIGHT INK
WOODBURY, MINNESOTA

Black Thursday: A Mrs. Frugalicious Shopping Mystery © 2014 by Linda Joffe Hull. All rights reserved. No part of this book may be used or reproduced in any manner whatsoever, including Internet usage, without written permission from Midnight Ink, except in the case of brief quotations embodied in critical articles and reviews.

FIRST EDITION
First Printing, 2014

Book design and format by Donna Burch-Brown
Cover design by Lisa Novak
Cover Illustration: Bunky Hurter
Editing by Nicole Nugent

Midnight Ink, an imprint of Llewellyn Worldwide Ltd.

This is a work of fiction. Names, characters, places, and incidents are either the product of the author's imagination or are used fictitiously, and any resemblance to actual persons living or dead, business establishments, events, or locales is entirely coincidental.

Library of Congress Cataloging-in-Publication Data
Hull, Linda Joffe.
  Black Thursday : a Mrs. Frugalicious shopping mystery / Linda Joffe
Hull. — First edition.
    pages   cm.
  ISBN 978-0-7387-3490-3
1. Murder—Investigation—Fiction. I. Title.
  PS3608.U433B57 2014
  813'.6—dc23
                                                    2014014326

Midnight Ink
Llewellyn Worldwide Ltd.
2143 Wooddale Drive
Woodbury, MN 55125-2989
www.midnightinkbooks.com

Printed in the United States of America

For Becky, who wrote the book on strength and grace while I wrote this book.

ONE

I, Maddie Michaels—AKA the estranged Mrs. Frank Finance Michaels, AKA Mrs. Frugalicious—should, by all rights, love Thanksgiving. I mean, what other holiday celebrates the bounty of fall and all there is to be thankful for *and* downright sanctions two of my favorite blessings—eating and bargain shopping?

Looking at the thirteen relatives seated at the dining room table I'd had to lengthen with both leaves and a card table, I reminded myself that Thanksgiving was, indeed, one of my favorite holidays.

Better, in less than four hours, I'd be setting out for an extra-special midnight savings expedition along with my Frugarmy (AKA fans of my website, MrsFrugalicious.com) to brave the late hour, low temperatures, and long lines for a local news segment on Black-Friday-on-Thursday-night deals.

"What a blessing to be here together." Joyce, my soon-to-be-ex-mother-in-law clasped her hands, drew them to her heart, and settled her gaze on me. "Amongst family."

My estranged husband, Frank; his father, Gerald; one of the nieces; and, if I wasn't mistaken, Spots, the runt-of-the-litter kitten Frank befriended when I moved him down to the basement after news of his infidelity surfaced, all nodded in a recalcitrant sort of agreement.

I took a deep silent breath.

This Thanksgiving was certain to be one of the most memorable ever—assuming I survived the actual feast itself…

"Eat up." Craig, my ex-brother-in-law-to-be, plopped a marshmallow-coated blob of sweet potato casserole onto my Wedgwood wedding china plate—part of a service for eighteen that was soon to be split into nine his and nine hers. "You could stand to gain a pound or two."

I'd have beamed at being called underweight for the first time in maybe ever, even by Craig (an enthusiastic chubby chaser), had the weight loss not been so hard won. After all, last year at this time, I was a happy, well-heeled housewife on the hunt for figure-flattering holiday wear to hide the extra ten extra pounds (okay, thirteen) I rationalized as part and parcel of the joys of motherhood and encroaching middle age.

I put on another five (okay, eight) during the dark days after Frank lost all of our money in a Ponzi scheme—a fact no one could know at risk of Frank also losing his job as Channel Three's on-air financial guru. When I finally stabilized at an all-time high weight, Mrs. Frugalicious began to take off.

Then all hell broke loose.

Nothing could have amped up my diet and exercise program more than finding out my husband lost not only the nest egg but his *mind* over the most unexpected of beautiful blondes.

And things only degenerated from there ...

I picked at a bright red indiscernible something mixed in with the sweet potato, butter, and pineapple chunks.

"I think Maddie looks great." Frank smiled and took a heaping bite of the sweet potato surprise. "And so is this, Mom."

Gerald nodded in agreement. "You've still got it, Joyce."

Joyce, whose eyelids had been *refreshed* so many times I wasn't sure they could close all the way, somehow winked in my direction. "Secret is the Red Hots."

Red Hots?

How, one might ask, had I ended up surrounded by my estranged husband's entire family, pretending to enjoy my soon-to-be-ex-mother-in-law's culinary concoctions?

I'd been asking myself the same question all day.

I'd agreed to one last simple Thanksgiving for the sake of our children. After all, our twin teenage sons, Frank Jr. (FJ) and Trent, had suffered enough upheaval over the last few months, and my stepdaughter, Eloise, was coming back for the weekend from college to yet another broken home.

A broken home we needed to be moving out of sooner rather than later.

I'd also planned on a delicious but economical[1] menu, including a small[2] bird suitable for five, when the boys asked if their cousins could join us for dessert. What that really meant was my brother-in-law and his daughters were somehow at loose ends and he was finagling a dinner invitation via the kids. It felt punitive for all concerned to say no. Instead, and to balance out the family equation, I called my sister in Fort Collins and talked her into making the drive for a second dinner with her husband and their kids.

With a new total of thirteen guests, I still planned to keep it simple,[3] as I advised my Mrs. Frugalicious readers. But as I looked around the table at the objectively attractive, dark-haired, blue-eyed Michaels clan, it was clear *simple* simply wasn't in the cards.

---

1. From my Thrifty, Thrilling Thanksgiving blog: There are four main ways to save on holiday groceries. 1. Coupon: If it's on your shopping list, there's probably a coupon for it in your Sunday paper, online, or via an app. 2. Buy in Bulk: Save big by picking up staples like butter, flour, sugar, and milk in bulk. 3. Buy Seasonal: Seasonal produce is cheaper, fresher, and suits the spirit of the holiday. 4. Shop Smart: Be sure to look for loss leaders and cherry-pick the best deals from each store. Keep in mind, the real cost of a meal isn't the turkey, but the little extras you pay too much for at the last minute.

2. Size Matters: Turkey experts recommend an 8–12 lb. turkey for 2–4 people, a 12–16 lb. turkey for 5–7 people, a 16–20 lb. turkey for 8–10 people, and a 20–24 lb. turkey for 11–13 guests. These estimates allow for some leftovers, so there is no need to waste money by upsizing.

3. While it's tempting to play hostess-with-the-Thanksgiving-mostest by making complicated, costly dishes, only turkey, stuffing, and cranberry sauce are "must-haves." Consider what's already in your pantry and keep it simple. If a recipe calls for a spice you don't have and don't expect to use much of again, you're probably better off looking for a substitute that's already in your pantry or skipping that recipe entirely.

First, Frank's parents' annual Thanksgiving cruise was abruptly cancelled en route to Ft. Lauderdale due to some unexpected civil unrest along the Panama Canal. A cruise they were to be joined on by Frank's sister and her children.

Before I knew it, the whole gang had somehow been rerouted to Los Angeles via Denver and, due to overbooking, had been awarded travel vouchers for the inconvenience of a flight back on Monday night.

Needless to say, they all turned up on the doorstep Wednesday evening.

They were barely inside when my sister called with word her whole crew had come down with food poisoning and were too sick to drive anywhere on Thursday, much less eat when they arrived.

As Frank's family settled in all over the house, I'd shut myself in my office, sat down at the computer, and prayed for a message from a long-lost, faraway friend in dire need of my immediate presence.

As soon as I could force my head off the desk and actually check, I discovered there really was an urgent email in my inbox after all. Anastasia Chastain, the field reporter from Channel Three, was planning an evening news piece on Black Friday bargain hunting. She wanted to know when and where I'd be shopping Thursday evening so she could talk local deals while Mrs. Frugalicious, AKA me, scored said deals on camera for the viewers at home.

Despite a house full of estranged relatives, disappearing was suddenly off the table—a table now covered with my mother-in-law's questionable holiday fare.[4]

---

4. Cooking from scratch is less expensive and (usually) tastier than anything you can buy ready-made.

"A toast." Barb, Frank's sister, held up her wineglass. "To making the very best of a bad situation."

Over the *here here*s and the clink of glasses, I began to silently list the reasons why breaking bread with Frank and his family *was* making the best of it and not the worst joke the universe had ever played on me.

Since Frank's major lapse of judgment, that was.

"Love these rolls, Joyce!" my son FJ said, adhering to his grandmother's insistence she was far too youthful to be called a grandma. Ever the diplomat, he slathered butter on a hockey puck roll and filled his water glass to prepare for the swallowing process.

Trent, FJ's identical twin, down to the Michaels blue eyes but with the lighter hair and stockier build of the men on my side of the family, stifled a laugh and followed suit.

With their bright, mischievous smiles—a far too uncommon sight these past few months—I had the first reason on my list:

1. Despite a genetic predisposition from my side, the kids needed and were reveling in the unexpected family togetherness.

"Maddie, these table centerpieces are as charming as they are clever." Barb looked admiringly at my admittedly fetching gourd, pinecone, leaf, and twig centerpiece.[5]

Joyce, who was equal parts feminist and pampered princess, and thus always leery of all things *crafty*, nodded. "So creative."

Heads bobbed in agreement.

---

5. Instead of store-bought Thanksgiving accents, go natural! Fall leaves and branches, acorn squash, pinecones, and other fall fruits that can be eaten later make attractive low-cost or even free décor.

2. The Michaels clan, known for speaking their minds, were clearly on their very best behavior.

"Green bean casserole?" Craig offered from beside me.

I took a grayish, crispy-topped spoonful, concealed it with my roll, and passed the dish along.

3. Since my meal would likely consist of a few slices of the twenty-six-pound tom turkey (for which I'd traded in my party-of-five bird) and the cranberry sauce I'd prepared earlier in the week, I wasn't going to put any weight on like I normally did every Thanksgiving.

"Good thing we had extra hands in the kitchen," Frank said, helping himself to a spoonful of gummy-looking mashed potatoes. "I can't imagine how Maddie could have pulled off a meal like this in midst of getting ready for her first TV appearance tonight."

He made an interesting point.

4. Other than something of a sticky marshmallow disaster in the kitchen and a pungent, lingering cooking aroma I'd have to Febreze away, my soon-to-be-ex-mother- and sister-in-law couldn't have shown up at a more opportune time to take over the kitchen and insist they whip up the Thanksgiving meal despite a shared lack of kitchen prowess.

"Speaking of TV," Craig said. "Is it really possible to get one of those forty-two-inch flat screens for two-fifty tonight?"

"First twenty people in line at Bargain Barn definitely will." The second I'd read Anastasia's email, I was on the phone with "Awesome" Alan Bader, local bargain outlet mogul and my first big advertiser.

Always at risk of being forced out of business by the box chains, he'd already placed an ad on my blog offering an extra 10% off the competition's pricing. When I let him know that I'd have a camera crew trailing me instead of live-tweeting like I'd planned, he upped the ante by opening at ten p.m. He also added a half-price sound system exclusively for Frugarmy members. "If everything goes well, people will be stuffing their cars full of incredible deals."

"Stuffing's just like I remember." Gerald helped himself to a second serving.

"It has to have been twenty years since you've made it, Mom," Craig said.

"Twenty-one," Joyce said. "Wasn't sure I'd get all the ingredients right from memory, but it all came back to me as soon as the popcorn started popping."

"It looks incredible," I said, marveling at a soggy, deflated kernel of bona fide Orville Redenbacher's mixed in with the breadcrumbs, onions, and celery.

"Try it, Maddie," Barb said.

Suddenly, all eyes were on me.

"Mom's popcorn stuffing is legendary," Frank said.

"You'll die when you taste it," one of the nieces said.

That's what I'm afraid of, I didn't say as I scooped up a small bite and checked to make sure my napkin was at the ready for a polite cough/spit. I took a silent deep breath, closed my nose in anticipation, brought the fork toward my mouth, and was about to bite the proverbial bullet when my text alert pinged.

Specifically, the alert the boys had set up for me to let me know when anyone commented on any of my blog posts at MrsFrugalicious.com.

Thanking the culinary gods for the last-minute reprieve, I put down my fork, grabbed my smartphone from my pocket, and read the title of the comment:

Thanks, But No Thanks!

The author, to my nonsurprise, was a certain CC, whom I'd taken to calling Contrary Claire due to her frequent negative remarks.

"Everything okay?" Joyce asked.

I wasn't exactly thrilled to have a gripe from my cyber naysayer on the one day of the year devoted to giving thanks. I was, however, grateful she'd given me a reason to locate my reading glasses and thereby avoid choking down Joyce's stuffing. "Contrary Claire is up to her usual nonsense."

"Ignore her," FJ said. "It's Thanksgiving."

"Totally," Trent, the other half of my teen tech support staff, agreed.

"I would if I could," I said, already halfway across the room and headed for my office on the other side of the front hall. "But I can't risk her disrupting anything more than a few minutes of dinner tonight."

5. Given my on-camera midnight shopping expedition, I had an excuse for my work issues to trump my personal ones.

———

I closed the French doors behind me, located my computer glasses, jiggled the mouse, and waited for the Mrs. Frugalicious home page to fill the screen.

Contrary Claire's comments were unnerving at first, but the boys argued I couldn't let them get to me because MrsFrugalicious.com hadn't arrived as a website until it had a dedicated stalker. It also helped that a flood of positive remarks always came in from my regular followers, burying whatever gripe she had that day.

Girding myself, I scrolled down past Bargain Barn's ad, below *Black Friday Frugasm*,[6] the post I'd written with tips and extra bargains for Frugarmy members who joined me to shop on camera, and read the sole entry in the comments section:

Dear Mrs. Frugalicious,

I, for one, plan to take a pass on tonight. For one thing, I already followed your advice and got two items on my list at Black Friday prices by going into Bargain Barn yesterday to pre-shop.[7] For another, the sound system is the only special addition that seems all that special. To be honest, this whole event smells of a scheme cooked up by you, your TV reporter husband, and Bargain Barn to line pockets with kickback dollars. Namely, yours. Thanks for offering me fifteen minutes of background fame, but I think I'll just stay home and cyber shop. Everyone knows the deals are way better online these days, anyway.

Break a leg,
CC

I put my head in my hands.

---

6. *Froo-gaz-m* (n.): A particularly satisfying bargain.
7. If there is an item from the Black Friday ads on your list, you may not have to wait until Black Friday to get it. Some stores will mark the item down in the days leading up to the big night. If it works, you can make your way through the sea of carts grabbing other bargains.

Had she really just accused Bargain Barn and Mrs. Frugalicious of being in cahoots, not only with each other but Frank?

How was it that CC, of all people, didn't seem to know we were in the middle of a divorce? Even if things were still hunky-dory marriage wise, Frank was too busy trying to keep his gig as Channel Three's financial guru in the wake of his professional pratfalls to ever think of suggesting me for a segment on his own station.

Fortunately, Anastasia Chastain had.

The unexpected boon of TV coverage would offer Awesome Alan Bader's generations-old family business a welcome leg up against the relentless threat of the all-powerful big-box stores. As for me, there was no denying the increased visibility and potential traffic to the website.

But *line my pockets with kickback money*?

The holes needed to be sewn up first.

Closing my eyes, I took a centering breath to regulate my blood pressure and tried to think of Contrary Claire, whom I pictured as thin, pinched, and in need of some kindness clearly missing from her life. I opened my eyes and forced myself to reread the post, mindful of the poor woman's right to her skewed opinion.

Once again, I was stopped by the word *scheme.*

What if other Frugarmy members checked the website before they left to go shopping, decided she had a point about the online deals, and stayed home themselves?

What if Alan from Bargain Barn saw the post?

I took another breath. It was unlikely too many people would take CC's rant all that seriously, but that wouldn't stop Alan from freaking out about the disastrous aftereffects of a TV crew filming in his otherwise-empty store on the busiest shopping evening of the year. And who could blame him?

My hands trembled as I began to type a response:

Dear CC,
Thank you for writing.

I promptly deleted that and replaced it with a less friendly, more direct, *I appreciate your concerns.*

Which sounded far too gratuitous.

I deleted the sentence and decided on, *I'm glad you were able to get Black Friday prices early with my tip on pre-sale shopping.*

Which sounded passive-aggressive. Because it was. I erased again, took a deep breath, and started anew:

Dear CC,

I really appreciate all the comments that come in to Mrs. Frugalicious, but sometimes I feel the need to respond with some qualifications, corrections, and/or additions.

This is one of those times.

Bargain Barn is an upstanding local business committed to providing the best prices and customer service. That is why they were the first store I thought of when Channel Three asked me (yesterday to be exact) to Black Friday shop on camera. There is absolutely no gimmick, scam, or kickback scheme involved. I simply got a message from one of the local TV stations (who coincidentally happens to employ my estranged husband) about doing a story of benefit to all of us in the bargain shopping community. I can assure you, the deals available tonight at

Bargain Barn are anything but hype—they are offering to meet or beat all competitor prices, for goodness sake.

As for MrsFrugalicious.com, I will only be gaining what I hope will be many more bargain shoppers looking to save money and share tips from the increased exposure.

I am truly sorry you'll miss the festivities. It's going to be a Black Friday to remember.

"Maddie?" Eloise, my stepdaughter, opened the French doors, rushed into the room, and filled my office with her fruity-floral perfume and usual sense of mild exasperation. "How long were the pies supposed to stay in the oven?"

"The pies?" I repeated, distracted by whether I should end by taking the high road with a *Happy Thanksgiving* or just sign off.

"Joyce said you said they needed to warm up together,[8] but that the pumpkin pie—"

"Is supposed to be served chilled or at room temperature."

Her dark, shiny curls bounced as she shook her head. "Not according to her."

"Oh dear," I said. "I'll be there as soon as I post this response."

"To that weird Contrary Claire person?"

"Unfortunately she decided tonight is some sort of marketing boondoggle and announced it on the website."

"No way!" Eloise looked over my shoulder at the monitor. "Why are you bothering to respond?"

"I'm just worried people will read it or—"

---

8. Save energy costs by making sure any items that call for similar baking temperatures go into the oven at the same time

"Just delete what she wrote."

"Delete it?" For the sake of fair blog journalism and a firm belief that by sharing and comparing bargaining tips everyone came out ahead, I'd never considered censoring anyone.

Even Contrary Claire.

Not her response to my Thanksgiving shopping tips: *Sure, some stores offer a free frozen turkey with $50 minimum purchase, but what they don't tell you is they're so deep frozen you could miss Thanksgiving waiting for the bird to thaw.*

Not her opinion about my Halloween savings post, in which I advised readers to consider less-expensive types of candy: *There's nothing gained by buying off-brands. The kids don't like them, they scare off the parents, and chances are the treats will just end up in the trash.*

Not her objection to a tip I'd passed along from the manager at an upscale women's chain, who told me it was company policy to accept all discount coupons for up to five days past the expiration date: *Didn't work for me.*

"Everything she said is totally lame," Eloise said.

"Other than she may have a point about online versus traditional shopping."

"She can't know for sure if she's not at Bargain Barn to compare," Eloise said with a touchingly sympathetic hand to the hip. "Right?"

"True."

"So press the delete button."

"I'm not really sure I—"

"Want a bunch of crazy lies on your web page?"

The pungent aroma of burning pie came wafting in from the direction of the kitchen.

"You better hurry and delete the comment," she said, "or there goes all the dessert."

"I suppose you're right." I sighed. "But I have no idea how…"

Eloise reached around me and began to tap away on my keyboard. "Simple."

———

"I just can't believe anyone would write anything so mean-spirited." Barb, no stranger to mean-spiritedness herself, shook her head.

"Cyber bully," Craig said.

"What goes around comes around," Gerald, who seemed to have a new penchant for clichés and catchphrases, mumbled through bites of extra-crispy apple pie.

Joyce eyed the plate of food she'd left out for me that I wasn't even pretending to pick at. "Why don't I just pop that in the microwave for you and—"

"That's okay," I said quickly, watching melting whipped cream drip down the burnt crust of the warm pumpkin pie she'd also placed in front of me upon my return to the table. "I'm afraid I've sort of lost my appetite for now."

"You know, Mom," FJ said. "Everything that wacko writes can be blocked."

"Probably not a bad idea," I said. "At least for tonight."

"We can make it so no comments can post without your approval," Trent added.

"That might be going too far," I said. "If I have to review and approve everything that comes in before it posts, my followers could miss a time-sensitive tip or deal."

"A missed deal is nothing if your personal safety is compromised," Joyce said. As Gerald, Craig, and Barb nodded in agreement, Frank furrowed his brow with what looked to be sincere concern.

"I can't imagine the woman is dangerous," I said. "She probably just has personal issues and goes online to vent and maybe escape real life."

"Escape is rarely the solution to dealing with life's little bumps in the road," Joyce said.

"Tempting though it may be," Barb added.

They shared a not-at-all surreptitious glance.

Before I could begin to process, much less respond, to their less than subtle statement about Frank's bad behavior and show of support for me, my real text alert pinged in apparent agreement.

The room fell quiet.

"Is it CC?" Trent asked.

A legion of nervous butterflies fluttered in my gut as I fished the phone from my pocket praying it wasn't an irate Contrary Claire, a freaked out Awesome Alan, or anyone else who might have been ruffled by the now-deleted post.

Anastasia Chastain scrolled across the display.

"Phew," I managed.

"Who is it?" Frank asked.

Not only wouldn't Frank suggest me for an on-air moment, my glib, camera-ready, soon-to-be-ex could barely crack a strained smile when I first mentioned I'd been invited to step out of the sidelines and into the TV spotlight—a spotlight I'd been only too happy to see shine on him all these years. Had we not been separated, I'd have been sensitive to his ego and asked for his blessing before accepting an offer to so much as mention Mrs. Frugalicious on any station, much less his.

Then again, times had changed.

"Anastasia," I simply said.

"Gotcha," he said, but with no sign of a grimace or scowl.

Having left my glasses atop my head, I didn't have an excuse to leave the room again, so I simply looked down and read the text:

NEED YOU AT BARGAIN BARN AN HOUR EARLY, READY FOR AN INTERVIEW.

With the word *interview*, a band of perspiration broke out at the base of my neck. I'd expected to play shopper with Anastasia providing the color commentary, not speak on camera beyond providing a quick sound bite or two.

"What is it?" Frank asked.

"She wants me there an hour early so she can interview me before the store opens."

"That's terrific!" Joyce said.

"Cool, Mom," FJ said.

"Figures Stasia would come up with a way to capitalize on the airtime." Frank actually smiled. "Gotta love that girl's ingenuity."

I dabbed at the beads of sweat that broke out across my forehead as well and forced my thoughts away from the recent past and onto my near future. "I should start getting ready."

"Will we all be on camera?" Eloise turned to check her reflection in the antique mirror that hung behind her. "Or just you?"

"I assume whoever's shopping with me will end up on camera."

"Maybe I should get ready soon too then."

"You're coming with?" I'd been Eloise's stepmother since she was a preschooler. I thought of her as my own, but I assumed she'd prefer to be home with the rest of the family she rarely got to see, instead of out all night with just me.

"I thought it might be fun."

"I'd love to have you along!" I said. "I could really use a helper."

"I'm thinking I'll tag along too." Craig raised an eyebrow. "I'd like one of those flat-screen TVs in my entertainment room."

"That's great," I said, not nearly as enthusiastically as I had to Eloise, and not wanting to think about what playboy Craig defined as *entertainment*.

"Can we hang at home and watch football?" Trent asked.

"We could keep an eye on the kids after they go to bed, too. Unless you want us to come with," FJ, the more sensitive of my sons, offered.

"No need," Frank said, as I'd have expected. He loved to encourage the boys, who were something of standouts on their high school football team, to watch the pros play whenever possible.

I didn't expect what he said next.

"I'm coming with too." He turned and made direct eye contact with me for the first time in months. "To help make sure they show your best angles and all that."

"I . . ." I was flabbergasted. He was well aware of the stage fright that had kept me from ever considering an on-air gig. He'd learned of it back when I'd served briefly as an intern at the station, fallen hard for him, and ended up married with twins—though not necessarily in that order.

"It's the least I can do," he said.

Even though there was no one more qualified, I hadn't considered asking for his assistance. Or anticipated his company…

"This is all so exciting." Joyce stood and started clearing the table. "Better get things cleaned up quickly so we'll be ready on time."

"You're coming along?"

"I just love a good deal," Joyce, whose idea of discount shopping was the reduced rack at Neiman Marcus, added.

"Really?" I asked, more than a little surprised.

"We're hoping you'll take us on a field trip to the grocery store while we're here," Barb said.

"Really?" I asked again.

"We want some pointers on how to do that extreme coupon grocery shopping."

"Nothing wrong with saving where you can." Joyce removed Gerald's plate just as he'd finished his last bite of pie. "Which is why we can't wait to experience our first Black Thursday!"

TWO

I certainly didn't expect this particular evening to be quite the way it was turning out, but despite a moonless night and the threat of snow flurries, a substantial crowd was already lined up along the sidewalk in front of Bargain Barn and weaving its way around the side of the building.

Anastasia was there when I arrived. She greeted me outside the news van with a makeup-preserving air kiss and gave my casual-yet-camera-friendly ensemble of dark pea coat, mauve silk blouse, black slacks, and matching accent scarf an approving once over. "I'd say this divorce is agreeing with you." She wrinkled her delicate, bobbed nose. "Except that those people heading in our direction look far too much like Frank not to be his parents."

We watched together as Eloise met up with Joyce, Gerald, Barb, and Craig, who'd followed us over to Bargain Barn in a second car.

"Not to mention his brother and sister." We weren't friends exactly, but given Anastasia was Frank's co-anchor apparent for *Frank*

Finance, the now on-hold national version of his popular local show, and so she was well aware of the particulars of our collapsed marriage. There was no reason not to tell her the latest developments in my ongoing marital saga. "His whole family showed up for Thanksgiving."

She raised an expertly plucked eyebrow. "Seriously?"

"Hard as that may be to believe."

Anastasia's heavily sprayed blond bob stayed firmly in place as she shook her head. "I can't believe you had them all for dinner, much less to tag along tonight."

"Lighting check," someone from the crew said.

Before I could explain that I hadn't exactly invited them for either event, Frank materialized from the news van holding a makeup kit and sponge. "You're a little shiny," he said, dabbing my forehead like a seasoned makeup artist.

"You could be a model!" Joyce said loudly, announcing the arrival of the Michaels gang. Her faux chinchilla coat (which I suspected wasn't faux at all) made an even louder statement. "Couldn't she?"

"Thin enough to be." Craig, whose taste in women ran to the pleasingly plump, scrunched his face a little.

Barb offered her hand to Anastasia. "We're here to watch Maddie's big moment."

"And pick up some cool deals while we're at it." Craig shook hands as well but looked wistfully toward the burgeoning crowd in front of Bargain Barn.

"None of this was my idea," I managed to mouth from behind their heads.

Anastasia gave me an *it's all good* wink.

"Maybe we should get in line and save a place for Maddie so she doesn't miss out on anything while she's being interviewed," Craig added.

"Great idea," Joyce said.

"No need," Anastasia said. "Alan Bader is letting us in the employee door early to film the crowds entering, so you'll be first in line."

"Awesome," Craig said. "Maybe I'll be able to get the TV *and* snag one of the sound systems."

"How can we be of help in the meantime?" Joyce reached into her oversized purse and pulled out two water bottles, a box of granola bars, and a pack of gum. "Anyone need a snack?"

"Ready when you are, Stasia," the cameraman said.

"Why don't you just watch and enjoy?" Frank, always the consummate professional (at least where his job was concerned) immediately whisked his family over to a spot behind the camera.

"They're all on their very best behavior," I whispered.

"No surprises there." Anastasia led me over to two X marks taped to the cement and stood on hers. "You ready?"

My pounding heart certainly wasn't. The first and last time I'd been on stage, much less in front of a camera, was in elementary school when I'd tried out to play the Dormouse but instead been cast as Alice in the third grade play. Needless to say, my understudy, Suzie Shultz, had taken over after the first performance—a memory I'd somehow managed to suppress until now. "I ..."

"You're going to do great," Frank said, returning to my side. "Just remember—"

"Feet shoulder-width apart, arms to your sides, lean slightly forward," Eloise said in a dead-on imitation of the instructions Frank had repeated ad nauseam on the drive over. "And speak a little louder and a lot slower than normal."

"Exactly," Frank said, handling being teased better than expected. "And put your cell on silent."

"Will do," I managed, managing to at least get the ringer on my phone turned off.

"I'll introduce the segment and introduce you," Anastasia said. "Then you take it from there."

"Great." My knees began to tremble.

"The camera senses fear," Frank whispered, "so think happy thoughts."

Happy thoughts…

Even though it was in my nature to be upbeat and generally positive, somehow I couldn't think about much of anything but that camera lens staring at me with its one skeptical eye.

I was thankful, however, that I'd doubled up my Lady Speed Stick with an extra swipe of Secret when the light went on and Anastasia instantly transformed from rosy-cheeked and pretty into a luminous, poised, intelligent beauty.

She leaned slightly forward, just as Frank had directed me, and assumed an expression of confident, serene intelligence. "While many of us haven't even started to fight over the wishbone, savvy local shoppers looking to cash in on early-bird bargains have already set up camp, quite literally, outside local retailers…"

The camera panned away from Anastasia and onto a scene that looked like a winter barn raising—complete with bundled-up shoppers lined up alongside the farm mural running the length of the concrete building.

"With the prices we're hearing about on everything from appliances to big entertainment systems, it's no wonder shoppers are clamoring to leave their cozy spots by the fire and bring the whole family out for the Thursday night bargains."

The next thing I knew I'd been guided/moved/gently shoved onto my X.

"Remember to look at Stasia, not the camera," Frank whispered.

A bead of perspiration rolled from the nape of my neck down my spine.

"With me today is Maddie Michaels, better known to many of you as local bargain hunting maven Mrs. Frugalicious."

To say my life flashed before my eyes would be a little overstatement and a lot Gerald-style cliché, but for one never-ending second, everything went white. Everything, that is, except the red-hot feeling in my ears and the sight of Frank reminding me to smile by pressing up the corners of his mouth with his thumb and forefinger.

I tried to force the panic stiff muscles in my face to follow suit as Anastasia continued:

"I love a good deal and I'm all for a fun family outing to help burn off that turkey and pie, but when I look at all the people gathered out here, frankly I'm awestruck and, I have to admit, a little overwhelmed…"

With the word *overwhelmed*, I locked my knees to keep them from buckling. I willed myself to not think about my disastrous turn as Alice in Wonderland. If only I'd practiced my lines in front of someone instead of the mirror. If only I'd been prepared to take on a lead role…

"It's all a matter of preparation," I finally said.

To my complete surprise, my voice didn't crack in the slightest.

Out of the corner of my eye, I could see people waving from the line, including my friend and business contemporary Wendy Killian from *Here's the Deal* magazine.

"Knock 'em dead!" Barb whisper-screamed from the sidelines.

Imagine the viewers are a group of friendly supporters, Frank had said during the drive over.

Fact was, they already were.

"Black Friday is a big, crazy shopping day and it starts earlier every year," I heard come out of my dry mouth. "But if you do your homework and come ready to get what you came for at the lowest prices, it's by far the best."

My smile morphed from forced to real when I caught sight of someone holding a sign: GO MRS. FRUGALICIOUS!

"You don't have to be a seasoned bargain hunter to take advantage of the incredible deals out there tonight if you follow these steps..."

I hadn't had time to panic about being on camera until I was about to go live, but instead of freezing completely, somehow I felt my shoulders relax, noted my hands were indeed at my sides, and realized I kind of liked the opportunity to reach an audience much wider than the band of dedicated bargain shoppers who frequented my site.

"To start," I said, with what felt like a little louder than normal voice, "go through all of the newspaper ads, online sites, and price-comparison phone apps ahead of time and figure out what you want to buy, where to go to get it, and in what order. Once you figure out where you're headed, 'like' those retailers on social media sites and sign up for their email lists to get extra coupons and last-minute deals."

Anastasia nodded thoughtfully.

"And don't limit yourself to the big-name chains. Some of the very best doorbuster deals this year are at stores like Bargain Barn, where you can combine Black Friday prices with Small Business Saturday shopping for a true win-win."

"All on Thursday night."

"Exactly." I smiled.

"So, figure out what you want, what you're going to pay, and the best place to go to buy it?"

"And be sure to bring copies of those ads so you know you're getting the right price, especially at stores offering to match or beat competitors' prices," I said. "Mainly though, you need to make sure you're comparing apples to apples. A big-screen TV that comes bundled with a video game system and DVD player may be a better value than a bigger TV that costs less at another store."

"Good advice," Anastasia said. "And what about preparing for the actual shopping itself?"

I couldn't believe it, but I was feeling a lot more like a seasoned professional than the almost-ex-wife of one. "If you're going to snag a highly sought after item or three, you're going to be out there for the long haul, so make your wait as comfortable as possible by bringing lawn chairs, blankets, coffee, water, snacks, and even games." As I stopped to take a surreptitious breath, Eloise gave me the thumbs up. "I also suggest you bring along fellow shoppers who are as excited as you are about Black Friday and leave those grouchy spouses home with the potentially whiny kids and sleepy babies who will only slow you down."

"Sounds like a plan," Anastasia said, having noted the THEY'RE READY INSIDE someone had jotted on a piece of paper and held up for her. "Thank you for that enlightening and incredibly useful information, Mrs. Frugalicious."

"Thank you," I said.

Anastasia smiled broadly. Her smile grew that much bigger when the camera faded to black. "I knew you'd be a natural."

"Atta girl!" Joyce said, rushing over to envelop me in a hug.

"Terrific!" Barb said, trailing behind them.

"Wow!" Frank said, nodding. "Way better than even I expected."

———

Even though I may have omitted a helpful tip or two[9] in the midst of it all, I pretty much felt, well … if not like I was a *natural*, at least totally energized by the first part of my interview and excited for what was still to come.

Spending Thanksgiving with my estranged husband's family was a definite departure from my original plan, but so was Black Friday in general. As such, having them along wasn't an entirely bad thing in that I had a bargain posse[10] made up of more than just Eloise. And Frank, despite all the water under our bridge, had really helped relieve what could have been a crippling case of stage fright.

---

9. E.g., check in via smartphone when you get to wherever you're shopping. Some stores have extra discounts just for mobile shoppers. Also, the all-important Black Friday is a bonanza for bargain shoppers, but no deal is worth carrying a balance on your credits cards until this time next year. Spend wisely!

10. If you shop with a posse of friends or like-minded shoppers, you can split up the store, guard carts, save places in line, etc. And then enjoy a post-shop powwow or brunch to show off your finds and compare your deals.

Any other lingering concerns about the evening, including possible negative fallout from Contrary Claire's short-lived gripe, also began to fade with Awesome Alan Bader's warm greeting at the side entrance of Bargain Barn. Not to mention the sheer exhilaration when he led us inside a store empty of shoppers. A store overstocked to the rafters with everything from closeout auto parts to zebra-striped, wall-to-wall carpeting.

"I can't tell you how much I appreciate having you folks here." Alan's eyes sparkled with a giddy, almost boyish excitement. "For once, the big-box outfits have to compete against us!"

I'd never actually met Alan in person, but felt I knew him from our friendly, borderline-flirtatious business conversations. That and his trademark commercials, which featured him—slick, stocky, and definitely cocky and always in a Bargain Barn polo—standing next to some prized horse, cow, or sheep and whatever appliance or furniture item he was trying to push. With his firm handshake, I was struck by how much better-looking he was in person. His hair, which I'd assumed to be dyed brown, was really salt and pepper. His signature gold bracelet and necklace, which seemed to shimmer on camera, were more smart than showy in real life. He was also a little shorter, but at least ten pounds thinner (confirming that old adage about TV and making me happy to have made my onscreen debut at an all-time low weight).

"How about we get you on camera before things get rolling, Alan?" Anastasia asked.

"Impromptu interviews aren't for me." He flashed a smile at me. "I think I'll leave the commentary to Maddie tonight."

"Don't you think we should set up the camera beside the front doors and back to the right ten feet or so, then?" Frank asked.

Anastasia did a quick scan of Bargain Barn's floor-to-ceiling, warehouse style aisles. "For starters."

"There's an even better view of the front doors from over there." Alan pointed toward the Customer Service counter where two sales-girls were putting out what had to be Black Friday maps[11] to help shoppers locate the specials set up throughout the store.

"Deal maps, I presume?" I asked, as the camera crew headed that direction to set up.

"For the specials advertised in the newspaper and some unad-vertised discounts on smaller-ticket items we've placed throughout the store," Alan said.

"Eloise, would you mind grabbing a few so we can figure out how best to divide and conquer?"

"No need," Alan said before Eloise could turn for the front coun-ter. "Just use your smartphone."

"You created a QR code[12] for tonight?" I asked, digging through my purse and locating my cell.

"And by keying FRUGARMY into the passcode I set up, Mrs. Frugalicious followers will be directed to the layaway counter for the stereo system," Alan said. "To sweeten the pot, they will get vouchers for another item of their choice without having to stand in a second line."

---

11. Many retailers have turned Black Friday bargains into a scavenger hunt of sorts, situating their best deals in seemingly random spots around the store. Video games may be hiding near car seats. A bin of $2 shirts could be over by hair care. If you can, check out stores ahead of time so you know where everything is.

12. Check to see if there is a Quick Response (QR) code to scan with your smartphone when you get to wherever you are shopping. Some stores offer extra discounts just for mobile shoppers.

As in a double frugasm? "Seriously?"

"Excluding the TV, which really wouldn't be fair to other shoppers since the supply is limited."

"Makes sense," Craig said. "I'll wait in the TV line if someone will get the sound system for me."

"Not a problem," Barb said. "As long as I can get two."

"Absolutely," Alan said.

"This is awesome," I said.

"Small token of my thanks for bringing the news crews and the shoppers here," Alan said in a chipper voice.

"Perfect," Anastasia said. "We'll be able to cover Mrs. Frugalicious, the Frugarmy, and the family shopping angles all at once."

"So I *do* get to be on camera?" Eloise asked.

Frank put his arm around her. "Day full of unexpected surprises."

"Incredible ones," I said. "But how will the Frugarmy know to—"

"I posted a message on your website," Alan said.

"You did?" I asked with more concern in my voice than I'd intended.

"About two hours ago." He moved closer as I scrolled down my web page to the *Comments and Last Minute Deals* section where, thankfully, there was nothing but a big bold CHECK IN WITH YOUR SMARTPHONES AT BARGAIN BARN TONIGHT FOR A DEAL WAY TOO GOOD TO BE TRUE!!! PASSCODE: FRU-GARMY.

"Brilliant," I said, as much about his offer as Eloise's insistence I block Contrary Claire's potentially toxic commentary. It must have been mere seconds before Alan logged onto my website.

He smiled. "I thought so."

"The Frugarmy will love it," I couldn't help but notice how good he smelled, in that woodsy/spicy/soapy kind of a way. "Thank you, Alan."

Our eyes met. "My pleasure."

"We need to get cracking," Frank said, turning to Anastasia. "Don't we?"

Alan furrowed his brow in what I could swear was an expression of *why exactly is he here tonight, anyway?* Anastasia looked up from her own cell phone at the sign marked LAYAWAY with an arrow pointing toward the back left corner of the store. "So the Frugarmy line will form where?"

"In Small Appliances. It'll switchback as necessary through the back aisles."

She pointed to the main corridor, which was lined with dishwashers, refrigerators, and ranges. "Any chance we could direct the line down one of the central thoroughfares instead?"

"They are way more open," Frank added. "For the camera and everything."

"Technically, that could impede other lines like the Blu-ray players also in that part of the store," Alan said. "But I suppose we could direct the Frugarmy line around toward the access aisle once it winds in and out of Linens."

Anastasia, despite wearing spiked heels, jogged down the main corridor of the store to the spot halfway to the back, where it intersected the center aisle. She looked around, turned back toward us, and nodded. "Works for me."

———

"This is fabulous!" Anastasia said watching the sea of shoppers rush through the front doors and immediately jostle for position. "Pure insanity."

"More like organized chaos," I said, watching a group of women confer over a Black Friday map, make assignments amongst themselves, and set off in different directions.

On Anastasia's cue and with the camera rolling, I walked over to Customer Service, picked up a map, pretended to consult it, and headed toward the Frugarmy line in Small Appliances. A line that, thanks to Bargain Barn's last-minute message on MrsFrugalicious. com, already spanned the length of the aisle, wound into Linens, and would soon be curling into the center corridor bisecting the store.

Alan (after some light arm-twisting by me) agreed to make a cameo at the register. He stood poised to ring up Customer #1 (who just happened to be Eloise). With the cameraman's nod, she gave her hair a meaningful flip and pretended to transact what were really my purchases. Barb, Gerald, and a suspiciously laugh-line-free Joyce smiled gleefully from behind her.

Anastasia and I stood to the left of the Layaway counter and provided color commentary.

"The most important thing to do on Black Friday is stick to your game plan," I said. "If you've done your research and have your shopping posse with you, there's no reason you shouldn't leave with most of the big items crossed off your list at the smallest possible prices." I felt like the crown princess of bargain shoppers, speaking to the TV audience but addressing the countenances of my loyal Frugarmy. "This isn't the time to worry about stocking stuffers and odds and ends that will just bog you down. Those half-off fuzzy slippers and sparkly holiday earrings will most likely be there early next week when the crowds have thinned, but that flat-screen TV definitely won't."

"Terrific!" Anastasia said, as the camera panned onto the people queued up behind the Michaels clan. "Next, we get customer reaction shots."

"Be there in a sec," I said as Anastasia, Frank, and the crew swung around to interview random shoppers at the less-crowded back of the line. Instead of following them, I headed straight down the aisle to meet and greet fans, friends, and clients like L'Raine, my former massage therapist, and Mrs. Piggledy, who, as a former big-top performer and co-owner of one of my favorite stores, Circus Circus, was both.

It took a full ten minutes of hellos and handshakes to work my way to them, just behind an end cap filled with toasters.

"Maddie!" Mr. Piggledy, her round, ruddy husband (made all the rounder by his bright red holiday sweater), appeared beside his wife. He gave me a big, squishy hug. "You're a star!"

"I don't know about that," I said.

"Well we certainly think so," he said, handing a customer pickup voucher to his wife. "We have a brand-new, state-of-the-art TV being delivered next week—thanks to you!"

"You have to be reveling in this wonderful manifestation of your hard work as Mrs. Frugalicious." Mrs. Piggledy was equally ample and, despite an affinity for flowing tops, denim skirts, and New Age rhetoric, bore more than a passing resemblance to Mrs. Claus. She gave me an even warmer embrace. "I knew that crazy person's note wouldn't keep anyone away from here tonight."

"I …" I looked to make sure Alan, who'd also stopped to press the flesh with a few customers after passing the register job off to real cashier, was out of earshot of Mrs. Piggledy's high but resonant voice. I lowered mine. "I was a little worried about that."

"No need. It wasn't up on the website long enough." A boxy-looking woman of about forty with a sweet face, bobbed hair, and neon pink sneakers who stood behind them embraced me as well. "I'm so excited to meet you in person, Mrs. Frugalicious. I'm a big fan." She took a camera out of her bag. "I can't believe my husband is in the TV line missing this! Will you take a picture with me so I can show him I met you?"

"Of course," I said.

She was about to hand the camera off to Mr. Piggledy when Frank appeared beside me. "How about I do the honors?"

"Frank Finance?" she said handing him the camera and swinging her arm around my shoulder. "OMG! I never expected to see you tonight! Aren't you two—"

Before I could pull him aside, look into the whites of his eyes, and confirm my suspicion—that he truly had been taken over by a kinder, gentler, more faithful being from a different dimension—Frank's cell phone chirped the theme song to the old seventies sitcom *All in the Family*.

"Looks like my mom needs me for something or another," he said, answering the call.

"And I need Maddie." Anastasia appeared beside us. "We're done getting shopper feedback and I have to take a quick potty break. Can you go with the cameraman so he can get tape of you in the voucher redemption line?"

"Sure."

"I'll be right there and we'll move on to interview folks loading goodies into their cars."

The next thing I knew, Anastasia had taken off toward the restrooms, Frank had joined his family, and I was being filmed pretending to wait for my purchases at merchandise pickup.

Resisting the urge to smile.

Feeling more hopeful about my career and future than I'd been since before …

A loud, booming crash echoed across the store.

THREE

"COULDN'T BE AN EARTHQUAKE," the woman behind me said. "Could it?"

"This isn't California," her husband said. "Something fell."

"Something really heavy," the guy behind him added.

The merchandise fulfillment clerk picked up his phone. "What's going on out there? My counter just shook like there was an explosion or something."

Anastasia appeared in the open doorway and beckoned the cameraman and me. "Follow me and keep the camera rolling!"

"What happened?" I asked, maneuvering around the people in line and trailing her through the open double doors and back into the store proper.

"They're saying a pallet slipped," she said, circumnavigating the horde of shoppers blocking the middle thoroughfare of the store by taking a sharp right into an aisle of strollers. "Off one of the upper shelves."

"Where?" I asked, as we made a left and started down the picture frame aisle.

"Everywhere," Anastasia said.

I figured she had to be referring to the onlookers blocking the ends of every aisle we'd entered, until I veered around a cracked, upended Hamilton Beach toaster.

And a Black & Decker.

"A pallet of toasters?"

My breath hitched with Anastasia's nod.

"Tell me they didn't fall anywhere near where the Frug—"

"A bunch of people are already helping the injured over there."

I'd already turned and was racing toward Layaway where Frank had gone to find his parents. Where I'd last seen . . .

"Eloise?" I shouted as though my voice could be heard from Electronics and over the ominous din of people surrounding the scene. "Frank?"

I reached the counter and the Frugarmy line, which was no longer a line but a bottleneck of stunned onlookers clustered at the end of a kitchen appliances aisle. There was no sign of anyone from the Michaels family, all of whom but Craig should have been somewhere near the back of the crowd given their spots at the front of the line when I left them.

"Eloise?" My throat constricted with panic as I fumbled for my phone, shot off a Where are you?? text to Frank, and worked my way around a dented Cuisinart box and an Oster four-slice model and into the cluster of people. "Joyce? Gerald?"

I was two people deep in the crowd when I got a return text: OMG! Where are you?

From Eloise.

I allowed myself a momentary breath of relief knowing it was her and not someone trying to locate next of kin using her phone. I texted back: At layaway. Looking for you.

We were coming to find you when it happened.

Who is we?

Everyone but Daddy and Uncle Craig.

Before I could type the *where* in Where are they? the man directly in front of me shifted to the left. On my tiptoes and looking around the frizzy auburn hair of the woman in front of him, I spotted assorted appliances, a slice of floor, and people tending to what appeared to be injured shoppers.

"Coming through!" I shouted, putting my hands together and using them as a wedge to push my way forward. "Mrs. Frugalicious coming through!"

The cluster of people parted long enough for me to step into what looked like the aftermath of an F5 tornado. I found myself staring in disbelief at a swath of damaged assorted collateral merchandise and shell-shocked shoppers, some with cuts and bruises. The injuries seemed minor in general, until I saw the distinctive tomato red of Mr. Piggledy's XXL holiday sweater through the legs of a group clustered together to the right of me.

He knelt down beside a silver-haired woman lying on the ground, her full denim skirt splaying around her like a flower.

"Oh, no!" I kicked aside a blender from a display that had toppled as well and rushed over in what felt like slow motion. "Mrs. Piggledy!"

"I'm okay," Mrs. Piggledy said. "I just twisted my ankle."

"I'm afraid it's broken," Mr. Piggledy said.

"It can't be," she said. "Not with Higgledy's commitment ceremony on Saturday."

"He and Birdie are supposed to tie the knot," Mr. Piggledy said by way of explanation about their pet monkey Higgledy and Birdie, the parrot from the mall pet store he'd fallen hard for. "Which is the last thing to worry about right now."

"Have to admit," Mrs. Piggledy said through gritted teeth and looking at the foot, which was already blackish-purple and starting to swell. "It sure hurts."

"I can't believe this is happening," Mr. Piggledy said, cradling his wife's foot. "One moment we were enjoying the spectacle of it all, and the next..."

"Appliances," Mrs. Piggledy mumbled. "Raining from the sky."

"It all happened so fast."

"So sorry, honey." Mr. Piggledy dried the tear rolling down his cheek with his sleeve. "I just couldn't get her out of harm's way fast enough."

"Oh my God," I said. "This is awful."

"Could be worse," Mrs. Piggledy said with more stoicism than I could possibly have mustered in her condition. "Much worse."

"I don't know how it could be much worse than—"

My voice was drowned out by the wail of sirens nearing the store.

Mr. Piggledy pointed around the corner at the cluster of people now tugging at the plastic rope and shrink wrap affixing boxes to what turned out to be a double-decker pallet that had slipped off the shelf.

Specifically, she pointed at the pair of neon-pink tennis shoes jutting out, Wicked Witch of the West–style, from underneath.

FOUR

THE NEXT FEW SECONDS sped by in a panicked, terrifying blur.

Alan Bader rushed over with a group of emergency personnel in tow. A paramedic beelined over to Mrs. Piggledy's side. A fireman went into the crowd to tend to those with cuts and scrapes. The rest of the shoppers—including Frank, who'd materialized right after the rest of the family—moved in to lend the tools and brute strength necessary to free the trapped woman.

I tried not to think about what shape she'd be in when they did.

"They'll have her out in no time," I said to a weeping Eloise, who was suddenly behind me with the rest of the Michaels clan, minus Craig, who'd texted to say he was being kept back on the other side of the store.

Joyce shook her head. "Is she a member of your Frugarmy?"

I nodded. "Everyone in that line was. I met her," I said, watching in transfixed horror as the emergency workers cut away rope and shrink wrap, freeing the upper row of boxes from the upper pallet. "I can't believe I didn't ask her name."

"She mentioned it," Mr. Piggledy said, "but with everything that's happened, I'm afraid I can't—"

"Katrina," Mrs. Piggledy said with a wince as the paramedic began to feel along the length of her shin.

"Katrina?" I repeated, trying to put a name to the woman with whom I'd so recently enjoyed a perfectly pleasant conversation. Was there any possible chance she could still be—

"Such a beautiful ballerina," Mrs. Piggledy said.

"She was a ballerina?" Barb asked.

"My wife's gone into shock," Mr. Piggledy said. "She's remembering the day she broke her foot back when we were with the circus. She was helping Katrina, the Fat Lady, out of the clown car."

"She was so incredibly lithe for her size," Mrs. Piggledy said as the EMT began to take her vitals. "And she always wore those beautiful pink toe shoes."

I couldn't bring myself to glance down at the neon tennis shoes jutting out from below the double-stacked pallet.

Just as the emergency personnel and helpers kneeled in preparation to lift, my eyes met Frank's for the first time in months.

"On three," one of the firemen said.

"Dear Lord," Joyce said. "Please let her be okay."

"With all the weight that fell on her?" Barb asked with a hint of her old tone and inflection. "No way she isn't toast."

FIVE

The gray-green pallor of Alan's horror-stricken face said it all.

"Absolutely flattened," someone said in a whisper, as though there were need for further confirmation.

Some of the stunned, shocked crowd averted their eyes and hugged loved ones. Those who couldn't look away inched closer to watch the emergency workers attempt to check for a pulse.

"Who is she?" I asked a shaken Frank, who'd returned to comfort his family.

"Don't know yet." He shook his head. "Her purse was just as squashed as—"

"It's my ankle, not my neck," Mrs. Piggledy said as the EMT proceeded to slide a backboard beneath her shoulders.

"I just can't believe this is happening," I said, kneeling to grasp Mrs. Piggledy's hand.

"Can't say we weren't warned," Mrs. Piggledy mumbled.

"Warned?" Mr. Piggledy asked, kissing his wife gently on the forehead.

"By Zelda, that new fortuneteller."

"Still thinks she's at the circus," Mr. Piggledy whispered from above her, looking that much more concerned. "Honey, are you sure you didn't hit your head when you fell?"

"I'm sure Katrina shouldn't have ignored what was in the cards."

"Which was?" I asked, now adding Mrs. Piggledy's possible head injury to my growing list of concerns.

"Be wary of too much of a good thing, or—"

"Kathy?" Rang out from behind us and hung heavily in the air.

I swallowed a sick wave of dread.

"Kathy?" The voice, male and plaintive, shouted again.

Again, there was no answer.

I was jostled as the crowd compressed to allow a man to push through and rush past.

He stopped abruptly beside the overturned pallet and glanced at the body, which was already covered except for a hint of sneaker and an inch or two of cuffed blue jean.

He crumpled to his knees. "Kathy . . ."

SIX

KATHY ECHOED DOWN THE aisles and hung in the impossibly heavy air. Her husband, I presumed, given the wedding band on his left hand, covered his horror-stricken face.

Looking anything but awesome, Alan knelt beside him and whispered words I didn't have to hear to know were heartbreakingly unbearable to receive.

"Back it up, folks," a police officer said, heading in our direction. "We're going to need to clear this area."

"I'm with her," I said, still holding Mrs. Piggledy's hand.

"And we're with her," Barb said pointing to me.

"You're all relatives of this victim?"

"I'm Frank Michaels from Channel Three," Frank said. "This is my mother, father, sister, daughter, and Maddie here happens to be my—"

"Whoever you are, I'll need you to take a step back so the stretcher can get through," he said to me before Frank could accurately quantify the current status of our relationship. "You too, sir," he said, offering a hand so Mr. Piggledy could hoist himself upright beside me. "You are the husband, right?"

"Forty-eight years, come June."

The officer nodded and directed his attention to me. "And you are?"

"Maddie?" A voice, familiar but definitely not anyone from the Michaels family, answered from behind me.

I turned and found myself looking into the familiar hazel eyes of another police officer.

Not just any officer, but South Metro rookie cop Griff Watson.

Griff Watson, the former mall security guard who had been with me when the manager of Eternally 21 collapsed, setting off a chain of events I still couldn't quite fathom. Griff Watson, the man responsible for saving me from my near-fatal brush with an unlikely, but decidedly homicidal, maniac. Griff, my friend, whom I hadn't seen since he was hired on the force.

The current circumstances more than marred what would have been a pleasant reunion, but his stocky, imposing presence—in official uniform no less—was definitely a comfort.

"Griff! I'm so glad they sent you."

"I told my partner we had to high-tail it over here as soon as the call came in," he said, with a slight nod in the direction of the other officer.

"Thank you," I said, in lieu of the hug I wanted give him—I couldn't exactly embrace an on-duty, on-scene policeman. Not even gruff but sweet Griff Watson.

"Thank L'Raine," he said. "Good thing she was right nearby when the incident happened."

"L'Raine?" I repeated, as blond, brash, bosomy massage therapist L'Raine appeared from the crowd and stood next to him. Although she didn't strike me as Griff's type per se, she certainly had his number handy, which I could only assume meant their relationship had blossomed since she'd begged me to introduce them a few months back. "Great thinking."

Griff nodded in agreement, confirming my suspicions with the vaguest hint of his dimpled smile.

At the same moment, Alan helped the shaken husband to his feet and led him over to the body. Neither were particularly tall, but the poor man looked a good six inches shorter with his shoulders crumpled and head down.

Joyce dabbed her wide-open eyes and hugged a teary Barb.

I bit the inside of my cheek to keep myself from crying.

Frank, who already had one arm around a sobbing Eloise, slipped the other around my shoulder.

Griff simply shook his head.

As we stood, numb and in stunned silence, Alan left the husband in the care of a fellow polo-shirted employee and made his way over to the linens aisle, where Anastasia Chastain and (more important) the camera had a nearly unobstructed view of the accident. Following a brief conversation, Anastasia and the cameraman, who had to already have enough footage for an Emmy-worthy report, packed up and relocated.

Alan stood dabbing his forehead with a handkerchief from his pocket as the stretcher made its way toward Mrs. Piggledy. With none of his trademark salesman-swagger, he followed behind, stopping beside us.

"Sir," he said, offering his hand to Mr. Piggledy. "I can't tell you how sorry I am."

"Accidents happen," Mr. Piggledy said.

"Not in my store." Alan shook his head. "Not like this."

Griff's walkie-talkie blipped and a scratchy voice announced: "Coroner's here."

Alan rubbed his temples. "This is just getting worse and worse."

"Why did they call in a coroner?" Joyce asked. "On the *CSI* shows they—"

"Call in a coroner on all fatalities to make a determination as to cause of death," Griff recounted, undoubtedly from his rookie manual. "Standard procedure."

L'Raine smiled like he'd recited one of Shakespeare's love sonnets.

The stretcher pulled up beside Mrs. Piggledy.

"Ready?" the EMT asked.

"I'll need to lead everyone out of here along with Mrs. Piggledy," Griff said, clipping his still squawking radio back onto his utility belt. "So the area can be secured."

"And I need to get back over there," Alan said, looking like he'd rather be headed anywhere else. He handed Mr. Piggledy a business card. "Please keep me posted on your wife's condition."

"No worries," Mrs. Piggledy said. "I'll be back on the trick horses in no time."

"But, honey," Mr. Piggledy rubbed her cheek, "you've never ridden the horses."

"Details," she winced, as she was loaded onto the stretcher. "Please come to Higgledy's wedding Saturday night," she announced to the crowd. "All of you!"

With the glimmer of his wife's usual sparkle, Mr. Piggledy looked ever so slightly relieved. "Everything's going to be okay."

Alan simply shook his head.

I felt almost as awful for him as I did for kind-faced Kathy and her grieving husband.

When he'd first contacted me about advertising on my blog, Alan spent our initial phone call proudly recounting the history of Bader's Bargain Barn, starting with its humble beginnings as his grandfather's five-and-dime. He talked about how his father had expanded into a small local department store. How he himself had worked beside his dad all the way through high school, growing the company into a discount retailer during his college years, and even getting an MBA to help keep his beloved family enterprise competitive in the cutthroat world of franchises, chains, and superstores—all of which not only anticipated but depended on Black Friday for their highest traffic and sales receipts of the entire holiday season. Including Bargain Barn.

"Is there anything I can do to help?" I asked.

"I don't know that there's anything anyone can do." Alan's shoulders sagged that much more. "Not sure how we can survive a hit like this."

Before I could think of anything else to say, Alan turned and seemed to be forcing his legs to move.

A few seconds later, I was following Mrs. Piggledy's stretcher down the central aisle. Making our way toward the awaiting ambulance, I couldn't help but feel like we were on a maudlin parade route. But instead of ticker tape, there were gasps, tears, and comments filling the air.

Oh God, is it her neck?

How bloody is she?

She doesn't look nearly as bad as you might have expected …

"Everything's under control, folks," Frank announced in his most dulcet newscaster voice. "If you'll all just step back, we need to let the paramedics get this lady off to the hospital so she can be fixed up as quickly as possible."

Somehow he managed to maintain an air of gravitas and still seem living-room-familiar as conjecture about the accident and the nature of the injuries died down and the inevitable whispers about spotting local celebrity Frank Finance began to swirl around him.

He's better looking in person than I expected.

Shorter though, huh?

They usually are.

Isn't that the wife he …?

Mrs. Frugalicious!

"This is horrifying," Joyce said.

I couldn't have agreed more. "What are people going to say when they wheel out—"

"They're going to have to take her out a side entrance," Barb said.

"That, or close down the store," Griff said.

Craig appeared at the juncture of the middle aisle and the main corridor.

"Honey!" Joyce threw her arms around him. "Thank God, you're safe!"

"Mom, I'm fine," he said eyeballing L'Raine, who, with a healthy extra thirty pounds in a lot of the right places, struck me as definitely more his type than Griff's.

"Do you really think they're going to close down Bargain Barn?" I finally asked, after Joyce decided she was satisfied by her visual scan of Craig.

"How can they not?" Eloise said. "There's a dead body totally lying over there."

We watched together in a kind of morbid silent agreement as the EMTs navigated Mrs. Piggledy's stretcher out the door and into an ambulance. Still, I couldn't help but think about Alan and the seemingly fatal collateral damage to his beloved family business.

"Isn't the accident scene pretty much contained now?" I finally asked, once Mrs. Piggledy was well on her way to the hospital.

"Yes, or it will be soon," Griff said.

"I don't mean to be indelicate or anything," Craig said, "but if they do close, how am I going to get the TV or any of the other stuff I was hoping to buy tonight?"

"Most people, at least in the Frugarmy line, didn't get to make any of their purchases at all," L'Raine added.

Despite how close L'Raine stood to Griff—or, more accurately, to his holster—Craig flashed a smile that said *concerned agreement* but meant *I like 'em blond and buxom.*

I watched as a group of women in telltale bargain shopping garb [13] rushed past us and disappeared into the crowd-free aisles on the west side of the store.

"It is the biggest shopping night of the year, and people have been gearing up for it for months." I glanced over at the register

---

13. Shoppers in the know dress in layers instead of bulky winter jackets, wear sneakers, and have water bottles and snacks in tow so nothing distracts from the important business at hand.

lines, where the cashiers looked downright confused about what to do next. "Not to mention the stores."

It wasn't even officially Black Friday yet and not only had a member of my Frugarmy died at an event I'd encouraged her to attend, in a line made up entirely of devotees to Mrs. Frugalicious, but my best sponsor might well have suffered a fatal blow in the process. To top it off, the ripple effect was sure to cause financial mourning in the form of lost jobs throughout the community. Bargain Barn employed a lot of local people.

"Do you think there's any possible way to keep the store open?" L'Raine asked.

"That will likely depend on how long they think it will take the coroner to assess the scene and how much manpower they need to keep things up and running while she does," Griff said like the old pro he'd eventually be. "I suspect they're mulling that over right now."

"I mean, if Bargain Barn dies, so do the jobs of a lot of innocent employees," I said.

"It's not like there's anything we can do about it," Eloise said.

Frank glanced at Anastasia and the Channel Three camera, now relocated just outside the main entrance door, and then over at a small cluster of women who happened to be pointing at me. "I'm not sure I agree."

History told me I had good reason to be both encouraged and concerned about the odd but enthusiastic twinkle in my soon-to-be-ex-husband's baby blues.

"We may not have manpower, but we definitely have media and Mrs. Frugalicious power," he said.

"Meaning what?" I asked.

Frank turned to the Customer Service counter behind us and picked up the store phone. "Meaning I really think we may be able to help keep a terrible tragedy from turning into total disaster."

SEVEN

FOLLOWING SOME ADMITTEDLY IMPRESSIVE walkie-talkie/cell phone/landline finagling between Frank, Griff, various emergency responders, and Assistant Manager Joe (left to negotiate after Alan expressed his fervent but seemingly futile wish to stay open, and then shut himself, the husband, and a police official into his office), a hasty but potentially promising plan to keep Bargain Barn operational actually did start to unfold.

The plan started with Channel Three taping while I, Mrs. Frugalicious, addressed all of Bargain Barn via the store PA system:

Attention shoppers. This is Maddie Michaels, also known as Mrs. Frugalicious. Thank you for your patience and calm in the face of this evening's unfortunate events. While a small portion of the store will, for obvious reasons, remain off limits, the staff of Bargain Barn is preparing to get the rest of the sales floor up and operational. If you have already made a purchase and still need to pick it up or arrange delivery, that line will be reforming

at Merchandise Pickup. If you were previously in a specific door-
buster special line, please show your number to the employees
and volunteers who will be standing by on the west side of the
store to direct you to its new locations. If you are a member of
my Frugarmy and were waiting in the line by Layaway, that
particular line will now be relocated…

Even as I spoke, shoppers seemed to be pouring into the store to sympathize, be part of the hubbub, meet me (per Frank), score abandoned electronic deals already sold out at some of the other stores (per me), and enjoy an extra 10% off their next purchase through December 24 (per Joe, the assistant manager).

As a result, the next hour was anything but a temporary lull [14] at Bargain Barn.

While emergency workers wrapped up their grim job in the yellow-taped southeast corner of the store, employees returned to their various tasks and posts, old and new, around the building.

The Michaels clan not only stuck around, but did so with an *in for a penny* spirit, starting with Frank. He trolled the aisles, reassuring shoppers everything was A-OK; non-answering questions about what had happened; and playing warm, comforting celebrity spouse. Barb and Eloise (who wanted to be as far away from the body as possible) joined the ranks of assistant to the assistant manager, helping to organize the newly formed lines. Craig volunteered to serve as a runner, fetching various small appliances for shoppers

---

14. There is typically a lull between the "Thanksgiving dinner at noon and get in line" crowd and the "let's just go see what's out there" people who may wait until Friday morning, but shopping during the quiet hours after the hot-ticket electronic items may have sold out can still pay off with great deals.

from the store employees on toaster-cleanup detail just inside the out-of-bounds area. Ditto that for Wendy Killian, from *Here's the Deal* magazine, who'd gotten her TV, locked it in the trunk of her car,[15] and joined in with the effort.

I didn't have the heart to tell Craig that his obvious ulterior motive—cozying up to L'Raine—was pointless since she'd volunteered for the same job to be close to the police activity.

Namely, Griff.

As I greeted shoppers at the front of the store and in range of the camera, Gerald and Joyce set up shop at the Customer Service desk as crisis counselors of sorts. Gerald offering soothing platitudes to still-rattled employees and needy shoppers alike:

This too shall pass.

Everything happens for a reason.

And Joyce took it upon herself to dole out "comfort snacks" from the cooler full of Thanksgiving leftovers she'd apparently stashed in Frank's car, *just in case.*

Curiously, or maybe because of the proximity of the TV camera, people seemed to be eating up both the words of comfort along with most of the horrid leftovers.

I was getting almost hungry enough to brave a hockey puck roll when a woman came up to me with a cart full of merchandise and a smile on her face. "Hi, Mrs. Frugalicious. I'm a huge fan!"

"Nice to meet you," I said, fighting a flashback of what had happened the last time someone had proclaimed themselves to be a big fan of mine.

---

15. Black Friday safety tip: Don't leave purchases visible in your car windows. Lock them in the trunk or, if possible, take them directly home.

"I just wanted to thank you for doing what you did to help keep the store open in the face of such difficult circumstances. My husband lost his job, but I think I'll be able to scrape together my Christmas list because of how much I'm saving tonight."

"Well—" I said, feeling good that despite going through a sobering experience, the Frugarmy wouldn't go home empty-handed. I glanced over at Frank, who nodded approvingly from beside Anastasia as the cameraman filmed our friendly interchange. "It's been a group effort."

"Could I please have your autograph?" she asked, reaching into her purse and pulling out a pen.

"Of course," I said, obliging the woman by signing the top flap of a slow-cooker box she held out to me.

As I thanked her again and watched her blend safely back into the crowd, Frank ambled over and smiled his charming smile—the one that used to melt my heart. Even though things were touchy between us, I couldn't help but appreciate all the hard work he'd done tonight.

We never get more than we can handle hung in the air, courtesy of Gerald, as our eyes met for the second time that evening.

"I told you people were coming in specifically to see you," Frank said.

"Maybe so," I said. "But it was your idea to—"

"If it weren't for you, your dedication to the people you care about, and your all-around resourcefulness..." He shook his head. "Amazing."

"Thank you," I said, genuinely touched by Frank's compliment.

"I'm just so sorry." He looked down at his worn designer sneakers. "If it weren't for me, you wouldn't have had to start all this bargain shopping in the first place."

"I really do love being Mrs. Frugalicious," I said. "I just wish tonight had turned out a lot differently."

"I just wish I'd acted differently. We wouldn't have to sell the house." His voice cracked. "Or liquidate our marriage…"

"I…" A swarm of what I thought of as my divorce butterflies, the ones I'd forced into hibernation, began to flit in my stomach and flutter toward my throat. "I don't exactly know what to say."

"I don't know how I could have been so damned stupid," he said, dabbing his eye with the back of his hand. "You're so incredible, and I'm such an incredible fool."

The last thing I'd ever wanted was to be was divorced and facing the possibility not only of single motherhood, but of being single for the rest of forever. Still, the water under our bridge was something of a raging river and this conversation—which always started with his claim that he'd truly been stalked and was "the pursued" in his illicit romance—always ended the same. "Frank, we've already been through this."

"I know. I know." His voice cracked. "But after seeing how much happier the kids are with the family here for Thanksgiving and then seeing how it can all slip away forever in an instant tonight—"

"Frank, I—"

"I made the absolute worst mistake of my entire life," he said.

As I nodded in agreement, my chest and back broke out in that familiar cold sweat.

"I'd do anything to erase all that happened and make things right for you again." He glanced over at the Customer Service counter, where Eloise had joined her grandparents to stand smiling in our direction. "For the kids."

"The kids..." I found myself repeating as the door to the executive offices opened.

And Alan emerged.

"I just wanted to let you know," Frank whispered as we took off together in his direction.

As Alan surveyed the store, he looked that much more grim, numb, and even more shell-shocked than I suddenly felt.

A touch of pink colored his otherwise gray cheeks.

I couldn't imagine what I looked like.

"What the...?" Alan asked.

"Maddie was worried about the collateral losses to Bargain Barn," said Frank, whose eyes were still uncharacteristically misty. "So—"

"So Frank came up with a plan to help keep the store open," I somehow heard myself saying like the admiring spouse I once was.

There was no missing the appreciation in his smile. "And people have been pouring in ever since."

"I can't believe this," Alan said, noting the lines, which were ten people deep at every register.

"It's pretty hard to fathom," I said, as much to Frank as Alan.

"So many shoppers..."

"If I've learned anything all these years in the newsroom, it's that folks can't ever really get enough tragedy or celebrity," Frank said. "Since we had Mrs. Frugalicious and Channel Three already on location, it just made sense to try and make the very best of an awful situation."

Alan's eyes narrowed as he spotted Anastasia and the cameraman standing by in front of Customer Service. "It's just that—"

"Anastasia told me you'd asked her to steer clear of the accident site and that you don't like to be on live TV," Frank said. "They won't be putting you on camera."

"I don't even know what to say," Alan finally did say.

Which made two of us.

"We're glad we could help with the store while you were trying to comfort the husband of the victim." Frank pulled a tissue from his pocket and wiped his nose. "How is he doing?"

"Not great." Alan shook his head. "We just sent him off in an ambulance of his own to the hospital. He's a wreck."

"Such an unthinkable accident," I said.

"Accident," Alan repeated, shaking his head. "We maintain rigorous safety standards. I insist upon the highest—"

"Mr. Bader," Griff's partner said, emerging from a nearby aisle. "They'd like to have a talk with you so they can get things wrapped up."

Alan nodded. "Yes. Of course."

"I'll wait here," Griff said, joining us while his partner and Alan started for the yellow-taped southeast corner of the store. "We're off shift when he gets back."

"Helluva night for a rookie," Frank said.

"Tell me about it," Griff said, looking as exhilarated as I'd ever seen him. "My partner says I'll probably never see anything like this again in my career."

"Let's hope not," I said.

"Glad I got the call, though," he said, looking away quickly, as if searching for L'Raine. She'd apparently phoned in the 911 to his personal cell phone. "But I'll be glad to call it a night soon too."

"Have they released the name of the victim?" I asked.

"Not yet," he said.

"But they've figured out what happened?"

"I overheard one of the firemen saying they thought the pallet was up there at an odd angle," Frank said. "The vibration from so many people lined up along the aisle and pushing against the shelf supports sent the thing off the edge."

"Officially, I can neither confirm nor deny," Griff said in true cop fashion. He looked around, ostensibly to check that his partner wasn't back in hearing range. "But between us, that's pretty much the general consensus."

EIGHT

AWESOME ALAN, WITH HIS full face and rosy cheeks, ran past a group of plump chickens playing hopscotch in the aisle and a baby goat gnawing at a zebra-print couch. He paused to pet the enormous garden snake slithering out of an open washing machine, but stopped entirely in front of a group of women wearing camouflage skirts and combat boots.

My Frugarmy.

They waved for the camera.

"This can't be happening!" Alan shouted in what sounded like Frank's voice, pulling battered, dented toaster boxes from their matching camo shopping bags. "Not in my store. Not tonight!"

The women opened their mouths like baby birds so Joyce, who'd appeared out of nowhere, could pour gray, lumpy, floury chunks down their throats from the gravy boat she held.

"Mmmm," one of the women said. It was L'Raine, and she was looking at a police service revolver in her hand.

"The secret is the Red Hots," echoed over the PA system, followed by, "Tragic accident cleanup, aisle one."

Eloise grabbed a mop and bucket, and we ran in slow motion—Frugarmy, animals, and Michaels family members alike—along a parade route lined with live-streaming flat screen TVs.

"We love you, Ms. Frugalicious!" someone yelled from the crowd.

"She's Mrs. Frugalicious, not Miz!" someone else yelled.

"Not if she divorces Frank!"

I waved and tried to shout Black Friday shopping tips over the crowd, but the only thing that came out was, "I can't confirm or deny!"

"Accidents happen," Barb said from what was left of aisle one, pointing to an almost-zipped body bag where a familiar pair of blood-soaked tennis shoes stuck out from the bottom. Barb turned to the counter beside her, loaded an entire loaf of bread into a giant multi-slotted toaster, and pressed the start button. "And then you're toast."

As *toast* echoed over the PA system and the heady scent of warm cinnamon, bacon, and eggs seemed to flood the store, tears ran down my face and dropped onto what I realized were the very same blood-spattered shoes. On my feet.

"No!" I tried to yell. "I'm not Kathy!" I tried to shout, but nothing came from my throat except the ping of an incoming text message.

———

I opened my eyes in a cold sweat, still trying to scream. Sitting up, I reached over to the nightstand for my cell phone and took a deep breath of the comforting but disconcerting aroma of cinnamon and bacon wafting through the air.

———

I tried not to process the surreal dream-meets-reality of sitting down to a post–Black Friday brunch[16] of bacon, eggs, and cinnamon French toast prepared by Joyce and accompanied by the other semi-early risers in the house: Barb, Gerald, Craig (who'd slept over on the family room couch after his ex picked up their kids early that morning), and Frank. Nowhere near ready to sort through my various feelings about Frank's midnight confession, I thought about hiding out in the bedroom all day. Since I'd eaten almost nothing in almost twenty-four hours, however, hunger had me quickly thinking otherwise. Instead, I decided to make my appearance in the midst of the hustle and bustle, figuring there'd be relative safety, at least conversationally, in numbers.

"Mr. Piggledy left me a message that Mrs. Piggledy was released from the hospital and they're on their way home," I said.

"That's a relief." Joyce took a gravy boat full of maple syrup out of the microwave and placed it on the breakfast bar. "I've been worried about her."

"Was her foot broken?" Barb asked.

---

16. There's (usually) nothing more satisfying than sitting down to a morning brunch or social gathering at the end of your shopping trip to wind down, compare bargains, and congratulate yourselves on a job well done.

"Mr. Piggledy said she left in a cast."

"What about her head?" Barb asked.

"I assume everything else must have checked out." My head, on the other hand, was still spinning. It was hardly surprising that a jumbled collage of last night's events featured prominently in my dreams, but had I really conjured up the syrup vessel I now held in my hand? "They've moved the commitment ceremony to the first-floor courtyard so Mrs. Piggledy won't have to negotiate an escalator, but it's still on and open to all tomorrow evening."

"Between their monkey and that bird?" Frank asked, stabbing his fork into a piece of cantaloupe from the platter next to him.

"Too weird," Craig said.

"But interesting," Barb said. "How often do you get invited to an inter-species wedding?"

"I can't wait," Joyce said, smiling lovingly at Gerald. "I think the whole thing is kind of romantic.

Gerald gave her a wink and speared a piece of bacon. "Love conquers all."

Last night's craziness had clearly left me a marble short. Not only had I joined the breakfast fray, I'd practically invited the Michaels family to the wedding (or whatever it was). I also found myself wondering if last night's heart-to-heart meant Frank might actually possess a fraction of his parent's knack for marital magic after all. Then again, I was so starved from barely eating all day that even the Joyce-prepared bacon looked divine.

So delicious, I barely noticed the measuring cups, flour, eggshells, and dirty mixing bowls littering my normally tidy countertops.

I was sure I'd lost it when I took a syrup-soaked bite of what had to be the fluffiest, crunchiest, softest, most delicately battered treat I'd had in years.

Joyce winked. "Not too bad, huh?"

"Wow!" I said.

"Secret is stale bread," she said. "I found some in the bread box."

Instead of spitting it out, I stuffed another bite into my mouth. "Delicious. Thank you, Joyce."

"My pleasure," she said. "I was too keyed up to really sleep, so I figured I might as well make myself useful."

One look at the dark half-moons under everyone but Joyce's eyes (no doubt thanks to a pre-dawn application of the makeup she never allowed anyone to see her without) and I had to appreciate just how incredibly useful the Michaels clan had been. "You've been so helpful, Joyce, and so has everyone else. I really can't imagine how things would have turned out had all of you not been at Bargain Barn, so willing to pitch in."

"Actually, I had one of the more promising evenings I've had in a while," Craig said through a mouthful of bread. "As far as attractive shoppers in need of comforting, anyway."

"Atta boy," Gerald patted his shoulder.

"Anyone in particular?" Joyce asked.

"Interesting you should ask. As a matter of fact—"

"The news is on," Frank interrupted. He pointed the remote at the muted TV in the corner of the kitchen and upped the volume before Craig could utter L'Raine's name. Which meant I was not now forced to fill him in on his gun-toting competition.

Anastasia couldn't have gotten even an hour's rest, but somehow she managed to look crisp and beautiful from behind the news desk.

"While everything appears to be back to Black Friday business as usual, it was quite a different story last night at Bargain Barn..."

"Does that woman ever sleep?" Barb asked.

"Not when she's got both the hottest story in town and a holiday weekend anchor slot," answered Frank.

The camera cut away from the live feed of Anastasia, and a pre-recorded close-up of my anguished face filled the screen. The camera angle widened to show Frank beside me as emergency workers circled the overturned pallet.

The food that was just starting to satisfy my intense hunger suddenly hardened to concrete in my stomach as I caught a glimpse of those pink sneakers.

I'd read the flurry of prayers and condolences that began to pop up almost immediately on my blog. I checked before I'd gone to sleep, and again first thing this morning after listening to Mr. Piggledy's message. Even though I knew the Frugarmy would still be sleeping off their shopping hangover, I'd hoped for something in the comments that had trickled in this morning about Kathy herself.

There was nothing of note.

"Authorities still haven't released specifics yet, but witnesses report that a double pallet of toasters slid from an upper storage shelf and, tragically, landed on a women waiting in line below." The camera zoomed in on Anastasia. *"Alan Bader, owner of Bargain Barn and a fixture in the Denver business community, has yet to make an official statement."*

"Have you talked to him since last night?" Joyce asked.

With Griff's definitive *can't confirm or deny* and Alan still behind the yellow tape when we left, I figured any remaining questions were best answered in the light of day. "I planned to check in with him this morning after brunch," I said, shaking my head. "I can't imagine he got much sleep."

Gerald let out a dramatic whistle, pointing at the TV, now showing a view of the overturned toasters, boxes, and small appliances that had littered the affected aisles of the store. "Not with a mess like that on his hands."

"As a television journalist, it's my job to present an unbiased report of the news vital to our community," Anastasia continued, the camera once again live in studio. *"But, as many of you may know, I happened to be at Bargain Barn doing a report on Black Friday with bargain-hunting consultant Maddie Michaels, better known as Mrs. Frugalicious, as the tragic events unfolded."* The studied concern on her face couldn't quite mask the *big scoop* gleam that had been in her eyes since the crash shook the store. *"I feel I would be remiss if I didn't mention how proud I was of my fellow shoppers who rushed in to assist the injured, the lightning-quick response of the South Metro emergency workers, and the above-and-beyond efforts of Mrs. Frugalicious herself. In the midst of the chaos and confusion, she not only stepped in to calm shoppers, but helped to coordinate efforts to ensure that people could get the items they had waited in line for hours to purchase."*

I stole a glance at Frank. He needed the good press way more than I needed to feel good about making the best of an awful situation. Instead of any understandable disappointment at the omission, however, he smiled what seemed to be a genuine smile.

"A star is born," he announced.

"On behalf of myself, Mrs. Frugalicious, and everyone who was at Bargain Barn last night," Anastasia continued, *"I would like to extend my condolences to the family of Mrs. Katherine Carter."*

With the surname Carter, I forgot all about anything else Anastasia was or wasn't saying.

Kathy *Carter.*

A photo flashed on the screen. Despite the makeup, jewelry, off-the-shoulder top, and slightly blurred glamour shot effect, I was looking at the very same heart-shaped face of the woman I'd met last night.

The Frugarmy member who'd met her fate a few minutes later.

Underneath the photo, her name written out in cursive was not *Katherine Carter* or even *Kathy Carter* but *Catherine Carter.*

The concrete in my stomach started to churn.

Catherine with a *C.*

CC.

———

I scuttled across the house to my office and powered up my computer. It couldn't be anything more than sheer coincidence that Cathy Carter shared her initials with my cyber stalker. Cathy was an enthusiastic member of my Frugarmy who'd met her untimely end by coming to Bargain Barn to enjoy special bargains. CC, AKA Contrary Claire, had made a point of saying she wasn't coming to Bargain Barn last night. Her exact words were deleted from my website, but they would likely be stored on my brain's hard drive forever:

Thanks for offering me fifteen minutes of background fame, but I think I'll just stay home and cyber shop. Everyone knows the deals are way better online these days, anyway.

I took a breath of relief and glanced at the comments and condolences now starting to stream in from the Frugarmy:

Love and blessings to all involved. —Susan H.

I was there last night and just wanted to say that Mrs. Frugalicious and her family were so terrific in the face of very difficult circumstances. —Randi T.

I missed the accident (thankfully) but was able to score some terrific deals anyway. —Lisa C.

Rest in peace, Cathy. —Ann S.

Absent, so far, was an snarky *I told you so*, or anything else for that matter, from the *other* CC. Maybe Contrary Claire went to bed early and was still sleeping in, or maybe she'd taken a last-minute, post-Thanksgiving, off-the-grid getaway, but one thing was for sure—she'd definitely be weighing in with something.

Then again, maybe she'd already tried to fire off her negative diatribe but was blocked by whatever the boys had done to my website settings.

All three kids were still sleeping, but I was too curious to wait until teenage-wakeup time. Instead, I went upstairs, knocked on Trent's bedroom door, and let myself in. For a split second, I wished I'd picked FJ, the tidier of the boys, thereby avoiding the minefield of laundry and sports equipment littering his floor. Either way, there was no missing the general boy funk permeating the air.

I nudged him awake. "Trent!"

"Sleeping," he finally mumbled.

"I have a question."

"Later."

"You blocked CC from posting, right?"

"Uh-huh."

"So, any comments she wants to post—"

"Have to be approved by you."

"And how do I know if she tried?"

"You get an email alert."

"That's it?" I said.

"Uh-huh," he managed.

"Thanks," I said. "And you need to clean your room when you wake up. It's a disaster."

"K," he grunted, rolled over, and was immediately back into his teenage sleep coma.

I headed back downstairs to my office to check my Mrs. Frugalicious email account. Other than a message from Wendy Killian from *Here's the Deal* commiserating about last night and wanting to know what happened after she finally left Bargain Barn, there was nothing of interest.

I dialed Alan.

To my non-surprise, and also relief, the call went straight to voicemail. The message I left, long and rambling, about how I hoped we'd been of help, how glad I was to assist with anything else, and inquiring as to how he was doing, would have been that much more awkward as a real conversation. Particularly since I tried my hardest not to mention the word *accident*, which had clearly seemed to bother him last night.

I'd just finished dialing him back with an addendum about Mrs. Piggledy's improved condition, since I'd completely forgotten to mention it, when I heard a bedroom door open and the shuffle of footsteps on the upstairs landing.

"Hey," I said, spotting Eloise on her way down the steps.

"What's up?" she asked, rubbing sleep from her eyes.

"Joyce made breakfast for everyone."

"So I smell," she said. "Bacon and eggs?"

"And French toast."

"It smells really good," Eloise said, scrunching her nose. "But what secret ingredients did she put in it?"

"I tried not to think about that," I said, not mentioning the stale bread part. "Everything was delicious though."

"Weird."

"Speaking of which," I said, "I just found out the lady was named Catherine Carter."

"From last night?"

With my nod, we shared a pained moment of silence.

"So awful," Eloise finally said. "But why's it weird?"

"It's just that her initials were CC."

Eloise raised a slightly too thin eyebrow. "Like your batsh— Uh, your crazy stalker CC?"

I nodded.

"But why would Contrary Claire spend months writing nasty posts, say she wasn't coming to Bargain Barn, and then just show up anyway?"

"And then proclaim she's a big fan who wanted her picture taken with me?" I asked. "Really doesn't make sense."

"Then why even think about it?"

"It's just that Contrary Claire hasn't weighed in yet."

"Probably because she's blocked," Eloise said looking over my shoulder at comments popping up on the website.

"But I haven't gotten an email alert that she's even tried," I said, glancing at my email again. "Not yet, anyway."

"Isn't her usual MO to comment after one of your blog posts?"

"Huh. Now that you mention it, everything she's written has been in response to something I've put on the website."

"Which means she probably gets an alert when you post something new."

"Then she responds accordingly?"

"So to speak," Eloise said.

"And if she hasn't seen the news yet, she might not think to check the website?"

"Exactly."

"That has to be it," I said. "The thing is, I really should post a condolence message to the Carter family and to everyone from the Frugarmy who was affected by last night."

"Once you do, you know CC is going to have a field day with it."

"True," I said, "but I can block any comments that—"

My text alert pinged.

"That's got to be Alan," I said as I picked up my phone. Then I looked at the message. "Oh dear!"

"Is it her? Eloise asked.

"Almost as bad," I said. "It's the realtor."

As in *my* realtor, the one who'd promised that having my extended family in town was no problem since Thanksgiving weekend would be dead where showings were concerned:

I HAVE SOME POTENTIAL BUYERS WHO ARE DYING TO SEE YOUR HOUSE. HOW DOES HALF AN HOUR FROM NOW WORK FOR YOU?

NINE

GIVEN THE NUMBER OF people sleeping, lazing, or generally enjoying (and by *enjoying* I mean *making a mess of*) every room in the house, I'd have preferred a message straight from CC's poisoned pen to a text about a rush-rush showing.

Tidying the kitchen after Joyce's brunch extravaganza was a half-hour job alone. Luckily I was able to negotiate a full hour before the realtor would arrive, which turned out to be just enough time to sound the alarm, rouse the teenagers, enlist my weekend lodgers in a mad scramble to pick up their various areas, and get everyone out the door.

We vacated en masse just as the potential buyers pulled up to the house.

As everyone gathered their various belongings, I managed to post a quick note on the blog:

Dearest Frugarmy,

As most of you now know, unforeseen tragedy changed both the mood and the mission last evening at Bargain Barn. I would like to express my sympathy to all of you who were affected and extend my deepest condolences to the friends and family of our fellow Frugarmy member, Catherine Carter.
Much love,
Mrs. Frugalicious

And then I added a small postscript.

P.S. If you know or are friends with Cathy, please feel free to share any memories or comments.

"I still don't see why we all had to leave," Eloise said as we left the house, echoing the general sentiment—at least from the kids, who'd offered suggestions from *just don't show my room* (Trent) to *we'll stay out of their way by watching the game down in the basement* (FJ) to *why do Uncle Frank and Aunt Maddie have to move out of this awesome house anyway?* (Barb's youngest).

"I told you," I said, "potential buyers can't relax and picture themselves living in the home if we're there." I had the women in tow, while the men took off for a local sports bar to watch more football.

"Those buyers had no potential," Eloise sniffed. "They didn't have a nice enough car to afford to buy the house."

"You never know," I said. After all, Frank and I had nice enough cars and couldn't afford to keep the place even if our marriage did have any hope of rising from the ashes.

"If nothing else, this showing was the perfect excuse to get Maddie to teach us how to be extreme couponers," Joyce said, as we pulled into a parking space at the grocery store.

On the one hand, the last thing I wanted to do was set foot in any store after last night, much less be teaching Joyce and Barb how to coupon on actual Black Friday.[17] On the other, there was nothing like the all-encompassing mathematical distraction of combining discounts, store specials, and little-known promotions to keep my thoughts from racing.

"I'm all about couponing," Barb said, her tone a little less convincing than her words. "I just wish I'd had a little time to put on some makeup."

"Tell me about it." Eloise fidgeted with the ponytail holder she'd had to put in her wet hair in lieu of a blow dry and flat iron. "At least you aren't at risk of running into like everyone you know from high school on the one day you're home looking like—"

"You look beautiful," Joyce said to Eloise. "A touch of lipstick and you're runway material."

Eloise rolled her eyes but smiled.

"We'll keep this on the down low as much as possible," I said, not relishing being seen in my own less-than-stunning ensemble of hot pink velour sweats and baseball cap. "And today I'll only be able to show you a few basics to get you started."

---

17. Groceries should be the last thing on a shoppers mind with all the bargains out there. While the big-ticket doorbuster items will likely be long gone by midmorning on Black Friday, retailers want your holiday business. Look for unadvertised store specials and markdowns throughout most stores.

"I'm ready!" Joyce said, reviewing the printout I'd given them of a blog I'd written a few months back about coupon clipping for beginners:

You don't have to be an extreme couponer to save 25–50% on groceries. Just follow the simple tips below and your grocery bill won't feel so much like a mortgage payment.

—*88% of all coupons issued can be found in weekend circulars, so pick up extra copies of the Sunday paper and use them!*

—*Clip coupons in multiples, but only on products you'll actually use or can get for less than zero by combining store specials with other offers. Remember, if you end up throwing a product out (or don't donate it to a worthy cause like a food bank), you've wasted money.*

—*Organize your coupons in a file by product type and expiration date.*

—*Before you set foot in a grocery store, research national and local online couponing sites that help keep track of where your coupons match up with the best sales. You can also download apps and get digital coupons on your smartphone.*

—*Know how much the items you buy most frequently cost when they are on sale. Create a price bible to make notes on the best pricing and keep it with you when you shop so you can stock up when prices are cheap.*

—*If you aren't brand loyal on a particular item, try store brands. They cost less.*

—Use those store loyalty cards! If you do, you'll not only save money, but stores share info with marketers who will pass along savings opportunities targeted specifically to your shopping habits.

Grabbing my coupon binder and price bible, I led Joyce, Barb, and Eloise toward the store and through the automatic front doors.

"Where should we start?" Barb asked.

Even though I didn't usually set foot into a grocery store on Fridays [18] and certainly not without having done my research, I'd come up with something of a plan for Barb, Joyce, and Eloise on the fly.

"Okay," I said, leading them over to the shopping carts. "If you're going to be a couponer, you have to not only be willing to change the way you shop, but the way you eat and plan meals."

Barb scrunched her nose. "Meaning what?"

"No more afternoon runs to pick up something interesting for dinner."

"I hate going to the store hungry, so I always plan ahead and shop for the week," Barb said.

"That's a start, but do you shop by what you feeling like eating or what's on special?"

"What I feel like having, I guess."

"That's a no-no too. So is that huge monthly trip to the local wholesale club for a giant jar of relish that will sit in the refrigerator uneaten for the next five years."

---

18. Many grocery stores start their weekly sales on Wednesday, and some will still honor the sales from the previous week—which can mean double the savings. Since many stores get produce deliveries on Mondays and Tuesdays, food is also fresh on the shelf.

"We always go through the snack chips and the bottled waters I buy there, though."

"At a four-thousand-percent mark-up?"

Barb looked incredulous. "What?"

"Bottled water by the case can wind up costing you more per unit than gas for the car because it takes about five bottles of water just to make the *plastic* for one bottle. You're better off purchasing a filter and drinking water out of a glass."

"We eat out almost all of the time," Joyce said. "So I don't waste money on almost any of that kind of stuff."

"Dining out is, by far, the least cost-effective way to eat,"[19] I said, although in her case, there was also a food palatability cost/benefit analysis to be considered as well. "If you want to save big on your food bill, not only should you mostly cook at home, but buy according to what's on sale with coupons—and then stock up while it's cheap."

"Good thing I'm living in the sorority house," Eloise said. "This couponing stuff hurts my brain."

"I'm going to make it easy," I said, particularly for Eloise who'd not only inherited the Michaels blue eyes and dark curls, but their penchant for bright, shiny, costly things. "Assume you have twenty dollars, then use whatever coupons you want from my binder to purchase the following staples and dinner fixings for tonight…"

I pulled a notepad from my purse, handed out pieces of paper and pens, and listed off the items: "Toothpaste, deodorant, yogurt,

---

19. At mid-priced chain restaurants like Chili's, Ruby Tuesday, etc., $40 a couple is pretty standard. Dinner out once a week at a similar restaurant over the course of a year exceeds $2,000.

any kind of beverage, at least a pound of meat/poultry or fish, a side dish, cereal, a vegetable, pain reliever, and one item of your choice."

"Let's roll!" Joyce said, a smile straining her taut cheeks. She opened my binder to the table of contents page.

"Just make sure you take the coupons that are closest to their expiration date and leave everything in order."

As Barb and Eloise joined her, I replaced the notepad and pens they'd handed back and grabbed my smartphone from my purse.

Eloise looked up. "Did she respond yet?"

There were no new texts or missed calls, but there were a few new emails, including two new potential advertisers.

Nothing from CC.

Nothing from anyone who wanted to contribute a remembrance about Cathy.

"Not yet, but it hasn't even been a half hour."

"Did who respond yet?" Barb asked, a fistful of coupons in hand.

"Her Mrs. Frugalicious stalker," Eloise said.

"Or anyone who knew Cathy Carter," I quickly added.

"You know Contrary Claire's gonna have a field day about last night when she does post something."

Joyce shook her head. "I really do find it hard to believe a person like that is harmless."

"She is now that everything she says is blocked," I said, putting away my phone and confirming that my favorite checker,[20] Yvette, was at her usual register on the far side of the store. Since I always

---

20. An effective couponer not only takes up extra time at the register but watches every transaction to make sure the discounts are being properly applied, so it's vital to develop a good rapport with the checkers at your local grocery store.

shared coupons and specials with her, I knew she wouldn't mind a few quick sample transactions along with my real one. "Let's meet and compare carts by aisle thirteen in, say, twenty minutes?"

"Sounds like a plan," Joyce said.

"Want to do this together?" Barb asked Eloise.

"Sure," Eloise said. "I guess."

I waited for the three of them to scatter throughout the store before heading toward health and beauty aids. Included in this weekend's promotions was a big-name national brand of deodorant at buy-one-get-one free (BOGO) at the store. (Someone in marketing was obviously sensitive to the perspiration and body odor needs of the nation's holiday hostesses in the face of the stressful onslaught of family). Since I'd also found manufacturer's coupons for the same deodorant online, I grabbed 4 at a cost of exactly $0.38. I made quick work of the rest of the list, including 5 tubes of a lesser-known brand of toothpaste in the small size for a $1.19 with a dollar off coupon for a total of $.95, two containers of yogurt on special, and a catalina[21] for $5.00 off my total order. Barb and Eloise had taken most of the frozen vegetable coupons with, but fresh green beans were on sale for 75 cents off a pound, so I bagged two pounds.

After filling my cart with sports drinks, multiple boxes of cereal, store-brand cold medicine, and a two-pound chub of ground turkey reduced for quick sale, I made my way to our meeting spot at the front of the store, where I figured I'd be waiting another ten minutes.

---

21. A catalina is a coupon that prints out of the machine next to the register. Don't toss them with your receipt without reading them over—they offer great manufacturer discounts!

Joyce was already there, checking her lipstick. "My stars," she said, spotting me in the reflection of her compact mirror. "All that for just twenty dollars?"

"Under seven dollars," I said. "That is, assuming I've calculated correctly."

"I'm impressed," she said.

"I could say the same," I said, glancing into her cart. One read-through of my tips and Joyce had a half-full cart that included the economical store-brand bagged cereal, coupon/ store promo combo on Rice-A-Roni, Greek frozen yogurt complete with coupon, and reduced bagged broccoli I'd determined to be the second-best value per pound in the produce department. "You're a quick study."

"Beginner's luck." She winked.

We stood together in silence for a beat.

"You know, Maddie ..." she finally said.

Judging by the consternation that crossed her face, I was fairly sure I didn't want to know whatever was coming next, and that the subject might well involve the one topic I'd tried not to discuss with anyone bearing the last name Michaels—aside from my children, of course—since the news of our split broke.

I just assumed Frank filled his family in on the particulars. Judging from their lack of commentary and abundance of good behavior since they'd arrived, there was little they felt they could say in his defense.

What if Frank truly meant what he'd said about making it up to me and the children? Difficult as our money troubles were, it was hard to blame him for being duped by a financial conman. Having a notorious public affair was a completely different story, though. I'd never forget, or even forgive, but could I move forward for the good of everyone if I thought he really could turn over a new leaf?

The divorce butterflies returned with a vengeance as Joyce took a deep breath…

Thankfully, my cell phone pinged.

"It's just my text alert," I said, both startled by the sound and grateful for the interruption. I swallowed the nervous lump in my throat and looked at the message.

WHERE ARE YOU GROCERY SHOPPING?

"It's Frank," I said.

Joyce nodded and seemed to almost smile.

SAVEAWAY BY THE HOUSE, I responded.

THAT'S WHAT I FIGURED.

WHY? DO YOU NEED SOMETHING?

STASIA DOES.

I hadn't thought to contact Anastasia yet since I knew she was on the air, but given her involvement in the story and the fact that her fiancé was acting police chief, Anastasia had to have the most up-to-the-minute information on what had happened and who exactly it had happened to. I WANT TO TALK TO HER TOO. I'LL CALL HER.

NO NEED. SHE'S ON HER WAY OVER TO YOU.

———

Anastasia materialized mere minutes later with a fresh cameraman in tow, and no sign, even up close, of the dark circles Joyce had quickly erased from under the rest of our eyes using makeup from the cosmetics bag[22] in her purse. "The producers were so impressed with how you handled yourself last night that they want to run a series of segments featuring Mrs. Frugalicious bargain shopping all weekend long!"

"How wonderful!" Joyce said.

"But I'm just at the grocery store to kill time while the realtor shows the house."

"Which will make a perfect segment for today," Anastasia said.

"You don't think viewers might see this as a little indelicate given what happened last night?"

"We're going to introduce the segment with a recap of last night and your role as a Good Samaritan in the aftermath," she said, with equal parts empathy and journalistic matter-of-factness.

Did she not remember that my last turn as a Good Samaritan almost landed me in prison?

"And what about Cathy Carter?" I asked.

"We'll run her photo along with the piece," Anastasia said. "We're also putting together a human interest bit on her, despite the fact that she really wasn't all that interesting."

"Meaning what?" I asked.

"She was forty-eight, married, no kids, lived in Denver less than two years, and was unemployed."

Which explained, at least in part, the lack of commentary on my website.

"You ready, Stasia?" the cameraman asked.

---

22. Luckily, or I'd have had to change one of the items on the ten-item list to a cosmetic. There are almost always great bargains to be found on makeup in the coupon section of the paper and online for various brands and retailers.

She nodded. "Ready."

Before I could ask Anastasia what she knew about Cathy's friends, what they thought of her, or even how the husband was doing, she smiled her megawatt smile.

And we went live.

"I've just caught up with Maddie Michaels, AKA Mrs. Frugalicious, who is trying to recover from last night's rattling events at Bargain Barn with a little retail therapy…"

"To the extent that's possible," I said, and once again—despite the baseball cap covering my not-ready-for-primetime hair—the camera zoomed in on me. But, unlike Barb and Eloise, also in the shot and looking like they wanted to die, my on-air endorphins kicked in once more. "And so did my mother-in-law, sister-in-law, and stepdaughter, who were helpful in keeping things under control last night. Since they wanted to learn how to save big on groceries while they're here for the holidays, I gave them a list of ten random items, a budget of twenty dollars, and full use of my binder and price bible," I said holding it up for the camera. "We are about to go through the checkout line and see how everyone did."

Yvette the checker smiled for her close-up and began to scan the items in the Barb/Eloise cart.

As the total climbed toward $20, I added some color commentary:

"They've done a nice job of using coupons to save money on deodorant, toothpaste, and cereal, which will ultimately keep them from going over budget, but they've made a couple of common mistakes that will keep their total higher than it needs to be. For one thing, pre-cut items—veggies, fruits, sandwiches—are always more costly, even on special. For another, convenience items like light bulbs tend to cost more at the grocery, so it's best to save that kind of coupon and use it at the hardware store." Yvette scanned the last of their items. "And brand-name cereal is approximately forty-three cents per serving while generic runs twenty cents, so unless you have a discount for more than half off, it's almost always better to buy the no-name brands."

"All great tips," Anastasia said, as the total rang up to a respectable $19.79 and the checker moved on to Joyce's purchases.

"Now, my mother-in-law here has a real knack," I said.

Joyce beamed as Yvette rang up her multiple tubes of toothpaste, the small 75%-off turkey in her cart, and a six-pack of sparkling soda for which she used a peelie.[23] Her total was teetering around sixteen dollars before coupons when two mistakes upped her total. "Greeting cards are very convenient, but they come at a two-hundred percent markup. Better to make them at home," I said, as Yvette rang up Joyce's last item. "And name-brand pain relievers are generally thirty to forty percent more than generics. Look for a sale on your store's brand, combine it if you can with any online coupons that reduce your overall total, and stock up then."

"Great tips once again." Anastasia said as Joyce totaled up to $14.37. "Now let's see the master at work."

The camera filmed as I unloaded my mostly full cart. "I generally try to shop on Tuesdays or Wednesdays to take advantage of store specials and/or double or triple coupon days, but by knowing what's on special, combining those deals with coupons in my binder,

---

23. Don't forget the blinkies (those automatic coupon dispensers in the store right beside the products) or the peelies (those instant coupons attached to the products themselves).

and keeping up with downloadable discounts, you'll always save, no matter when you shop."

The camera zoomed in on the register readout as I handed over my coupons. As Yvette scanned, my total plummeted precipitously from an original grand total of almost $40.

The crowd that had gathered around us began to clap when they saw the register readout:

$6.89.

"Outstanding," Anastasia said. "From Saveaway, this is Anastasia Chastain, with Mrs. Frugalicious and some great grocery shopping tips."

———

"You're gonna be as famous as Dad soon," FJ said, helping to unload the groceries while I prepared to put them away in the spare basement bedroom I'd converted into a stockpile room [24] for my ever-growing supply of non-perishable food, health and beauty aids, and housekeeping supplies.

"Maybe you'll get rich enough that we can keep the house," added Trent, whom I'd also enlisted to help after sending Joyce, Barb, and Eloise to their various quarters for some long overdue rest.

"It would be nice if we could, guys, but we really don't need this much space, anyway." I ran a feather duster across the boxes, cans, and bottles already lining the shelves, circled the expiration dates

---

24. The one room every single prospective buyer commented on as a top-five favorite feature of the house. It was also the one room I'd really miss when the house finally sold.

on each item, and put everything away by category. Divorce or no, I was saving so much by couponing that tapering off for the inevitable move made little sense. Particularly given the financial strain of paying the mortgage while it lingered on the market waiting for that buyer who not only *loved the house* (as the current lookie-loos had written on the comments clipboard) but drove a car that corresponded with the healthy checkbook that might allow them to buy it. "At least Mrs. Frugalicious is getting some positive exposure in the midst of everything."

"Speaking of which," Trent said. "Heard anything from Contrary Claire yet?"

"Not yet," I said, folding and putting away my reusable [25] shopping bags. The blog continued to fill with condolences and comments from Frugarmy members, many of whom had been at Bargain Barn. But none of them bore the initials CC or claimed to be a friend of Cathy's.

"The lady who died had the initials CC," Trent said to FJ.

"Seriously?" FJ asked.

"Isn't that weird?" Trent said.

"Did Eloise tell you that?" I asked.

"I heard Joyce telling Dad," Trent said.

"So Contrary Claire hasn't tried to post anything about what happened last night?" FJ asked.

"Not so far," I said. "I'm thinking maybe she hasn't heard about it yet."

"But it's been all over the news," Trent said. "And so have you."

---

25. Reusable bags are not only good for the environment and carry way more than plastic bags, but they often earn bag credits.

"She must have gone out of town or something," I said.

"Could be." FJ knit his brows in just the way my brilliant, beloved, and long-departed grandfather used to when he was putting the facts of a case together for trial. "Unless CC and Cathy Carter—"

"Can't be," I said, trying to ignore the growing dread I couldn't totally shake. "It has to be a coincidence."

"Does it?" FJ asked.

"CC made a point of saying she wasn't coming to Bargain Barn."

"But what if she did anyway?" Trent asked. "Wouldn't it be kinda cool if—"

"Trent, there's nothing cool about someone dying," I said.

"No." Trent looked mildly apologetic. "But—"

"But, if she did show up," FJ said, "and then the pallet just happened to fall on her of all people, you kinda have to wonder if there's a connection."

My phone chirped from the paper goods shelf behind Trent.

"It's Alan Bader," he said turning to look at the display.

"Got it," I said, lunging across the room.

"Alan," I answered, stopping myself from launching into an immediate breathless diatribe in which I repeated the entire message I'd already left on his phone.

"Sorry I haven't been able to get back before now." Alan's voice was hoarse and his tone subdued, like he'd been sedated. "The investigation didn't wrap up until six this morning."

"Did they at least figure out what happened?"

"No," he said definitively.

"No?" My growing confusion only increased. "Frank said he'd overheard the emergency responders saying something about the pallet being at an odd angle. That they were thinking the vibration from so many people lined up along the aisle and pushing against the shelves sent it off the edge."

"That's what they're saying," he said.

I sensed something in Alan's tone. "But you don't think so?"

"I don't know how it happened, or why it happened, but a double decker pallet doesn't just fall of a shelf," he said, his voice suddenly steely. "Not in my store."

"Meaning what?" I asked.

"I don't care what anyone says," Alan said. "This was no accident."

TEN

I swore I'd never set foot in the South Metro Police Station after my last visit as an overnight guest in their no-star accommodations, but not long after talking to Alan I found myself walking through the glass doors and into the hot, crowded lobby.

The last thing I wanted to do was get in the middle of another investigation, but given Alan's certainty the accident was anything but accidental and my uncertainty about the CC/Cathy Carter connection, how could I not let the authorities know there might be more going on than met the eye?

Even a pair of eyes belonging to a trained investigator.

I took in a breath of the stale body odor and paper-tinged air and walked up to the uniformed policewoman at the front desk. "Detective McClarkey, please."

"Your name?" she asked, her eyes on the paperwork in front of her.

"Maddie Michaels," I said.

"As in Mrs. Frugalicious?" she asked, looking up.

"That's me." I managed an awkward smile as she looked me over with an expression that said either *I heard all about last night* or *I remember the last mess you were caught up in* or *I'm a fan of your website*. My best guess was some combination of all three.

"Can I let him know what this is in regards to?"

"I have some information I wanted to bring to his attention about the events at Bargain Barn."

She picked up the phone and pointed me toward the waiting area. "Have a seat and I'll let him know you're here."

"Thanks," I said, heading for the cleanest of the dingy, gray plastic chairs.

To avoid making eye contact with the man across from me, wearing a trench coat, a comb-over, and what appeared to be nothing else, I pulled out my phone and checked my Frugalicious email. As I expected, there was still nothing from CC or anyone claiming to be Cathy Carter's friend.

Which Trent, FJ, and I all agreed was definitely weird.

While I was at it, I fired off a note to the Frugarmy inquiring into mom-and-pop store specials for Small Business Saturday. Anastasia wanted to meet first thing in the morning, but even with the recaps of the accident and its aftermath, the tribute to Cathy, and Anastasia's assurance that viewers would see me as a Good Samaritan, I couldn't just show up somewhere and shop as though nothing had happened.

Better the Frugarmy made the call about where we should go.

A few minutes later, the wood partition separating the reception from the processing area of the station swung open, and, like déjà vu all over again, Detective McClarkey ambled into the room.

"Maddie Michaels!" he said, this time with genuine warmth and no hint of the suspicion that tinged my first (and certainly my second) visit to the station. "Wrong place at the right time again?"

"Sure seems that way," I said, somehow emboldened not only by his overly firm handshake, but by his whole handsome, blue-eyed, graying crew cut, square-jawed detective vibe. Not to mention the corduroy sport coat I'd never seen him without.

He offered a crooked but not unattractive smile and a friendly, *we're in this together* wink as he motioned me to follow him. "Seems like just about everyone was at Bargain Barn last night."

"Tell me about it," I said, following him on a familiar serpentine path around the metal desks.

"Did I hear Frank Finance was even on hand for the festivities?"

Considering he'd been there when Frank's marital misdeed had revealed herself, the detective's curiosity wasn't entirely surprising. "He came to help me out with my TV appearance."

He stopped briefly at the coffee pot. "Aren't you two in the middle of a divorce?"

"The holidays complicate things," I said, waving off another opportunity for a steaming hot cup of tarrish-looking brew.

"I hear you there." He shook his head. "I have to pretend I can stand the sight of my ex from now through New Year's for the sake of the kids."

I began to sweat thinking of the potential loneliness and discord I had to look forward to in my future holiday seasons. The sweat ramped up as I looked into the interrogation room with its imitation wood grain table, banged up chairs, two-way mirror, and the inherent supposition of guilt. Luckily, Detective McClarkey stopped short and lead me into his glassed-in office instead.

"Have a seat," he said.

As I hung my handbag on the back of the chair, he reached into his shirt pocket for a mini-tape recorder.

"Here we go again," I said.

"Department policy."

I nodded and took a long, slow centering breath.

"I'm speaking with Maddie Michaels," he said, pulling a paper and notepad toward him from across the desk. "Is that correct?"

"Correct."

"And what is it that brings you in today?"

"Well…" I paused to take a deep breath. "As you know, I was at Bargain Barn as part of a Channel Three feature on Black Friday shopping during and after the events that occurred in the store last night."

"By Black Friday, you mean Thursday, correct?"

"Yes," I said. "The Bargain Barn sale, along with many others, started well before midnight on Thanksgiving evening."

"And by *events,* please describe exactly what you mean?"

"I was in the store when a pallet of toasters fell and killed a woman now identified as Catherine Carter," I said as officially and factually as possible. "Alan Bader, the owner of Bargain Barn, told me the event was determined to be an accident."

Detective McClarkey nodded.

"So it *was* ruled an accident?" I asked.

"I can neither confirm nor deny until the official report is released," he said. "But, from what I'm hearing, things are pretty clear cut."

"Alan Bader seems convinced there's more to the story," I blurted as much as said.

Detective McClarkey jotted a note. "How so?"

"He claims there's no way a double-decker pallet could have slipped with the safety procedures he has in place at the store."

"If I were him I'd be scrambling for a different scenario too."

"Why's that?"

"Awesome Alan's not gonna be so *awesome* when the lawsuits start rolling in from everyone who got a nick, scratch, or thinks they may be able to cash in and make a buck."

My stomach began to churn anew.

I'd assumed Alan's flat initial response to his bustling store was the result of stress, shock, and fear about the potential revenue loss. I hadn't really thought about the inevitable litigation. Particularly from the distraught and now hospitalized John Carter, Cathy's husband.

It was certainly one explanation for Alan's strong aversion to the word *accident*.

"As soon as the report is official, it'll be up to Bargain Barn's insurance adjusters to do any further digging."

"So that's it?" I asked. "Case closed?"

He looked up. "What else you got?"

"It's just that…" I took a deep breath. "I'm sure it has to be an awful, unfortunate accident just like everyone is saying, but there's just one thing…"

"Which is?"

"My online heckler."

"Your online heckler?"

"In the last few months, this person popped up and has been making snarky, critical remarks about practically everything I post on Mrs. Frugalicious."

"Your website?" he asked.

"Yes," I said pulling out my phone. I pulled up my website and scrolled through all of Contrary Claire's messages, recounting the one I'd erased word for word and how the boys had blocked future messages. "That is, until today."

"I get that she's an annoyance, but why exactly is it so suspicious to you that she hasn't commented about last night?"

"Her initials are CC," I said, pointing to a comment she'd made complaining about her grocery store refusing to allow a particularly obscure combination of coupons I'd specifically said might or might not work together. "As in Cathy Carter."

"Hmm." He raised a bushy eyebrow. "So you're thinking the deceased and this online heckler could be the same person?"

"CC said she wasn't coming to Bargain Barn last night, but as the hours tick by and there's no comment from her, I can't help but wonder…"

Detective McClarkey jotted a note.

"I mean, the story's been all over the media since last night and there hasn't been a word from CC since Cathy's… incident."

"Didn't you say you'd blocked her though?"

"I'm supposed to get an email with a preview of her comments so I can decide whether to post or not, but there's been nothing to post," I said. "I even wrote a condolence blog this morning, but there was no response. Not even from anyone who seemed to know or be friends with Cathy Carter."

"I see," he said.

"And, according to Anastasia, she was fairly new in town and kept to herself, so that fits too."

"Interesting," he said.

"I thought so," I said.

Neither of us said anything for a second.

"If CC and Cathy Carter are, in fact, the same person, and she did meet her end at Bargain Barn, I have to wonder if Alan Bader might be right that there's more to the story than a random pallet of toasters falling on an innocent bystander in his store."

"As in, she was such an unpleasant person, someone knew she was going to be at Bargain Barn and timed it just right so they could sneak unnoticed up onto an upper shelf and crush her by pushing a double pallet off the edge?"

"I know it seems far-fetched, but it really is a little strange that the person who happened to die last night just might be CC as opposed to, really, anyone else in my Frugarmy."

Detective McClarkey put down his pencil. "Agreed."

"So you think it's worth looking into too?" I asked.

He raised his caterpillar of an eyebrow once again. "Sure you want us to?"

"Why wouldn't I?"

"Maddie," he smiled kindly, "there's no doubting what a great job you did with the DeSimone case, and for that I'm incredibly thankful. I'm still sorry I didn't believe you much sooner, but what are the odds you've chanced into two homicides in the past three months?"

"Not great, I'll admit, but—"

"But if, for the sake of argument, you're right and it was the case that CC not only is Cathy Carter but also the victim of foul play designed to look like an accident while in line at Bargain Barn, who do you think would be the most likely suspect, or even suspects?"

"Judging by all the comments to her negative posts, there could be a number of people who might feel inclined to let her know how out of line she's been." The butterflies flittering across my stomach began to migrate toward my throat. "Although I can't really imagine that anyone in my Frugarmy would go so far as to try and kill her over something like that."

"Me either," he said.

"Whoever might have done such a thing would need a much more compelling motive."

"Exactly," he said, turning off his tape recorder. "Like, for example, someone whose business she was threatening with her criticisms, perhaps?"

My heart began to pound harder than it had since the last time I'd been at the South Metro Police Department being accused of a crime I didn't commit. "You're not trying to imply that I ... Why on earth would I tell you she was my heckler and implicate myself if I—"

"Maddie, you're the last person I'd suspect, but I'm not heading up this particular investigation. If I pass along what you've told me, I have no way of controlling what the detective in charge will think or decide to do with it."

"So you think I'd end up as the prime suspect again?"

"A group of highly trained investigators have looked into the incident and the victim and have ruled this to be an accident." He patted the back of my hand with his. "No sense looking for trouble where there isn't any."

"But ..."

"I'll definitely give you a buzz if I have any further questions." Detective McClarkey pressed the erase button on his tape recorder and winked. "So don't go fleeing the country or anything."

ELEVEN

WHILE FLEEING THE COUNTRY for somewhere warm and tropical where no one could possibly find out I'd just made a fool of myself at the police station sounded appealing, I couldn't even figure out how to sneak past the boys on the way to the relative escape of my bedroom.

"What did Detective McClarkey say?" FJ asked, deigning to look up from the Xbox as I walked past.

I stopped and recounted the conversation.

"The primary suspect?" Trent's incredulous voice boomed across the family room. "Again?"

"Shh!" I said, not at all interested in having him broadcasting the details of my near-predicament in the form of a wake-up call to the relatives, all of whom were napping in various locations throughout the house. "Detective McClarkey knows I had nothing to do with what happened."

"That's a relief," Trent said.

"What does he think happened, though?" FJ asked, pausing the game.

All I could think about, beyond finishing my conversation with the boys and stumbling upstairs for my overdue nap, was why I hadn't stayed out of this mess by putting myself down when everyone else had gone to catch up on their shut-eye. I'd not only be close to caught up on sleep by now, I'd have avoided making a complete idiot out of myself in front of Detective McClarkey.

I wouldn't have felt the sting of his *don't go fleeing the country* sign-off yet again.

"The detective said the incident's been ruled an accident and there's no reason to look into it any further." At least he hadn't given me a patronizing pat on the head and called me Nancy Drew.

"And he didn't think it was weird that CC hasn't said a word since Cathy Carter died?" Trent asked in a modulated, but still booming voice.

"He thinks Cathy Carter was crushed by accident and that Awesome Alan's just having a hard time accepting it because Bargain Barn will be facing a mountain of negligence lawsuits."

"Seriously?" Trent asked.

"Even if CC and Cathy Carter turn out to be the same person?" FJ asked.

"If CC and Cathy are the same person, she was directing so much of her criticism at me that if someone did kill her, I look like a prime suspect."

"Like you were so mad because of her complaining that you tried to off her?" FJ asked.

"Something like that," I said, my head spinning with the mere thought of it.

"It sort of makes sense when you think about it," Trent said.

"Trent!" FJ and I said in unison.

"Well, you did block her emails," Trent said. "Which, technically, makes you look even guiltier."

"Never mind we did the blocking for her," FJ said.

"Wouldn't that kind of make us accessories?" Trent asked.

"Oh lord!" How unbelievably stupid had I been to march down to the police station with my flimsy, self-incriminating, novice suspicions?

"How could Mom even know CC would change her mind and come to Bargain Barn, much less plan out how to off her if she did?" FJ asked.

"Good point," Trent said.

"I have no idea what Contrary Claire even looks like or who she is in real life," I added.

"So no worries." FJ smiled.

Trent nodded in agreement.

Thank goodness Detective McClarkey agreed with them or I'd have been right back at the top of South Metro's suspect list like I'd been when the police thought I was responsible for the death of Eternally 21 manager Laila DeSimone, the other person who'd managed to unceremoniously drop dead right in front of me.

I sighed.

"So what now?" Trent asked.

"I take my nap, we forget about all this, and the authorities remain unconcerned about who Cathy Carter was or wasn't."

"That's cool, I guess," Trent said.

FJ shrugged. "Whatever."

Before they could un-pause the Xbox, I heard a rustle and footsteps from the basement, where most of Frank's family were bunking for the weekend.

"Boys," Joyce called, making her way up the stairs. "Do you need a sandwich or some cookies or something to tide you over until dinner?"

"FYI," I whispered, before scampering off to the safety and quiet of my upstairs part of the house. "Unless there's a fire, consider my door to have a DO NOT DISTURB hanging from it until I wake up."

I made it to my bedroom, locked myself in, detoured for a quick stop to the bathroom, and was milliseconds into enjoying that divine moment of pillow-meets-head when I heard the faintest of pings coming from inside my zipped purse.

I sighed, sat up, and forced myself out of bed and across the room to silence my smartphone for a few hours.

I was definitely disturbed when I spotted the email that had popped up in my Mrs. Frugalicious inbox.

All's well that ends well.
Regards,
CC

TWELVE

SEEING AS A CALL to Detective McClarkey or even Griff was tantamount to writing my name at the top of the police department World's Stupidest Suspect list, I spent the evening hiding out in my bedroom, where no one would question me about the lines of concern etching my face. I pretended to be down for the count when Frank knocked lightly to check in, and again an hour later when Joyce left what appeared to be a turkey casserole outside my door.

I could no more force down her grayish, gooey concoction than sleep with *all's well that ends well* running on an endless loop through my head. Especially given that the message, which contained nothing more in the way of elaboration or explanation, was signed *CC*.

Meaning the accident was truly just that and Contrary Claire was alive, well, and definitely someone other than Catherine Carter—albeit someone who had risen beyond penning dismissive comments about my blog topics and on to dismissing the life of another human being?

The sheer callousness of it all struck me as shocking.

Even for her.

But now I had an email address—cc@coupclip.com—which I Googled.

Nothing in particular came up.

I put the URL into my browser.

When the only thing that came up was one of those vague guides to similar website addresses, I thought about replying to CC's comment with a one-liner: *Who are you?*

Instead, and having thought better of it, I found myself doing the only other thing I could think of to herd the thoughts milling around my brain like a bunch of wayward alley cats.

I started a spreadsheet,[26] titled a tab *Questions & Answers*, and typed: *Was the accident really an accident?*

Hypotheses and corollaries began to sprout from there.

1. Yes. If the accident really was an accident, as the police concluded, and the pallet of toasters had been placed improperly on the upper shelf at Bargain Barn, then there is no more to the story.

Except for the eerie message in my inbox. And the question of who had left it. An exceptionally cold Contrary Claire who was gloating over having stayed home?

---

26. While they may take a bit of doing to create, there is no better tool for keeping track of the best prices and the best places to shop for the items you buy most than a set of spreadsheets that are easy to read, maintain, and update.

Why would anyone send such a comment in the first place unless they hated sweet-faced, friendly Cathy Carter and wanted her gone?

Which led to the more likely answer to my question.

2. No.

Maybe I couldn't call Detective McClarkey, but there was one person I could contact—someone who needed to know about the existence of the email and its seemingly malevolent message. Someone who wouldn't arouse suspicion by reporting my findings to the police.

Since it was the middle of the night and phoning was only for true emergencies, I fired off a text to Alan Bader. I hoped the message was insistent but not alarming enough that he'd feel he needed to contact me before morning:

CAN YOU PLEASE GET BACK WHEN YOU HAVE A SECOND? THERE'S SOMETHING I'D REALLY LIKE TO RUN BY YOU.

As soon as I pressed send, I immediately felt less alone with my suspicions and began adding questions to my spreadsheet, ones Alan would surely ask when we did talk.

Questions I wanted answered ASAP.

Were Catherine Carter and CC (Contrary Claire) the same person?

1. Yes. If so, then she couldn't possibly have sent an odd message after her demise. Right?

2. No. If not, then who was CC and why was she happy Cathy Carter was dead?

3. Maybe?

I exhaled deeply.

Either Cathy and CC were the same person and both had been murdered and someone pretending to be CC sent me the message for reasons I couldn't yet begin to grasp, or Cathy was dead and CC was alive but hated Cathy enough to kill her and gloat over it.

Or…?

As my head swam with convoluted possibilities, the Frugarmy continued to write in with tips about local businesses offering Small Business Saturday specials. Despite a few good ones, I was growing that much more uncomfortable about doling out bargain shopping advice on camera as if nothing had happened at all. I minimized the window on what I'd intended to be a spreadsheet (but was really evolving into a loose flow chart of possibilities) and tried to zero in on a few of the better suggestions.

And then a certain Barbara M. wrote in with a perfect idea:

We all know Black Friday weekend is about scoring great deals and bargains, but what about the rest of the year, when we depend on small stores and establishments to add flavor to our community in ways that mass-market retailers simply can't? Instead of trying to save pennies on Small Business Saturday, I vote for forming a cash mob[27] where we band together and spend an extra dollar or two at one of our local shopping districts.

I immediately forwarded the contents of the message to Anastasia, who was sure to appreciate the community spirit of it all as

---

27. A group of shoppers who band together to spend money and thus stimulate the economy of a small area, locally owned store, or group of stores.

much as I did. Stopping short of coaxing the Frugarmy to form an actual cash mob after the events of the previous evening, I posted:

Thanks to Frugarmy member Barbara M.'s terrific suggestion, I've decided to spend Small Business Saturday shopping on Main Street in downtown Littleton. I'd love it if she and any other interested shoppers would care to join me tomorrow morning to show our appreciation for our local retailers.

With a workable plan suddenly in place for my Saturday segment with Anastasia, I turned back to the far more murky business of adding more questions and answers to the spreadsheet:

Was Cathy Carter, whoever she was, murdered?
1. No.
2. Yes.

I went ahead, put a presumptive red line through NO. Which led to the most important questions of all:

Who killed Catherine Carter?
Why?

My text message alert pinged.

Reaching for the phone to look at the text, presumably from Alan, I wondered how I'd thought he could possibly be sleeping either. Instead, I found myself faced with a different question from a completely different insomniac.

Can't sleep. Been watching a late-night rebroadcast of you on TV and thinking about our conversation last night. Any chance we could continue it?

The text, from Frank, sent the divorce butterflies fluttering toward my throat. There was another ping.

IT MEANING THE CONVERSATION ...

And then another.

IT ALSO MEANING US ...?

After a few minutes of hyperventilating, which did little to calm me or the butterflies that had migrated and settled into my brain, I found myself staring at a new spreadsheet.

Actually, more of a Benjamin Franklin Decision T.

On one side of the document I listed reasons why I didn't want to get divorced in the first place:

Negative effect on the kids.

Splitting up a household and family that was supposed to be forever.

Emotional turmoil.

Increased financial difficulties.

Legal bills.

Lonely, difficult holiday seasons for years to come.

Lonely, difficult non-holiday seasons for years to come.

Mrs. Frugalicious becomes Ms.

Online dating.

Divorce sucks.

On the other side of the page I listed the single reason I felt I had to go through with it:

Frank's affair.

My text alert pinged again:

YOU AWAKE UP THERE?

Instead of answering, I closed my laptop and put my head down on the pillow.

THIRTEEN

"No Frank or Michaels-family entourage this morning?" Anastasia asked as we met up on Main Street in Historic Downtown Littleton—once a pioneer town south of Denver proper, now a charming suburban shopping area filled with locally owned shops, galleries, and cafés.

"They all slept in," I said, marveling at how I'd somehow managed to sneak out of the house unnoticed for my morning on-air duties.

I was also wondering how long Frank stayed awake waiting for a response I wasn't ready to give.

And I was assuming Awesome Alan, who hadn't gotten back yet, was still asleep too.

Along with CC…

"They may have slept in," Anastasia said, noting the growing group of shoppers amassing around us, "but your Frugarmy certainly seems to have mobilized."

Which was a whole other problem.

Considering true bargain shopping wasn't on the agenda and given the peril they'd faced the last time I'd summoned the troops, I was more than a little taken aback by the four or five dozen people drinking coffee from the local café while they waited for the stores to open.

A few of whom were already in front of the camera being interviewed for pre-shopping color commentary:

Mrs. Frugalicious handled things so well after that awful accident the other night, I became an instant fan. —Jennifer G.

I'm not much for big-box stores or Black Friday mayhem, but when I heard about Small Business Saturday, I came right over. —Kara K.

As Anastasia smiled and gave me an *isn't this great?* wink, I scrutinized Kara K. and the others to see if they looked in any way familiar.

As the owner of Laura's Organic Pet Care, I understand the challenges facing small businesses, so I came out to support my fellow independent business owners. —Laura F.

Historic Downtown Littleton is the best! I come here whenever I get the chance. —Candy P.

I couldn't help but feel a little suspicious, and not just by the somewhat obvious plants from the Chamber of Commerce disguised as Frugarmy members that were (understandably) promoting their own interests. I'd watched enough crime dramas over the years to know that any of the people being interviewed or standing in the crowd might well be Contrary Claire herself. Killers often returned to crime scenes or events associated with their crime to gloat and gauge reaction in the aftermath of what they'd done...

I glanced into my purse for what had to be the hundredth time that morning and checked my cell phone.

There was still no further word from her or Alan.

Anastasia, on the other hand, always had the latest word. If only her fiancé weren't the acting chief of the South Metro Police and she herself wasn't a bloodhound for any and all things newsworthy, I'd have grilled her about potential new developments the moment she stepped out of the news van.

"Anastasia?" I asked, settling for what I hoped would be some nonchalant but useful brain-picking.

"Stasia," an assistant producer called before I could. "We're ready for you now."

And the next thing I knew, I was once again trying not to blink before the unblinking eye of the TV news camera.

"Good morning from Historic Downtown Littleton. I'm here with my special correspondent Maddie Michaels, AKA Mrs. Frugalicious," Anastasia started, her expression morphing from animated to serious. "As all of you who've been following our reports know, this Black Friday weekend was darkened by the terrible accident both Maddie and I had the misfortune of witnessing late Thursday evening."

The camera light clicked off while they ran a taped montage of Bargain Barn, the overturned pallet, and the mayhem that followed, as well as a dated glamour shot they'd been running for the past day and half of Catherine Carter.

Anastasia let out a huge yawn. "Two days without sleep is start-ing to hit me."

"I hear you," I said.

"I guess we'll rest when we're dead," she said checking her teeth for lipstick and tucking a stray strand of otherwise perfectly coiffed hair behind her ear. "Were you going to ask me something?"

"I was just wondering if there'd been any new information about Cathy?"

"Not really," she said "Other than—"

"Live in three, two, one . . ." the assistant producer said.

"We extend our deepest sympathies to her family and loved ones," Anastasia said somberly, while I merely nodded along in agreement and wondered what it was she didn't have the chance to tell me. "Fortunately, hope springs eternal, particularly on this bright, clear morning thanks to Mrs. Frugalicious and the group of her followers, better known as the Frugarmy, who've joined us today for Small Business Saturday."

Cheers rose from the group behind us.

"As you can tell, these shoppers are not only devoted, but un-daunted by crowds, lines, or the unexpected. In fact, they've come out en masse, cash in hand, to support our local businesses."

"Woo-hoo!" someone shouted.

"I have to admit," Anastasia grinned and turned to me. "I don't think I'd ever heard of Small Business Saturday before this week-end."

"That's not surprising" I said, surprised I'd already become so accustomed to being on camera that, despite wearing a coat, scarf, and gloves for the clear, cool, but not frigid morning, I wasn't per-spiring in the least. "Small Business Saturday was actually started as a business promotion by American Express in 2010 to boost spending at locally owned retailers, many of whom dreaded the Black Friday shopping weekend, knowing they'd likely be overlooked in favor of big chain stores with larger marketing budgets and huge doorbuster specials."

"Sounds like an all-around win-win," Anastasia said.

"Especially since Small Business Saturday has become something of a national movement boosted by consumer interest in buying local and supporting small businesses," I said. "With local establishments comprising nearly eighty percent of the total businesses here in Denver, the money we spend locally has an immediate impact on our community."

"With so many wonderful restaurants, bakeries, boutiques, and craft galleries, I can't think of a more perfect location to boost our economy," Anastasia said.

"There are many terrific stores to support all over the city," I said. "When I found out we were going to be taping today, I deferred to the Frugarmy and received a number of great ideas, which I've listed on my website."

"That's MrsFrugalicious-dot-com, right?"

"Yes. Thank you, Anastasia," I said. "And I have to give credit for the idea of shopping on Main Street to Barbara M., who suggested we all band together and patronize the various businesses together in what's become known as a cash mob. I'm hoping she's here today so I can thank her personally."

The camera panned the crowd.

No one stepped forward.

"Barbara?" Anastasia asked again. "Are you here?"

An awkward silence followed. It was only broken when my cell phone, ringer on and just in range of the mic attached to my collar, pinged.

And pinged again.

Luckily the clock almost simultaneously struck nine, the doors to storefronts began to open, and the Frugarmy dissolved as shoppers rushed into the various stores. Anastasia quickly signed off.

"Gotta be sure and turn your phone every time from now on," she said as soon as the camera light went off and the cameraman took off to tape the shoppers mob a nearby clothing store. "I mean, tomorrow."

"I'm so sorry," I said, not wanting to add insult to injury by pulling my cell from my pocket but too itchy not to glance at the message, which just had to be from Alan.

And it was.

Can you come over to the store ASAP?

"Do we have a plan for tomorrow?" I asked.

"Just waiting for time confirmation on Cathy Carter's memorial service at the North Suburban Community Church tomorrow morning," she said, finally divulging what had to be that mysterious bit of information she didn't get to share before the camera turned on. "We're all going."

"All?"

"You, me"—she paused to yawn again—"and the cameraman."

FOURTEEN

I wasn't at all convinced that having Channel Three news tape us at Catherine Carter's memorial service was (as Anastasia insisted) not only in acceptable taste, but the ideal way to let viewers know we cared about the deceased and her family.

Then again, I wasn't sure about much of anything as I left the Frugarmy on Main Street and raced over to Bargain Barn. Was Contrary Claire incognito amongst the cash mob? Was the email a hoax and she was, in fact, dead? Why hadn't Barbara M., who'd suggested we all shop together in the first place, bothered to show up? Why did Alan want to see me ASAP?

I didn't have to wonder about the last question for very long since Alan was standing outside the entrance to the store as I pulled up.

"Mind if we talk out here?" he asked, opening the door to my car and jumping in the passenger seat. "The walls have ears, if you know what I mean."

"Okay," I said, but I wondered if *he* was okay as I pulled into a nearby parking space and killed the engine.

He certainly didn't look okay.

Alan's eyes were bloodshot, his hair unkempt, and his beard well past the five o'clock shadow stage. His wrinkled, semi-stained, Bargain Barn polo and khakis told me he hadn't changed anytime recently. And, seeing as his woodsy, spicy, soapy smell had given way to a somewhat less pleasant undertone, I strongly suspected he hadn't showered, either.

"It took me all night . . ." he said, confirming my overriding suspicion that he hadn't slept or been home at all. "But I figured it out."

"You've figured out what happened?"

"I've devoted my career to being on top of everything there is to know about competitive business models, corporate strategy, sales techniques, and hostile takeovers." He shook his head. "Never in my wildest dreams did I imagine they'd go this far."

"They?" I asked.

"I haven't figured out how they pulled it off, and I don't know which one of the big-box outfits is behind this," he said. "But I will."

My head, already throbbing, began to spin. "You think one of the chain retailers—"

"They haven't been able to kill Bargain Barn, so they resorted to the next best thing."

"Killing a shopper in your store?"

"In the middle of the Black Friday shopping crush," he whispered as though someone in the parking lot could possibly hear through the closed windows of my car. "As brilliant as it is cold-blooded and evil, don't you think?"

All I could think was that the suggestion of a corporate "hit" or whatever it was he'd convinced himself had happened, fell somewhere on the spectrum between sleep-deprived delusion and stress-induced temporary insanity.

"They figured the *accident* would not only scare shoppers away, causing receipts to go down on the most crucial night of the year, but simultaneously put a taint on the store forever." His voice cracked. "Not to mention making us uninsurable."

"But Alan, I—"

"You," he said, not pausing long enough for me to contribute my two cents. "If it weren't for you, they'd have already succeeded."

"Me?"

He managed a weak smile. "Because of you, your Frugarmy, and all the TV coverage, we still had the best Black Friday receipts we've ever had."

And Frank, I didn't say, even though he was the one who really deserved the thanks. I would have panicked had he not talked me off the ledge late Thursday night.

"It wasn't until the next morning, when the store went dead and stayed dead, that I figured out what had to have happened. I mean, who wants to spend their Thanksgiving shopping in a store hexed by tragedy?"

"Alan, I'm sure shoppers will be back in droves once the commotion dies down."

"By that time Bargain Barn will be so devalued and broke from paying out on lawsuits that whoever is behind this will have bought me out for pennies on the dollar."

"Have you spoken to the police about all of this?"

"They've already tied things up with a neat bow and don't want to hear about it." He pulled a handkerchief from his pocket and pretended to blow his nose while he surreptitiously dabbed tears from the corners of his eyes. "So I really can't until I have some firm evidence."

"Which I may have," I said, thinking of CC's latest message.

He looked up.

"I got an email."

"What kind of email?"

"Here's the thing…" I took a deep breath of the stale car air. "There's this person who's constantly making critical comments about everything on my website."

"You mean that CC person?"

"You know who she is?"

"I saw her comment about not coming to Bargain Barn on Thursday night."

"I was hoping you hadn't," I said.

"I was a little bugged until I noticed that she seemed to have something to say about almost everything you've posted lately."

"She's definitely been a nuisance, but I honestly didn't think all that much about her either. Not until I heard the victim's name."

"Cathy Carter," he said.

"Kind of coincidental they share the same initials, don't you think?"

"Very," he said.

"Unfortunately, the police don't seem to agree."

Alan's eyes widened. "You've already spoken with them?"

I sighed and recounted my interview with Detective McClarkey, his suggestion that opening the investigation might well cast suspicion directly on me, and my decision to tell Alan about the email I'd received yesterday afternoon before approaching them again.

"And you say this email was signed CC?"

I nodded.

"And what exactly did it say?"

I took a deep breath. "All's well that ends well."

I waited for Alan to process everything I'd said and start asking the questions I'd been asking myself since yesterday afternoon:

So you think CC actually is Cathy Carter and someone got mad enough to kill her, or she's a homicidal maniac who happened to target a woman with her same initials?

And a few I hadn't thought of yet:

This doesn't exactly jibe with my theory, but I have to say it's a relief to think Big Box Brother isn't out to get me.

"There's only one possible conclusion," Alan finally said after what felt like an interminable silence.

"Which is?"

"They must have been tracking my every move these past months, knew I was doing an advertising push on your website, and set me up."

I was now sure that lack of sleep and stress had sent Alan off the rails. "By having CC heckle me?"

"Or at least figuring out who she was and somehow enticing her to go to the store so they could—"

My cell, sitting face up on the console between us, began to ring. We both looked down as *Frank Cell* appeared in the display.

"I'll get that later," I said, without picking up the phone or allowing myself to wonder what he wanted.

What I wanted.

Alan now looked as perplexed as he did wild-eyed. "I have to say I was kind of surprised to see him and his whole family the other night."

"It was something of a surprise to me too," I said.

"Aren't you two in the middle of a divorce?"

"Yes," I said, nodding. "But it's complicated."

"Got it," he said, almost as dismissively as Detective McClarkey had.

"I wish I did," I said, in reference not only to my marital situation, but to Alan's seemingly reality-challenged theory of corporate espionage, greed, and murder. "In any case—"

My text alert pinged.

I looked down, dreading a repeat of last night's text from Frank.

Luckily, it was Anastasia:

Carter memorial service confirmed for tomorrow at ten am.

Alan, who had once again reflexively looked down when I did, simply nodded.

"You already knew about the service?"

"The husband was in no condition to plan anything," Alan said. "And considering his wife was killed by corporate scumbags bent on destroying *my* business, I felt like I had no choice but make the arrangements for the Carters."

"You arranged the memorial service?"

"It seemed like the right thing to do," he said reaching for his handkerchief again.

"Alan, that was exceptionally kind of you," I said, touching his shoulder and thinking about my own culpability. After all, Cathy

Carter, whoever she was, would still be alive if I hadn't recommended she shop at Bargain Barn Thursday night.

"I couldn't possibly have put together my own wife's funeral." His voice cracked. "I barely made it through that day."

"Your wife . . . ?"

He nodded.

"I'm so sorry," I said, feeling the utter hollowness of the only words I could think of to say. "I had no idea."

"It's been almost ten years," he said as though it was both forever ago and yesterday.

I was trying to figure out how to politely inquire about what happened when Alan spotted a pair of shoppers who'd stopped outside the store and began to compare something on their smartphones.

"Damn it," he said, "they look like secret shoppers."

"Secret shoppers?" I asked.

"Sent by whoever's behind all this," he whispered, opening the car door and sliding out. "Let's talk later."

FIFTEEN

My plan had been to pass along my information to Alan, let him go to the police with it, and, as Detective McClarkey advised, not look for any more trouble. Instead, I sat in my car watching Alan size up what looked like garden-variety shoppers before slinking past and disappearing through the employee entrance to the store.

Clearly, lack of sleep and stress were working against Alan's mental equilibrium. It was awfully far-fetched to believe a corporation would be so desperate to put a single-location family-owned business, even one as established and prominent as Bargain Barn, out of business that they would "accidentally" kill off a shopper. But, as I thumbed through my emails, stopping at the message from CC, I was glad to have a place to start, theory-wise.

On the unlikely assumption that a *mystery* corporation had been tracking Bargain Barn's moves, they would likely know about his advertising push on my blog. The problem was, this shady entity (whoever they were) would have to have been aware of CC's negative posts, managed to locate her right after she trash-talked Bargain

Barn, and then somehow convinced her to go out and shop there just so they could kill her off.

Somehow, it didn't quite add up.

If—and it seemed awfully iffy—CC was some sort of plant in the first place, it was theoretically possible that Alan and Bargain Barn were being set up to fail. Albeit in one of the oddest, twistiest ways imaginable.

I still couldn't quite get my head around the details, but one way or another, I felt even more sure that whatever happened wasn't just an unfortunate, untimely accident.

While I figured I'd leave the investigating of murderous corporations to my new partner in solving a crime no one else believed had been committed, I did have an email address that, in the hands of someone with some actual technical savvy, could very well be key to everything.

I picked up my cell and texted FJ:

IS THERE ANY WAY TO LOCATE WHO OR WHERE AN EMAIL CAME FROM?

My return message pinged almost immediately.

MEANING YOU HEARD FROM CC?

I DUG UP AN OLD EMAIL, I wrote, not wanting to worry him with the real details. I WAS HOPING YOU MIGHT BE ABLE TO TRACK WHERE IT CAME FROM.

IT'S NOT LIKE I'M A COMPUTER CSI GUY, came back. BUT I CAN TRY.

THANKS, I wrote, forwarding the cc@coupclip.com address and wondering how long the process might take.

BUT NOT TILL WE GET BACK HOME.

WHERE ARE YOU? I asked.

SOME PEOPLE ARE COMING TO SEE THE HOUSE AGAIN.

THERE'S ANOTHER SHOWING?

DAD SAYS TO LISTEN TO THE VOICEMAIL HE JUST LEFT YOU.

I exited my text messages, went to voicemail, and listened to the message I'd planned to leave unplayed, at least for a while:

Maddie, the realtor just saw you on TV and figured this was a good time to have another showing on the house. We need to make ourselves scarce, so I'm taking the gang to lunch and a movie or something. I'll have everyone back before I have to go into work this afternoon. They're all planning to go to that wedding at the mall except Eloise, who says she wants to go but needs a car right after to meet up with some friends. I told her that since you'd need to take two cars anyway, we'd figure it out with her.

———

Since my first priority—heading home for some long overdue rest—wasn't exactly an option for a while, I settled for the next best thing: a mind- and body-rejuvenating trip to the gym.

Despite a recent workout-related near-death encounter, I somehow managed to maintain a commitment to semi-regular exercise. It didn't hurt that Xtreme Fitness had given me a free[28] member-

---

28. Don't be afraid to turn lemons into lemonade when things go "wrong" at a restaurant, service, or retail establishment. Reputable businesses have procedures in place to keep customers happy and coming back. Whether it's a free appetizer on your next visit or a full refund if you're not satisfied, it's worth letting management know when you're not happy. But don't forget—you'll almost always get more bees with honey.

ship for my "troubles," including a lifetime gold membership at Xtreme Challenge, their upscale sister facility.

The new gym not only offered state-of-the-art equipment and exercise classes, but upgraded members received spa treatments at 25% off [29] and a locker, complete with nameplate, to store their workout clothing.

I pulled into the parking lot and went inside.

"Welcome, Mrs. Michaels," the young woman at the front counter said as she scanned my gold-rimmed card. "I've been watching you on TV! I can't believe that lady *died* at Bargain Barn. So awful!"

"I'm hoping a little exercise will give me some relief from the stress of it all."

"I'll bet you could also use the complimentary fifteen-minute Thanksgiving detox chair massage we're offering today after your workout."

While the gesture was nice, I usually passed on their special promotions—primarily because of the awkwardness near the end where the masseuse or aesthetician tried to up-sell the service for another fifteen or thirty minutes (at the regular rate), chargeable directly to your house account.

On the other hand, if someone had told me my safe, cushy, seemingly blissful life as the well-heeled wife of Channel Three's respected Frank Finance Michaels was not only going to come apart at the seams, but that the career I'd developed while trying to keep things together would put me in the midst of not one but two suspicious deaths…

29. While spa treatments can be an ill-afforded luxury, they make ideal gifts. If you find yourself entitled to a discount you won't be using, reap the savings by purchasing the service for someone else.

"What do you have open?" I asked, figuring I'd still have time to shower, get home, and hopefully catch a quick nap before Higgledy the monkey's evening nuptials.

"Let's see," she said looking at the master calendar. "We have a twelve forty-five, and it looks like Susan's coming in at one. Oh, and we have L'Raine coming on at one thirty. She—"

"L'Raine from Xtreme Fitness?" I asked. Not that there could be another L'Raine who happened to be both a massage therapist and work for the Xtreme chain.

"She's usually at our other gym, but we have her on schedule today because of the promotion." The counter girl asked, "Should I book you with her? She's one of our very best."

If L'Raine was, in fact, seeing Griff as I suspected, the last thing I wanted to do was spend fifteen minutes trying *not* to pump her for any pillow talk tidbits she might have gleaned from him about Cathy Carter or Bargain Barn. If she wasn't, she was likely headed on an evening date with my brother-in-law, another topic that wasn't exactly relaxing to think about.

"One thirty is a little long to wait. How about the one o'clock?"

She smiled. "Perfect."

And, thankfully, *perfect* pretty much summed up my next hour.

I slipped into yoga pants and a T-shirt, headed for an elliptical machine, and plugged my headphones into the satellite radio dock. Willing my mind to relax while my body got in gear, I somehow managed to block out everything but working up a sweat to Classic Soul radio.

I spent the first nine minutes of my chair massage having the knots worked out of my neck and shoulders and even had a few preliminary thoughts about what I might eventually say to Frank before I had to politely pass on the offer to extend my massage to a full sixty minutes.

By the time I'd showered and was presentable enough to walk out of the gym, I even had something of an opening for a discussion with Frank. *I really don't know that I can ever fully recover from the nuclear bomb you've dropped on our marriage, but given we will always be co-parents to our terrific kids I'm willing to at least consider the possibility of trying...*

I even managed to circumvent an awkward hello with L'Raine, who was turned away from me and busily working her thumbs down the spine of whoever had taken the one-thirty slot as I made my way out the front door and over to my car.

I started the engine and backed out of my space. As I began to exit the lot, I happened to spot a silver sedan just nondescript enough to be an unmarked police car. Inside, a stocky young man with a close-cropped goatee and a uniform was keying something into his phone. His cap hid what I suspected was a rookie crew cut and obscured his cute, boyish face to the point where I couldn't be positive. Still, it didn't take a seasoned investigator to figure out it was Griff.

I may have bumbled my way through the DeSimone investigation (and once FJ got back with some information, I'd be well on my way to doing the same with another), but it wasn't hard to deduce that Griff and L'Raine had to be an item.

Clearly he'd dropped her off for work and was in the lot sending a message before he took off toward the police station or wherever it was he was heading.

Not that it was any of my business, but somehow, she hadn't struck me as his type when I'd introduced them at her request a few months ago.

As for my business, I wanted and needed to talk to him, but I definitely couldn't.

He looked up and spotted me as I rolled by. Considering his car was in an empty row practically facing mine, I also couldn't just drive off.

Instead, I pulled up along beside him, willed my heart to stop thumping, and rolled down my window.

Griff smiled his dimply smile. "Twice in two days!"

"What are the odds?" I smiled back. "Do you work out here now, too?"

"Actually—" His police radio bleeped. "Hold that thought," he said, answering the call with a string of acronyms and abbreviations.

"Are you going to Higgledy's commitment ceremony tonight?" I asked as soon as he hung up, not necessarily wanting to hear exactly why he was at the gym, even though I'd asked the question in the first place.

"I'm afraid I already have plans," he said. "Glad I ran into you here, though."

Before I could manage a *So you and L'Raine, huh?* he added, "Since I missed you down at the station."

"How did you know I was at the—"

He smiled and shook his head. "Turns out cops are like a bunch of gossipy school girls."

"Apparently so."

"I heard you were there and talking to McClarkey, but I never heard exactly why you'd stopped by."

I wanted to fill Griff in more than anything. He'd know exactly what to think not only of the email I'd received from someone signing off as CC, but of Alan's crazy but increasingly plausible story.

Which was the problem.

If Alan was right that whoever was behind this was dangerous, ruthless, and had connections, I couldn't risk the story becoming stationhouse gossip.

"It was dumb of me to have gone running down there," I said. "I just wanted to let someone know about the coincidence between the name of the person that died and this person whose been a pest on my website."

"Doesn't sound dumb to me," Griff said.

"I wouldn't have said anything. It's just that she goes by CC."

"Seriously?" Griff asked immediately. "Like Cathy Carter?"

"Yeah. But Detective McClarkey assured me the incident was an accident and there's nothing more there."

Griff shrugged. "He's the boss."

"Definitely," I said, wishing I could say more.

As I was wondering what Griff would make over the *All's well that ends well* message, his radio bleeped again.

"Speaking of which," he said.

"McClarkey?" I felt my face flush with his nod.

"Gotta run," he said. "But if anything else comes up, be sure and let me know."

"I will," I said.

"I mean it," Griff said. "McClarkey is a smart detective, but he can be a little hard to talk to sometimes."

"You think?" I asked.

"I know," he said.

"Good to see you again," I said.

"You too," he said, flashing his sweet dimpled smile. "With any luck, maybe we'll make it a hat trick."

———

As luck would have it, FJ and Trent hadn't gone with their father to lunch and a movie (or even down the street to their friend's house) but had lingered in the driveway playing basketball just long enough to hear the wife of the couple that had come through sniff and say something along the lines of *Bigger isn't always better.*

Because the prospective buyers were in and out, both boys had gotten to work trying to track where the email from CC had originated.

"So we entered the email address on this site that tells you who it's registered to," FJ said, sitting behind the desk in my office. "But for a registrant, we only get 'Domains by Proxy.'"

"Which means what?" I asked.

"The owner's name is blocked," Trent said, still clutching a basketball under his arm. "Which is sort of common."

"But we did figure out another thing or two," FJ said, staring at the computer monitor.

"Like what?"

"The email message came from a different account than the comments from CC on your website."

"And did you look into *that* email address?" I asked, trying to sound calmer than I felt.

"Address*es*," Trent said. "There were like three or four different ones."

"As in, CC was writing from more than one email account?"

"Sure looks that way."

"And they were all blocked too," FJ added.

"All of them?"

Trent nodded.

If emails were coming from various sources all claiming to be Contrary Claire, it was suddenly way more likely that CC somehow stood not for Cathy Carter, but Conniving Corporation.

Crazy as it still felt.

"Thanks, guys," I finally said. "I need to make a call or two."

"Before you do," FJ said, pulling up my email and pointing to the message from cc@coupclip.com. "You wanna tell us what's really going on?"

"I'm just trying to figure out who CC actually was," I said, still hoping I sounded relatively nonchalant.

"Mom," Trent said, and in that drawn out exasperated teenager way. "We saw the new email."

"But I have my own—"

"Password?" FJ asked. "You used to use some variation on the words *frugal* or *bargain*, but now you use one of the cat's names and a number from one to five."

"*Applebee4* ring a bell?" Trent asked.

"You shouldn't be trying to open my private emails in the first place!"

"We wouldn't," FJ said, "under normal circumstances."

"But we were worried," Trent said.

Why had I thought the boys could track down CC's web address but wouldn't think to crack my apparently rudimentary password combinations? "You still shouldn't be snooping on my email account."

"But it's okay to snoop into CC's?"

Touché. I kept that comment in my head.

"So, what is going on?" FJ asked.

"I'm not sure yet."

Since it was useless to try to keep anything from the boys, I proceeded to fill them in on everything from the suspicious nature of the accident to the various theories about CC's identity.

"Seriously?" Trent asked when I finished.

"Interesting," FJ said, pulling up MrsFrugalicious.com. Trent and I watched as he logged into the admin section and began to peck away on the keyboard. "CC's comments did start appearing right about the time Bargain Barn began to advertise," he finally said.

"So Alan is on to something?" I asked.

"Maybe," Trent said.

"We'll keep looking into it," FJ said.

"I really appreciate it," I said as the door from the garage squealed open and the combined chatter of various Michaels family members echoed through the front hall.

"Listen," I said, lowering my voice with the sound of approaching footfalls. "Everything I've told you or that you guys find out is entirely between us for right now. Okay?"

"No problem," FJ said.

"What about Eloise?" Trent asked, in his less than quiet indoor voice. "I mean, she's part of all of this, too."

"I don't want to get her all worked up and then have to send her back to school tomorrow worried before things get figured out."

"And she will get all worked up and worried," FJ said.

"True that," Trent added.

"I just think it's better to give her the all-clear message once it really is all-clear."

"Hey there," Frank said from outside the door to my office. He entered the room smiling, almost expectantly, as though he'd been listening and thought he'd heard something he wanted to hear. "What's doing?"

He stopped beside a framed snapshot of himself. Taken in happier times during a family trip to Hawaii, I'd left the photo on my bookshelf for "Feng Shui purposes" at the realtor's insistence. When I compared the current humbled Frank with the tan, handsome, cocky man I'd fallen in love with, and then glanced over at the boys who looked so much like him, I realized the anger I'd held all these months was giving way to something else.

What that something was, I couldn't entirely say.

Not yet.

"Nothing to report," I said.

———

There was plenty to report to Alan, however.

As soon as I shooed all three guys out of my office, I dialed his number. When he didn't answer, I left a voicemail followed by a text, both with a generic *call me when you get this* message.

Just in case.

I needed to rest before I had to gear back up for the Higgledy-Birdie nuptials. But hoping Alan would get back sooner rather than later and too keyed up to actually close my eyes, I turned to my computer, opened my spreadsheet program, and updated my *Questions & Answers* spreadsheet instead:

Why would CC write to me from as many as four different email addresses?

1. She had various emails and simply used whichever one struck her at the moment she felt compelled to write.

2. She was crazy.

3. She wasn't a she at all, but a big corporation bent on bankrupting and taking over Bargain Barn.

As Alan's theory rolled around in my head, I logged onto Mrs. Frugalicious. I checked for any noteworthy follow-up comments and returned the business correspondence that had been rolling in over the past two days (including no less than six advertising inquiries, all of whom mentioned they'd seen me on the news and wanted to do business).

I emailed back with advertising rate cards and was just finishing up a response to the message Wendy Killian from *Here's the Deal* had left on Friday when my phone rang.

My stomach flip-flopped when I read *Payphone* on the caller ID, but I figured it had to be Alan calling me from a "safe" phone.

"It's Alan," he said, confirming my suspicions. From the traffic noise and what sounded like wind in the mouthpiece, I assumed he was calling from the last remaining coin-operated gas station phone in the whole city. "Returning your call."

"I'm not sure what to make of this," I said by way of hello. "But CC was writing from four different email accounts."

"Did you say four different emails?"

"And the message I got last night was different from the other three."

"Holy," he said, over a honk. "This confirms everything I thought."

"Maybe so," I said. "But why would CC, whoever she or they might be, send that last email? Wouldn't it just make more sense to let the accident be an accident?"

"That's been nagging at me too," he said.

"Don't you think its time we alert the police?"

"Not yet," Alan said. "Whoever's behind this is clearly ruthless. If they get wind that we've given the police what at this point are only leads—"

"Okay," I said, not entirely sure that was the right course of action. "But—"

"But I plan to spend the rest of the day holed up here in the office viewing store security tape from Thursday night."

"There's tape?"

"Not from up high enough to see how that pallet fell, but there has to be something or someone of interest."

———

Before I finally, blessedly, rested my head for a long overdue nap, I posted a message on MrsFrugalicious.com:

Dearest Frugarmy,

As most of you know we lost one of our own under the most awful of circumstances. If you are a friend or relative, a fellow shopper from Bargain Barn, or just want to support the family of Cathy Carter, please join me in celebrating her life and commitment to bargain hunting at the North Suburban Church tomorrow morning at 10 a.m.

With love,
Mrs. Frugalicious

SIXTEEN

The processional music was already playing when we arrived and split up into twos and threes to fill the random remaining seats among the plastic palm fronds and flowers in the central courtyard of the South Highlands Valley Mall. I managed to wave to a few familiar current and former mall employees before the "Wedding March" began to filter through the speaker system and we all stood.

Bedecked in a tiny veiled wreath and perched on the shoulder of Pete from Pet Pals, Birdie the parrot started down the aisle toward a grinning, tuxedo-clad Higgledy the monkey.

Joyce stood beside me, dabbing her eyes. "I just love weddings."

"Me too," I said, although I couldn't quite shake off thoughts of the funeral I'd also be attending in the next twenty-four hours. Still, the inherent joy of a commitment ceremony, even one as surreal/ absurd as to unite two different species, was a welcome diversion.

Birdie hopped from Pete's shoulder onto the flower-covered perch beside her grinning, love-struck groom. This was an odd diversion, but admittedly a touching one.

Mr. Piggledy—complete with Bible, black robe, and online minister's license—joined the happy couple at the altar.

"I'm glad you finally got some rest this afternoon," Joyce whispered.

"Me too," I repeated. I'd slept through my alarm and finally awoke hitting my snooze button in the middle of a dream where I was being pecked by a squawking parrot. "It's been a challenging few days."

"Don't you mean months?" Joyce whispered.

I glanced back at Barb, seated behind and to the right of us with her kids and Gerald, and Eloise and the boys in front and to the left, and wondered how, despite effort on my part to avoid being alone with my mother-in-law, I'd veered off to leave a present at the gift table [30] and ended up sitting with her.

"Months," I managed to agree.

"Dearly beloved, we have come here on this crisp fall evening to surround Higgledy and Birdie with our love and best wishes for the journey they've chosen to embark upon together. While this may be the first ceremony of this type you have witnessed, its purpose, like all commitment ceremonies, is to celebrate deep spiritual union." Mr. Piggledy paused to smile lovingly at the happy couple and then

---

30. Yearly US spending on pet supplies exceeds $50 billion! Shop smart for your pet by comparison shopping and checking out the web for manufacturer's discounts, weekly deals, and printable coupons. And don't forget online auction sites for deals on durable pet supplies like beds, carriers, toys, and the like.

at Mrs. Piggledy, who was dressed in mother-of-the-bride pink chiffon and a matching pale pink cast, and was seated in a flower-covered wheelchair parked in the front row. "From myself, my wife, and the bride and groom, we thank you for being here tonight. We are truly blessed to be able to celebrate this passage in the presence of so many good friends and family."

A woman wearing the dark green blazer bearing the SHVM crest that signified her position as the new mall manager stood off to the side of the altar. She smiled and blew a kiss to the happy couple.

"Higgledy and Birdie, despite your individual differences, you share love, loyalty, and trust, which are the foundations of a lasting and happy union…"

Out of the corner of my eye, I saw a look of what seemed to be consternation cross Joyce's tight face.

"And with your commitment, trust, and uncanny ability to communicate with each other, I know your life together will be full of joy, satisfaction, and peace."

"Frank…" Joyce whispered under her breath and into my ear.

I held mine, dreading what was coming next.

"Who brings this monkey to be given into this union?" Mr. Piggledy asked.

"I do," Mrs. Piggledy said, her wheelchair beside Higgledy.

"And who brings this bird to be given into this union?

"I do," said Pete from Pet Pals.

"I don't believe what an absolute dumb shit he was," Joyce whispered in my ear.

Had I'd really just heard Joyce, who *never* swore, utter such a pointed slur (no matter how accurate) about the Michaels family pride and joy? "Did you just call Frank a—"

"Marriage is the magic of two hearts joining as one," Mr. Piggledy continued. "It creates a new light and space within which you both will live beyond your soon-to-be-shared cage…"

I couldn't believe I'd spent the better part of a week trying to avoid being alone with Joyce, anticipating what she might say in defense of her wayward son and what I might say in response, only to have her come out and completely bash him during a wedding.

Mr. Piggledy turned to the candelabra behind him. "Higgledy and Birdie, the two candles now lit before you symbolize each of you individually. The larger candle, still unlit, is to symbolize your unique union."

At Mr. Piggledy's cue, Higgledy climbed into Mrs. Piggledy's lap and Birdie hopped back onto Pete's shoulder. Pete pushed the flower-covered wheelchair over to the candelabra.

"Fire! Fire!" the bird said in her guttural, pre-recorded-sounding avian voice and flapped her wings.

A charmed *ahhh* went through the crowd as Higgledy slipped a comforting arm around his bride-to-be.

"May the eternal flame of your love continue to burn brightly for as long as you both shall live," Mr. Piggledy said.

"You know Frank cries to Barb on a regular basis?" Joyce whispered as Mrs. Piggledy and Pete helped their respective pets light the unity candle. "And he must be a glutton for punishment, because she does nothing but assure him he's getting what he deserves."

"I don't know what to say," I finally said, as Pete and Mrs. Piggledy returned to their sides of the aisle and a salesgirl I recognized from Whimsey's Accessories stood and made her way to the microphone.

"I didn't know what to say when my darling Gerald stepped off the curb, either."

My heart, already thumping, began to pound in my chest. "What?!"

"Dear," Joyce said in a tone that was equal parts comforting and condescending, "they all do it at one time or another."

I glanced back at a blissfully unaware Gerald, who, despite his present mild senility, had been as upright and respectable as he'd been handsome and dashing.

The salesgirl began to belt out an a cappella version of Mariah Carey's "We Belong Together."

"Men will be men," Joyce added, smiling in her husband's direction. "Let's face it. They're just weak at their core."

"But…" I finally managed despite feeling like my mouth dried shut.

"But you've certainly been playing it just right."

"Joyce," I whispered, "I haven't been 'playing it' at all."

"Kicking him to the curb without kicking him out of the house so he'd see what he'd soon be missing forever was brilliant." She patted my knee lightly. "I've never seen that boy so utterly down and out."

I pinched myself to make sure I wasn't really just having a dream in which my cheating husband's mother bad-mouthed her son at the commitment ceremony of a primate and a tropical bird. "Given our finances, it wasn't like I've had a whole lot of choice in the matter," I whispered, feeling the sting from my own pinch.

"You certainly do now."

"Meaning what?"

The song ended, the salesgirl returned to her seat in the front row, and Mr. Piggledy returned to the makeshift pulpit.

"Higgledy, do you take this bird to be your partner, to share your life openly with her, to love, honor, and comfort her, in sickness and in health for all time?"

Higgledy hopped up and down and emitted an undeniably affirmative *hoo-hoo*.

"Birdie do you take Higgledy to be your partner, to stand beside you always, in celebration and sadness, for richer and for poorer, to love and to cherish, for now and forevermore? If so, say I do."

"I do," she mimicked.

"I love you both," Joyce whispered. "And I want what's best for everyone."

"Which is what?" I asked, more confused than I'd been in months.

"The giving and receiving of rings symbolizes our love for one another, which like the circle, knows no end, but given the unique nature of our ceremony—and something of a tendency for escape on the part of both of our participants—we've opted for matching tracking bracelets."

A man wearing a veterinarian's lab coat stood and approached the altar bearing a pillow with two animal tracking devices.

Joyce flashed the giant marquis diamond I remembered Gerald giving her for their thirty-fifth anniversary. "It was well worth the temporary trauma."

"Temporary trauma?" I heard myself repeat as the veterinarian began to affix the bracelets onto the ankles of Higgledy and then Birdie. "You got that ring as an apology gift?"

"Not to mention my convertible, a pair of opal earrings, the condo in Palm Springs, and our annual Thanksgiving cruise," she said. "All of which have given me great satisfaction over the years."

"Higgledy and Birdie, please face each other."

Since they couldn't exactly take each other's hands, Higgledy grasped the edges of Birdie's wings.

"Oh Lord, give Higgledy and Birdie the willingness and patience to fulfill their commitments to one another and fill them with freedom and happiness even while sharing cages."

He turned to the audience.

"Will each of you do all that is in your power to encourage them in their commitment and to support them in the promises that they make here today? If so, please indicate by saying *we will*."

"We will," the audience said in unison.

"You have Frank over a barrel," Joyce whispered.

"May this day shine forever in your lives. May you give cheer and strength to each other. May your life together be a source of inspiration to yourselves, your families, your friends, and to all whose lives you touch."

"This is no time for a divorce," she continued quietly.

"With the promises they have made to one another, and by the power of their love, I now pronounce Higgledy and Birdie to be joined in spiritual union. You may kiss the bride."

"Kiss! Kiss!" Birdie said.

The crowd was already clapping and hooting as Higgledy leaned in and planted a wet one on Birdie's beak.

Mr. Piggledy beamed. "Ladies and gentlemen, I'd like to be the first to introduce Mr. and Mrs. Higgledy and Birdie Piggledy!"

———

"Are you all right, dear?" Mr. Piggledy asked as I made my way through the receiving line and stopped to give him a congratulatory hug.

"You look pale," Mrs. Piggledy said from beside him. "Maybe you should sit down."

"I'm fine." That was, if being downright shell-shocked and numb was fine. I leaned down to hug her. "I'm just glad you're okay. The ceremony was amazing."

"Wasn't it?" She gazing admiringly at Mr. Piggledy. "Went off without a hitch even with my bad wheel."

Mr. Piggledy beamed. "If I learned anything in my years at the circus, it's to expect and be prepared for the unexpected."

I grabbed a plastic pineapple from a passing waiter with a drink tray and toasted that thought by sucking down the tropical, rum-infused concoction.

Gerald led Joyce out to the dance floor and they began to tango together in what seemed to be perfect step.

What if Frank was, as she said, *over a barrel* and guaranteed to behave *as long as we both shall live*? Would it be easier to stay married knowing I had a new, improved version of the man I'd fallen in love with rather than face an unknown single future?

The rest of the evening was a blur of music, rum drinks, jungle-themed appetizers, and small talk.

That was, until everyone gathered to watch Birdie climb onto Higgledy's shoulder, and with the help of Pete and Mr. Piggledy, cut the cake.

And Barb appeared out of nowhere beside me.

"You okay?" she asked, as Birdie pecked lovingly at the first piece in Higgledy's outstretched hand.

"Fine," I said, adding, "I hear the cake is supposed to be fantastic. Banana chocolate chip with banana filling."

"I can't wait to try some," she said spinning around to face me. "And, by the way, I know you're not okay."

I grabbed another beverage from a passing waiter. "Why's that?"

"I know my mother got to you."

"Got to me?"

Barb looked into my eyes. "Definitely."

All I could think to do was take a nonchalant gulp of my drink.

"I'm not sure why she decided she needed to lay it all on you in the middle of a wedding." Barb shook her head. "But I suppose time is of the essence."

"She told you she was going to talk to me?" I asked, not even attempting to mask the incredulity in my voice.

"I could tell just by looking at your reaction as she whispered into your ear during the ceremony."

"And you also know *what* she told me?" I asked, locating the nearest restroom since throwing up suddenly seemed to be in the realm of possibility.

"I'm guessing *men will be men* and *temporary trauma* ring some bells."

"I just can't believe she—"

"Told you about Dad's indiscretions, or that she told me?"

"Either." My voice cracked. "Both."

"Believe me, I was more than a little shocked to find out that Dad ..." She hung her head for a second as if to regain her composure. "But I really wished I'd listened to her and not gotten divorced myself."

"Your husband was playing around?"

"As she said, they all do. Although I can't say if that's why Craig got divorced, for the record." She sighed. "But I should have just let him know he'd best keep it in his pants, and then forgiven him."

"But—"

"I could have reaped the spoils like Mom did." She looked over at the dance floor where her young daughters were clustered together on the sidelines. "And the kids wouldn't have suffered nearly as much."

"At least my kids are older," I said, which sounded weak even to me. The truth was, a single day didn't go by where I didn't wonder if they were doing okay with all the upheaval, past and future.

"Maddie, Frank acted like a royal turd, but he does love you and your kids more than anything." Barb said. "When you think about it, it's not the worst idea in the world to let him keep proving it to you over and over."

I shook my head. "This is all so—"

"Anti-feminist and hard to swallow?"

"For starters." I took a deep breath. "Even if I could see myself forgiving or at least moving on with Frank, this whole notion of him showering me with guilt gifts for the rest of our lives is not only a little hard to fathom, it's hardly an option given our current—"

"*Current* being the key word," she broke in.

"Meaning what?" I asked.

"My brother seems to have a way of always landing on his feet, is all."

"Maddie!" Eloise appeared in front of us, pointed to her cell phone, and sighed dramatically. "It's like almost nine and if I don't get out of here in the next half-hour, I'll miss everything and then I leave tomorrow and I will hardly have gotten to hang out with my friends this break and then we'll probably be moving by the time I come home again and—"

"I'm pretty much ready to go," I said.

"I'm ready now," Barb said. "I'll grab the girls. If you can drop us off, you'll have the car and everyone else can say their goodbyes and come home in the rental car without rushing."

"You don't mind?" I asked.

"My feet are killing me and it's already way past their bedtime."

"Thanks, Aunt Barb," Eloise said to both of us as I tossed her my keys.

"No problem." Barb winked. Before she headed over to corral her girls, she whispered into my ear, "And don't cause yourself any more problems when you don't have to."

———

It turned out everyone else was ready to leave anyway, which was great, as my feet were also killing me by the time we started across the mall toward the second car. Not to mention my head.

"Cool wedding," Trent said.

"Commitment ceremony," FJ said. "Animals, particularly those of two different species, don't exactly have equal rights under the law."

"Do you think they should?" I asked, tongue-in-cheek, of course, but with a mind toward FJ, who'd always had a generally more sensitive nature.

He shrugged. "If you want to get married, you should be able to get married."

"Especially if you're going to have a wedding like that," Trent said. "The mall chicks were hot and those rainforest-themed appetizers rocked."

"The deviled eggs with the seeds or whatever on them were really good," FJ said.

"So were the fried bananas."

"I have a question," I said as Gerald and Joyce strolled ahead of us, hand-in hand and just out of hearing range. "About the opposite of marriage."

"Oh jeez," Trent said. "Here it comes."

"Seriously," I swallowed hard. "How do you guys feel like you're holding up in all this?"

"Well," FJ said. "This divorce thing totally sucks."

"I'll admit I kinda hate that you and Dad are splitting up, and I really hate that we're selling the house," Trent said.

"But we get it," FJ said in an octave slightly too high to be truthful. "I mean, what choice do we really have?"

We walked in silence past Macy's, Things Remembered, and PacSun while I fought the urge to cry and the boys thought whatever else they were thinking but weren't willing to say.

"You okay, Mom?" FJ finally asked as we exited the doors to the north garage.

"Fine," I said, even though I wasn't.

I was even less fine when I reached my car.

———

Eloise handed me a neon green sticky note. "This was on your windshield."

Clearly she'd already shared it with Joyce, Gerald, and Barb, who all seemed frozen in place, their eyes huge and awaiting my reaction.

Joyce's face was the Botoxed equivalent of a terrified question mark.

I read the handwritten, all-caps message and knew there could be no doubt it was intended for me:

I'M STILL ALIVE, BUT IF PUSH COMES TO SHOVE AGAIN, SOMEONE ELSE MIGHT NOT BE.

SOMEONE LIKE YOU.

SEVENTEEN

I stood beside Detective McClarkey as one officer dusted for prints and another dropped the Post-it into an evidence bag. Never mind that pretty much everyone in the Michaels family had already handled the note.

"And you say you got that email from this CC person, when?" he asked.

"Yesterday," I said, scrolling through my phone until I located the email and handed it to him to see. "Exactly forty-five minutes after I got home from the police station."

"*All's well that ends well*," the detective repeated, reading the message.

Gerald nodded in seeming agreement.

"I told you that CC person was dangerous," Joyce said.

With my car currently at the center of a CSI investigation, any hopes I'd had of speaking to Detective McClarkey out of the earshot of an opinionated audience vanished. I'd barely been able to convince

Joyce that a discreet call to the police station was preferable to dialing 911 and having the police cars arrive with sirens a-blazin'. There was no convincing anyone (particularly Eloise, who insisted that none of them were going to leave my side) that it really was okay to squish any, much less all eight of them, into the rental car that seated five and go on home.

"We'll make sure she's safe." Detective McClarkey said, looking at me. "I'll personally make sure."

"I should hope so," Barb sniffed.

I should have been furious at the detective for dismissing me the way he had yesterday, but he looked so contrite and even worried now that I couldn't help but feel ever so slightly gloaty.

"I'm sorry, Maddie," he said rubbing his hands through his graying crewcut. "There's little doubt *this* was an accident."

"It was all by design," I said. "At least according to Alan Bader."

"Meaning what?" McClarkey asked.

I hated having to unload the whole story when Alan hadn't even wanted to go to the police, but a Post-it with a death threat counted as solid proof for me. Considering the killer decided to leave the message on my windshield while I was chauffeuring a car full of relatives, it wasn't like I had much of a choice, either.

"At first, I was sure Alan was insane or at least profoundly sleep deprived, but he really thinks the accident was engineered by a corporation determined to devalue Bargain Barn and take him over."

"Murderous corporate raider?" Joyce asked.

"Sick, huh?" Trent said.

"You knew about this?" Eloise looked that much more distressed.

"Mom asked us to do a little bit of cyber-snooping for her," FJ added. "We found out that CC was writing from different email addresses."

"You boys did a nice job," Detective McClarkey said before anyone else could chime in.

"The whole idea that a corporation would mastermind something of this nature still seems outlandish to me, and I'm not saying I buying it entirely, but after we realized the emails weren't coming from the same place..."

"This whole situation is really freaking me out," Eloise said, her voice husky with the threat of tears.

"It's okay, honey," Gerald said, putting his arm around her. "It's okay."

"Not if Maddie's in danger, it isn't," Barb added.

"I presume you'll be providing a security detail for her from here on out?" Joyce asked.

"Folks," Detective McClarkey said holding up his hand. "I know you're worried and concerned, and I assure you I'll do everything in my power to make sure Maddie is taken care of, but I need to hear the whole sequence of events first so I can determine exactly what needs to be done."

"Of course," Joyce said.

"From her," he clarified. "In fact, since they're about done looking over the vehicle—"

"Doesn't it need to be impounded or something?" Trent chimed in as another police car pulled up and a detective in Dockers and a sport coat stepped out to join us.

"I think we have what we need," Detective McClarkey said, with a patience belied by the annoyance in his face and body language.

"And now that Detective Ross, who headed up the Bargain Barn investigation, is here, we do need that detailed statement from Maddie, so I'm going to ask the rest of you to take the cars and go on home."

"Should one of us hang back?" Joyce asked. "Just in case?"

"No." McClarkey managed a tight smile. "That won't be necessary."

———

What was necessary was a full retelling of the whole story for the lead detective, starting with CC's snarky comments on my blog and working my way to the note left on the car.

Detective McClarkey stepped in with the details about my visit to the station, again apologizing to me and re-explaining his motivation to not make me look suspicious for no reason.

When I'd finished, Detective Ross nodded, put his pencil and pad away, thanked me for the thoroughness, assured me they'd keep me out of harm's way, and (no doubt based on my history) asked me to please do the same.

In addition, I agreed not to discuss the case beyond filling in my family, but as the detectives conferred for a few minutes, I pulled out my phone and sent a text to Alan, who I felt also deserved to be updated.

SOMEONE LEFT A NOTE ON MY CAR WHILE I WAS AT THE PIGGLEDY WEDDING AT THE MALL.

WHICH SAID?????

I'M STILL ALIVE, BUT IF PUSH COMES TO SHOVE AGAIN SOMEONE ELSE MIGHT NOT BE. SOMEONE LIKE YOU.

Oh, lord! Are you okay?

Yes, but i'm afraid i had to call the police.

There was a delay. Then he replied, Of course.

At least the police believe us now.

It's a start.

I'm sure they're going to want to talk to you.

I'm sure you're right.

Alan, I really am so sorry about all this.

"Maddie," Detective McClarkey said, heading back in my direction.

Alan texted back. Maddie ...

Before I could read the rest, there was a screech of tires on pavement as a Mercedes came around the corner and pulled up beside me.

Frank's Mercedes.

He jumped out of the car.

"Maddie!"

EIGHTEEN

BEFORE I KNEW IT—and to the consternation of Detective Mc-Clarkey, who appeared to be interested, if not eager, to make up for yesterday by escorting me home—I was sitting in the passenger seat of Frank's car.

I was also nursing a headache that felt a lot more like a whole-body ache.

Somehow the reality—that there really was a killer, and that he/she/it knew where I was and what kind of car I drove—began to hit me in full force as we made our way home.

And apparently it was also hitting Frank, who made a point of thanking the detectives, assuring them that we lived in a gated community so there was no need to post an officer right outside the house, and going so far as to actually snap me into my seat belt.

"Let's get you home," he said.

Without questioning me about how I was feeling, what I was thinking, or otherwise demanding anything out of me conversationally or otherwise, he patted my leg and started the car.

We drove in an oddly peaceful silence all the way home.

The silence was crushed the second we stepped into the house and entered the family room to find the entire Michaels gang seated on the L-shaped sectional, waiting for us like a news-hungry press corps.

"Have they figured out who left the note?"

"Do they have a cyber team assigned to CC yet?"

"Are there officers posted outside the house?"

"How soon do you think there'll be an arrest?"

"The police are in the process of reevaluating Cathy Carter's accident in light of the note," Frank announced. "And we're not supposed to talk about anything we do or don't know to anyone but each other."

"What about Maddie's safety?"

"I'll make sure of it."

"But—"

"But Maddie's exhausted," he said firmly.

"Probably starved though too," Joyce said. "Can I make you a sandwich, honey?"

"I think I'm okay," I managed before Frank put his hand on my back.

"We'll debrief more in the morning," he said. "She needs rest."

With that, he waved off the family and directed me toward the front hall and up the stairs.

"I'm just going to make sure everything's secure in here," he said following me into the master and heading toward the bank of windows on the east wall, where he began to check the locks.

"I'd like to take a shower," I said.

"Go ahead," he said. "I'll be right out here."

"Okay," I said, more meekly than I intended, continuing on toward the bathroom and closing the door behind me.

When I emerged nearly a half hour and a hot shower later, Frank was not only still there, as promised, but he'd turned down my side of the bed.

"Let's get you tucked in," he said, reaching for my hand.

For the briefest of seconds, I flashed back to a time not so long ago when heading to bed with my husband was a pleasant, mundane, utterly normal part of my daily routine. "Frank, I—"

"I like the pajamas, by the way," he said leading me over to put my phone on the charger and slip under the sheets.

The pajamas, black with white polka dots and purchased on clearance at Macy's using a 20%-off coupon and a $20 customer loyalty rebate, had cost a total of $4.99. Given Frank's preference for nightgowns on me, they not only represented a true Frugasm dealwise, but my newfound freedom to wear whatever I wanted to bed.

"Thanks," I said.

"You're welcome."

I pulled up the covers. "I'm good, now. I think."

"Great." He sat down on the edge of the bed. "But I'm not going anywhere."

"Frank," I sighed. "I really do appreciate every thing you're doing, but—"

"But now you're in danger," he said.

"Not here, not in the house."

"Look, Maddie. I know you way too well to think you'd even consider trying to work things out with me without a lot of thought and consideration, but I can't live with myself if I don't do everything in my power to make sure you're safe and sound while you're thinking about it."

"This feels awkward," I said. "I feel awkward."

He smiled his charming crooked smile. "Just think of me as your bodyguard."

For the briefest of moments, I allowed myself to remember what it was like when we did share the bedroom. How safe and protected I'd felt with him beside me in the bed at night. I couldn't help but muse about how much easier it might be to just give in and give Frank another try. Righteous anger or no, my future would be that much less up in the air. And the kids would certainly be happier.

Wouldn't they?

I took the deepest of breaths.

"Can I take that as a yes?"

"It's an, I'm thinking about it."

"Good," he leaned forward and kissed me gently on the forehead. "Because I'm not taking no for an answer. Not tonight, anyway."

As I rubbed absently at the spot where his surprisingly cool lips met my skin, he stood, took a few steps and sat down in the over-stuffed chair beside the bed.

"Maddie," he said, pulling a throw from the arm of the chair over himself. "I really am just so, so sorry for all of this."

"I know," I said.

"Time for some rest," he said, leaning his head against the back of the chair and closing his eyes.

Somehow, despite how tired I was, I couldn't get settled in, much less sleep.

Instead, I grabbed my cell phone. Not allowing myself to check Mrs. Frugalicious or the associated email account, I remembered that I hadn't read the addendum to Alan's last text.

It simply said:

No need for apologies.

As Frank began to snore softly, I wondered how many times he would have to apologize and how long it would take before I could finally forgive him.

While I feared the answer was never, the events of the evening, starting with Joyce's startling admission and suggestion, definitely had me thinking I had to at least give it a try.

NINETEEN

I woke to the uncertain reality of my not-quite-estranged husband snoring in a familiar *puh-snort* pattern from the chair beside me, a police-processed car in the garage, an at-large murderer who felt inclined to leave an ominous neon Post-it on said car, and a pending memorial service for Cathy Carter, whoever it was she turned out to have been.

As I slipped out of bed and began to tiptoe toward the bathroom and what I hoped would be a little peace and quiet while I prepared for the morning ahead, the landline rang.

And, once again, things grew just a bit more uncertain.

———

"So there's an offer on the house?" Anastasia, luminous in funereal but camera-friendly dark blue, asked as the cameraman checked out the lighting in various spots around the vestibule of the church.

"The realtor called this morning and there are some very interested buyers having a second look as we speak."

"I don't see why all of us had to rush to clear out again if they've already seen it before," Trent said, yawning and fidgeting with the tie I'd handed him to wear in the latest mad dash to get out of the house. "I mean, I wasn't even at Bargain Barn Thursday night, and I never met this woman who—"

"Safety in numbers," said Joyce, who stood with Barb, Gerald, Craig, and various grandchildren in a cluster just behind the camera. "Until they figure out what's going on with that horrid note and everything, we stick together."

"Joyce!" Barb said. "You know we're not supposed to talk about—"

"All I said was, until *they* figure it out," Joyce said. "It wasn't like I said—"

"Half the people here are cops," Anastasia, the only person outside the family who'd overheard Joyce, whispered conspiratorially. Given she was a journalist and she was engaged to the acting police chief, she would (and already did) know what had happened last night. "I guarantee you're as safe here as you would be at the police station."

I'd definitely spotted a couple of black and whites parked out front, which translated to an extra uniformed officer or two inside, but as I looked around, I couldn't help but notice the number of "regular" couples, one or both of whom were dressed in outfits that could easily conceal a weapon.

A quick conversation with Alan Bader might have made me feel more confident that they actually were plainclothes cops and not corporate assassins, but I hadn't spotted him yet among the growing crowd.

Eloise shook her head. "Do we really even have to sell the house at all if you and Dad are like talking and stuff?"

"It's not quite that simple," I said.

The Michaels gang, including Frank, who was once again dabbing makeup on shiny spots I'd missed in my haste to get dressed, all smiled like it was exactly that simple.

Even though she had to be confused about what was going on, Anastasia just smiled.

The showing had us rushing around to clean, get ready, and get out of the house, which left no time for a morning debrief. On the way over, however, I assured Eloise and the boys, who had come in my fingerprint-dusted vehicle, that the police were in the process of figuring out what had really happened. I also let them know that Frank was committed to keeping everyone in the family safe, particularly me, until the police could complete their investigation.

While I didn't go so far as to say we were back together, there was no getting around the fact that Frank spent the night in the master bedroom for the first time in months—even if it was in a chair.

I decided it best not to elaborate or explain the situation, but just added that there was nothing to be done now but be cautious, let the authorities do their job, and let things take their course.

Eloise, seated beside me in the car, seemed content with my explanation. So did Joyce, Gerald, Barb, and Craig, who'd ridden with Frank and had (I assumed) been filled in on the way as well.

"Found our spot," the cameraman said, pointing to the area just between a huge multi-colored spray of sympathy flowers and a tribute table lined with photos of Catherine T. Carter, some with her husband. In the pictures he was, if not handsome, infinitely more bright-eyed and nice-looking than the grief-stricken man I'd seen the night of the incident.

"Everyone should probably go sit," Frank said to the family, watching the crowd of mourners swell. "Looks like it's going to be standing room only."

"We'll save seats for you," Joyce said, already mobilizing everyone toward the doors into the sanctuary.

"Near the back would be best," the cameraman said. "So we can get an over-the-shoulder shot or two of Maddie and Stasia mourning at the service itself."

"You ready, Maddie?" Anastasia asked

"I suppose," I said. "It still feels awkward to be broadcasting from the memorial."

"Clearly, there are a lot of people here grieving for Cathy and her husband," Anastasia whispered. "It's our job to bring closure to all the viewers at home who couldn't be here, but are feeling the same way."

"You should also think of it as reporting from the scene of a continuing investigation," Frank continued. "Which is really what it is after last night."

"Exactly," Anastasia said.

At the very least, there was no denying how many people had and were continuing to show up, including Wendy Killian from *Here's the Deal* magazine, whom I spotted on the front steps.

Typically in jeans and a nice if unremarkable top with her hair pulled back in a tight, severe ponytail, she entered the church looking somehow decked out. Her dress was appropriately black, but form-fitting and showed off her toned, almost sinewy, arms and her slim athletic figure.

Wendy accepted a program, saw me, and made her way over in anything but sensible black stiletto heels.

"Maddie!" She enveloped me in a perfumy hug.

"Thank you for coming," I found myself saying, as though I were one of the bereaved.

"I'm just glad to be able to pay my last respects." A tear fell from the corner of her eye as she glanced at a shot on the tribute table of Cathy Clark holding a kitten. "How are you holding up through all of this?"

"It's been a helluva weekend," I said, which was as honest as I was currently at liberty to be.

We hugged again.

"Ready when you are, Stasia," the cameraman said.

"I should get out of your way," Wendy said as we moved to our places. "The show must go on."

"Couldn't have said it better myself," Anastasia said, as Wendy blended into the growing crowd. "Ratings haven't been this high since summer, when..."

I swallowed the sudden lump in my throat while Anastasia had the decency not to utter *when you were almost killed* and whatever else she might have been inclined to add.

"Look," Frank said, motioning toward the glass entry doors.

Anastasia and I turned and the camera swerved in time to catch a black limo pull up in front of the church.

The car door opened and Cathy Carter's husband emerged looking grimmer and even more gray than he had Thursday night. With him were a grief-stricken older couple and a middle-aged man I presumed were the extent of Cathy's extended family.

All had red-rimmed eyes and matching noses.

"Those poor people," Frank said as they entered the church, were immediately greeted by a minister, and whisked off through a side door.

"Do you think the police have filled them in on what happened last night?" I asked.

"They're probably waiting until after the memorial," Anastasia said. "Especially with all the buzz this morning."

"The buzz?" I asked.

"I hear there's been a break in the case."

I looked around once again for Alan. If the police had gone to talk to him after last night's sticky note, which they had to have done, chances were he'd spent the rest of the evening filling them in on what he knew, or at least suspected, about a big corporation being behind the death of Cathy Carter.

"What kind of break?" I asked.

"A big one."

Meaning Alan had been right after all? "As in?" I persisted.

"Still classified, so I don't know," Anastasia said. "But something's going to go down soon."

"How soon?" Frank asked.

"Not sure," Anastasia said. "But from all the back-and-forth calls this morning, I'd say very."

———

"This is Anastasia Chastain and Maddie Michaels reporting from the North Suburban Community Church, where services will soon be underway for Catherine T. Carter…"

Much as I might have hoped to transform into Anastasia's camera-ready, appropriately glib weekend sidekick, Maddie Michaels, AKA Mrs. Frugalicious, I felt far too distracted by everything to do much more than survive the segment.

While Anastasia gave a teary account of the somber mood amongst the crowd and stepped over to the photo display, I somehow managed to maintain my composure, sharing a sound bite or two about the horror of Thursday night's "accident" and Alan Bader's generosity in organizing the memorial to help ease the grief of the Carter family.

Alan finally showed up while I was on the air and immediately got swept into the last-minute arrangements with an official from the church. I had hoped to get close enough to confirm that even though he looked like his old dapper self in a dark double-breasted suit and pressed white shirt, his eyes would belie a night's worth of filling in the police.

As the camera taped me hugging various members of the Frugarmy, including Mr. Piggledy, who'd come to pay his respects on behalf of Mrs. Piggledy, Higgledy, and their new "daughter-in-law" Birdie, all I could think about was what exactly the big break in the case would be.

And did Alan already know about it?

If he did, then he had come to the memorial with confirmation of both his safety and his sanity.

But what if he didn't?

Was he also circulating through the crowd wondering who was truly a mourner and who was there under false, potentially fatal premises? Not to mention the still unanswered question:

Who was Cathy Carter?

———

Catherine Theresa Carter, Cathy to her friends and family, was a woman who loved hobbies …

According to her beloved husband, John, she worked from home as a freelance bookkeeper and enjoyed a variety of interests over the years —everything from knitting, ceramics, and beading to taking in rescue dogs and, at one point, breeding sugar gliders. Recently, Cathy became increasingly interested in two hobbies in particular, cooking and couponing clipping.

Sniffles echoed through the overfull church while the minister paused, either for effect or to check his notes.

Cathy didn't dabble in her interests. She dove wholeheartedly and with great gusto into whatever she did, reveling in her ability to have delicious gourmet meals waiting for her husband after a long day at work. Meals for which she'd paid only pennies on the dollar …

From my seat in the back row between Anastasia and Frank, I watched Cathy's husband, John, put his head into his hands.

It was in pursuit of both of these hobbies that the Lord, in his infinite wisdom, determined it was time for Cathy to return unto his loving embrace …

Up front, someone let out a big choking sob.

It is often difficult to understand the Lord's plan at times like these—a woman who wants nothing more than to save a few dollars goes down to her local retailer, stands in line enjoying the Black Friday fanfare like so many of us do, and the most unthinkable of accidents occurs.

As Frank, whose arm was draped loosely onto the back of the pew, gave my shoulder a comforting squeeze, I tried to will Alan, who was seated in the front row of the opposite aisle, to look up and in my direction.

He continued to stare at his feet.

Never mind that we were too far away from each other for him to see much less interpret a meaningful look or hand signal from me asking *Do you know what the heck is going on?*

The minister took a step back and "Angel" began to play on the loudspeaker.

As Sarah McLachlan's haunting voice floated up toward the abstract stained-glass windows of the nondenominational church, I couldn't help but sniffle. That and scan the crowd, noting that Wendy Killian and Mr. Piggledy had joined the Michaels' two rows of pews with Wendy beside Craig and Mr. Piggledy next to Gerald. Other familiar faces from Thursday night dotted the church, some of whom had introduced themselves as Frugarmy members at various points throughout the weekend. The others, the ones who'd never said a word, all somehow looked that much more suspicious for not making themselves known.

Were the camera not set up discreetly but directly behind me, I might have considered sending Alan a quick FYI text. To avoid a TV clip of me callously plinking away on my cell phone during the most watched local funeral of the year, I sat trying not to feel like I was trapped in a bad dream filled with sad music, sadder readings, and a heart-wrenching lack of friends, co-workers, or acquaintances on hand to share touching or funny stories about their friend Cathy Carter.

While the minister reiterated bland platitudes about Cathy's happy life as the only daughter of already deceased parents and her devotion as a wife, needlecrafter, lover of animals, and budget gourmet cook, I listened for anything that might give me some clue as to whether she really was simply the victim of bad luck. Was there any way she could also have had an alter ego known as Contrary Claire, online heckler and malcontent? With adjectives like *sweet, honest, thoughtful, kind,* and the utterly nondescriptive *nice* being repeated, it seemed unlikely.

Or was the utter lack of information that much more suspicious?

Cathy seemed like a perfectly friendly soul, but her eulogy had her sounding even more sweet and bland than vanilla ice cream.

And that was before the minister added:

In recent months, her interest and success in saving money as a couponer had her donating a variety of low-cost and free nonperishables to local shelters…

As people turned to smile at me and Frank patted me softly on the back, a pretty, heavyset woman of about thirty-five lumbered up to the stage, adjusted the microphone down, and tucked a loose strand of dark hair behind her ear.

"A few months back, Cathy and I telecommuted together on a project," she said.

I found myself sitting up a little straighter, hoping for something about Cathy. Anything from *while she could be a little opinionated* to *I can't believe she warned me against going to Bargain Barn Thursday night.*

"She couldn't have been nicer or easier to work with," the woman said. "Which is why I thought I should read this poem by Maya Angelou in her honor."

As she launched into a touching reading of "When I Think of Death," I was increasingly sure Alan was right about everything and Cathy not only couldn't have been CC, but had to have been chosen as an unfortunate pawn simply by virtue of just how bland a person she'd been.

I glanced briefly over my shoulder and noted the cameraman standing a few steps back from the camera.

Seizing the opportunity, I leaned down, planning to fumble through my purse for mints or a tissue and somehow tapping out a quick text to alert Alan.

I rifled past my wallet and gum, located my cell, and turned it over.

There was already a text message waiting for me.

It was from Alan:

Meet me at the stairwell doors at the back north side of the church right after the minister starts his final announcements and the reception begins.

———

"I found something on one of the store security cameras," Alan said leading me down a set of stairs toward the basement of the church. "A person stepping down from an upper shelf a minute or so after the pallet fell."

"That's huge!" I said, feeling my first real sense of relief since that sickening crash on Thursday night. I was also breathless from ducking out of the service, rushing from the front vestibule, through a side door, and down the north corridor to meet up with Alan.

"Except that the tape was fuzzy and came from a perimeter camera in an area that shouldn't have been accessible from where the pallet fell," he said, leading the way down a darkened hallway across the west side of the church.

"What did the police think?"

"They spent most of the night trying to determine whether someone could have worked their way across the upper shelves of the store and shimmied down in that particular area undetected."

"And?"

"That it wouldn't be easy, but it wasn't impossible."

"Which means there's a suspect now, too?"

"Not yet," he said. "The tape still has to be officially analyzed and all that jazz."

"Anastasia seemed sure something was about to go down."

"I bet the big break she was talking about already happened. They just need to process the tape and hopefully we can wake up from this nightmare," he said, pushing open a door marked EXIT. "Not that I've had much, if any, actual sleep in the last few days."

Up close, there was no missing the dark circles under his eyes. "I hope you can get some rest soon."

"That's my general plan," he said propping open the door.

I drew in a breath and squeezed my eyes shut to adjust to the juxtaposition of brisk temperatures and bright sunlight.

"So you're leaving for home now?"

"Not yet," he said, pulling a BMW key fob from his pocket, but looking toward the stretch limo that had ferried the Carter family to the memorial and was parked alongside the back of the church. "I thought I'd follow John home and get him settled first."

"That's so kind of you," I said.

"It's the least I can I do."

"But isn't he inside, at the reception?" Which was where I was supposed to be so Anastasia and I could wrap up by having a word with him. I was now bordering on overdue.

"His aunt, uncle, and brother are going to greet well-wishers, but the poor guy is still pretty heavily sedated and in no frame of mind to talk to much of anyone."

"I can't imagine," I said.

The sadness in Alan's eyes had me swallowing back tears.

As we started for the limo, a police cruiser appeared from a side street and pulled into the far entrance to the lot.

"Doesn't it seem like there's an awfully heavy police presence this morning?" I asked, mostly to break the heavy silence. "Despite it all."

"Until they figure out who killed Cathy Carter, I'm probably the only one who's safe." He sighed. "And that's only because they're trying to kill my business instead of me personally."

"I'm sorry to say you may be right."

"I'm the one who's sorry," Alan said, his voice teary and sounding oddly reminiscent of Frank. "First I get Cathy Carter killed, then I drag you into this disaster." He shook his head. "To know I've put you in harm's way …"

"Maddie?" The unmistakable voice of Frank himself echoed from behind us.

Alan looked startled as Frank bolted out the back door, ran over to us, and put a protective arm around my shoulder.

"The last place you should be is out here! It's not safe."

"I haven't let her out of my sight," Alan said.

"I'm fine, Frank," I said. "We're just waiting for John Carter. He's not going to the reception and Alan's planning to follow him home to make sure he gets settled in okay."

Frank nodded his approval.

"Alan also found some incriminating video tape that may be important in—"

Before I could finish my sentence, the police cruiser pulled up and blocked the limo. The driver's side and passenger doors swung open, and none other than Detectives McClarkey and Reed flew out of the car.

"Mr. Bader, put your hands up and lean against the side of the car," Detective Reed called.

"Me?" he said faintly.

Both detectives had their guns out to show they definitely meant him.

"But I …" he said, turning around and putting his hands against the glass of his otherwise spotless car. "I …"

"Alan Bader, you're under arrest for the murder of Catherine Carter."

TWENTY

"I CAN'T BELIEVE THIS is happening," I said to Detective McClarkey as Alan Bader was cuffed, read his rights, and loaded into the back of a patrol car by Detective Reed. "He can't be…"

"Where did Mr. Bader say he was heading?" Detective McClarkey asked.

"To John Carter's house, so he wouldn't be alone while his family was at the reception."

"And he asked you to come with him?"

"No."

"But he did call you out of church to meet him?"

"Yes, but—"

"But it's a good thing your… Mr. Michaels came out when he did," Detective McClarkey said with a brusque nod of acknowledgment to Frank. "I can only imagine what Alan had planned for you."

Frank held me that much tighter. "You think he planned to abduct her or something?"

"Or worse," Detective McClarkey said. "I think she's been getting in the way of his plans."

I felt ill. "I just can't believe that Alan—"

"Neither could I until all the pieces started fitting together," Mc-Clarkey said.

"Pieces?"

"I began to look into a few things after our conversation down at the station the other day."

"Like what?" I managed, watching the lookie-loos trickle out of the church, spot the disturbance, and make their way over to investigate the police activity.

"Like why a big corporation would run a single-location family store out of business by resorting to murder in the first place."

"If you destroy both the reputation and the profit margin of a store like Bargain Barn on the busiest night of the year, and in the midst of media coverage, they're as good as gone," I said.

"I've certainly seen some crazy things done in the name of greed," Detective McClarkey said. "But why would a big, deep-pocketed corporation take such a huge risk when they could simply open up nearby and advertise all sorts of specials that would have shoppers flocking to the new store anyway?"

"I don't know," I said.

"Did you know that Alan Bader is in the midst of a contentious divorce?"

"I knew he was a widower."

"He's that, too," Detective McClarkey said. "But apparently wife number two got used to a certain standard of living she has no intention of compromising, and she's rejected any and all reasonable alimony offers."

"So you think he was trying to devalue his business to keep her from getting her big settlement?" Frank asked.

"It sure looks that way."

Frank *whoa* whistled. "Not un-clever."

Detective McClarkey shook his head. "As though there's such a thing as a clever way to get divorced."

"But if his business dies, then he loses everything too," I said. "Right?"

"He wasn't trying to kill the business, just suppress profits for a period of time to show his assets were nowhere near what his wife is demanding from him."

"By playing Russian roulette with Bargain Barn?" I asked.

"Why did he shut himself away in his office with Cathy Carter's husband and leave the fate of the store in the care of an assistant manager?"

"To comfort a man whose pain he understood only too well?" I said.

"Or to hide out while all hell broke loose around him," McClarkey answered.

"But—"

"But we kept the store open," Frank said, finishing my sentence.

"And Bargain Barn had the best Black Friday receipts they've ever had," I added.

"Which is why an arrest had to happen ASAP," Detective Mc-Clarkey said. "Particularly after the note on your car threatening Maddie."

Frank glanced into the back of the patrol car at Alan, hands behind his back, awaiting transport to a jail I knew far too well.

"What a sick plan," Frank said.

I swallowed the giant lump that had formed in my throat. "I still don't get why would Alan stage an accident then insist it was a crime."

"Easy," McClarkey said. "Remember what I told you about the flood of negligence lawsuits he'd be facing?"

"If it's a murder, then Bargain Barn isn't at fault," Frank added.

"Exactly."

"But what about the tape?" I asked.

"Alan couldn't prove when it was made. He claimed it was from right after the accident, but that particular security camera was older and the date stamp hadn't been programmed in. Besides, the image was too grainy to tell who the person was."

A police officer emerged from the door where I'd exited the church. Behind him, and flanked by two additional officers, was John Carter. His expression was equal parts deep distress and sheer confusion.

I had a feeling it matched mine.

"Did you know Alan not only organized, but underwrote the memorial today?" I said as Anastasia and the cameraman appeared in the doorway and began to film John and his small entourage of family members being led over to the waiting limo.

"Even more interesting," Detective McClarkey said as John paused to look over at the patrol car where Alan awaited transport, shook his head, and slipped inside the limo. "Did Alan tell you how his first wife died?"

"I didn't get a chance to ask," I said.

"An accident," he said.

"What kind of accident?" Frank asked as I fought back tears watching the vehicles take off together, each man headed toward his own personal hell.

"An accident in the warehouse of Bargain Barn," Detective Mc-Clarkey said.

"At the store?" I heard myself ask.

"She was *accidentally* pinned beneath a front loader."

"Seriously?" Frank asked.

"The file's been sitting in our cold case cabinet for years," Detective McClarkey said.

"Meaning you have evidence tying Alan to both crimes?"

He nodded. "We do now."

TWENTY-ONE

"I'M JUST GLAD MADDIE is safe and sound," Joyce said as we filed from our various cars back into the house. "Thank goodness!"

"Why is it always the nice ones you have to watch out for?" Barb asked.

Frank sniffed. "Never trusted the guy."

"I don't think I've ever watched someone I know get arrested," Trent said, tugging off his tie.

"You weren't there when Toby Torrance got caught with booze after the football game last year?" FJ asked.

"Oh, yeah. I forgot about that."

"Now that there's nothing to worry about, can I have a car?" Eloise asked. "I really want to see my friends for a couple of hours before I leave tonight."

"Shouldn't we have a proper goodbye supper before we send you back to all that dorm food?" Joyce asked.

"That would be great," Eloise said. "But I don't want you to go to any trouble."

"Maybe we can order pizza or something?" FJ asked.

"That way no one has to cook," Trent added.

"I do have a coupon for twenty dollars off any order over fifty at Leonardo's."[31]

"All I know is we need to eat early," Frank said. "Say, five thirty, so we have time before I take you to the airport?"

"Perfect," Eloise, the boys, and I all said in unison.

As she accepted Frank's car keys, the boys headed toward their never ending, purportedly ever-evolving Xbox game, and the rest of the family began to disperse throughout the house, I made my way into the entry hall. The realtor had jotted a note on the comments pad I'd left on the front table.

Thank you for opening your lovely house on such short notice, but the buyers have decided to go in a different direction.

"Everything's coming up roses," Gerald said from the kitchen to Joyce or whomever it was he was talking to.

His words seemed to hang in the hallway as I went into my office, powered on the computer, turned on the TV to drown out the family noise, and closed the French doors behind me.

Cathy Carter's killer was behind bars.

We were all out of harm's way except for the one person who, by his own admission, was safe in the first place.

My marriage was no longer on the brink of collapse.

Other than a still-necessary offer on the house, everything *was* coming up roses.

I sighed.

---

31. It seems obvious, but never throw away coupon mailers without leafing through for deals on goods, services, and entertainment. Great deals and found money await.

If only the roses didn't feel quite so thorny.

My situation with Frank, while on a better track, had a long way to go to be called ideal again. We needed to sell the house and soon, so the buyer's pass was a disappointment. What bothered me most though was I hadn't even for a second considered that Alan Bader could be anything more than the victim of horrible bad luck or—if his sleep-deprived, distress-induced theory had proved true—the target of corporate evil doing.

But a double murderer?

I still couldn't believe the kind, sensitive man I'd been working alongside was not only a cold-hearted sociopath, but one with Oscar-worthy acting skills.

Could he really have had plans to do me in next?

I logged on to my computer and found myself scanning through the growing messages and sharing the shock, outrage, and general horror about the arrest. Ditto on my emails, where, mixed in with the mounting *How could he?* notes was a message from Anastasia.

The subject line read *Cyber Monday:*

Maddie,

Can you believe this day? Just when we thought things couldn't get any more shocking or sensational ... wow!!!

Sorry we didn't get to talk in the midst of everything, but since Cyber Monday is meant to be a day to stay at home and shop, I was thinking that I'd really like to tape tomorrow's segment from your house. I'm planning to have the crew there tomorrow morning at ten a.m. to tape us talking online tips. We'll run the segment on the noon news in conjunction with any updates on the Bargain Barn story. Sound like a plan?

Still reeling from this morning,
Anastasia

Reeling was the key word, all right.

I hadn't expected to have a camera crew traipsing through my house, but given the weekend had been nothing but a series of unforeseeable and unexpected events, why not tape from the comfort of home?

I sent Anastasia a confirmation email and then tried to distract myself by jotting Cyber Monday bullet points for both the Mrs. Frugalicious blog and my morning interview:

* Make a list: It keeps you on track and prevents unnecessary impulse buys like accessories or add-ons that eat into your discounts.

* Do your research in advance: Many merchants announce their online offers ahead of Cyber Monday. Check top coupon sites for a roundup of deals available as well.

* Pre-shop: Some marketers will try and make a regular price look like a bargain so before you start loading your cart, do some comparing at sites like pricegrabber.com, eBay, and local stores—particularly when you're shopping for high-priced items with options and features.

* Find free shipping: Steep shipping and handling costs quickly cut into your cyber savings.

* Read up on returns: Return shipping and restocking fees can be an unexpected and unwelcome expense, so know the policies for sending things back.

I managed to stay semi-distracted with the task at hand—but only until I wrote the next bullet point:

* Practice safe shopping: Don't be fooled by a deal that seems too good to be true. Do a search on the name of a particular website to see a record of prior consumer complaints.

Somehow, I couldn't imagine feeling entirely safe about shopping ever again.

I'd certainly been fooled by Alan and his best advertiser and friendly client act, both online and in-person.

*Check the Better Business Bureau to see if the site you want to visit is accredited. The National Retail Federation's CyberMonday.com also has a list of legitimate retailers offering Cyber Monday discounts.

Detective McClarkey was right—a legitimate retailer might not be above an elaborate scheme to depress Bargain Barn's profits so they could be acquired at a low price—but why resort to murder?

*Secure your purchase by only entering credit card details on pages that use SSL security. To make sure you're on a secure page, check that the URL for the page begins with "https://" and not "http://." That "s" lets you know the site is secure.

Bargain Barn sold all types of high-tech equipment, from televisions to video cameras. What were the chances that they didn't know how to set the date and time on their own store security camera?

Setting aside the Cyber Monday tip list I'd started, I turned back to my computer and opened the *Questions & Answers* spreadsheet.

The spreadsheet I'd made specifically to share with Alan.

Alan, who insisted we not bring the police into it until we had enough information for them to believe our story.

His story.

My first question, *Was the accident really an accident?* had apparently been answered.

As was *Who killed Cathy Carter?*

I created a new tab, titled it *Alan Bader: Guilty As Charged* and began to list every suspicious thing I could think of about our interactions over the past few months.

Contacted Mrs. Frugalicious, invested in advertising, and established a preferred customer relationship for the purposes of manipulation.

Made too-good-to-be-true Black Friday deals to entice Frugarmy to his store.

Sweetened the deal when he learned Channel Three was coming but made sure to stay out of the spotlight himself.

Created deal maps to get shoppers into a certain organization and order.

Snuck away at an opportune moment, climbed into the rafters in an out of the way corner of Bargain Barn, scrambled across the store, and pushed pallet off upper shelf.

Disappeared into his office with victim's husband after the pallet fell.

A: To comfort John Carter in light of the tragic loss of his own wife?

B: So he wouldn't be available in the aftermath of the incident and Bargain Barn would necessarily have to close?

Somehow, both options still stumped me for some reason.

So did the news report that then preempted the all-in-one-weights-and-cardio-training-system infomercial that had been droning away on my small office TV.

Not surprisingly, Anastasia Chastain appeared on the screen.

"I'm here in front of the South Metro Police Department, where local businessman Alan Bader of Bargain Barn is being held at this hour on suspicion of murder. His dramatic arrest took place earlier this morning in the midst of the memorial service for his alleged victim, Mrs. Catherine Carter..."

Tape rolled of the arrest scene itself, including me in conversation with Detective McClarkey amid the gathering crowd. The clip ended with John Carter, his face a mask of confusion and distress, as he stopped to glance at Alan in the back of the patrol car.

The news report went live again outside the police station.

"We were all shocked by Mr. Bader's arrest, none of us more so, I'm sure, than the Carter family." The camera angle widened as Anastasia turned to a familiar gray-haired lady standing beside her. "With me is Cathy Carter's aunt, Louise Carter."

"We came straight from the memorial down to the police station," said a stoic, but clearly angry Aunt Louise. "How could Mr. Bader have done such a horrible thing?"

"A question I think we're all asking right now," Anastasia said.

"If only John and Cathy had headed home from Thanksgiving at our house like they'd planned."

Like they'd planned?

"They weren't planning to go shopping?" Anastasia asked as though reading my mind.

I upped the volume on the television.

"Cathy said she was tired from eating too much turkey and they were turning in early. I can't imagine why they decided to stop by one of those wretched, crazy sales instead…"

Instead of heading straight home, Cathy Carter—who wasn't and couldn't have been CC since Alan was, but coincidentally happened to have the same initials as CC—suddenly happened to decide, for no particular reason, to go shopping on Black Friday at none other than Bargain Barn?

That, or Cathy *was* CC and had spent months writing nasty posts saying she wasn't coming to Bargain Barn, and had gone so far as to announce she was headed straight home after Thanksgiving dinner, then just showed up at Bargain Barn anyway? Not to mention proclaimed she was a big fan and wanted her picture taken with me when she got there?

I turned to my spreadsheet.

Were Catherine Carter and CC (Contrary Claire) the same person?
1. Yes.

If so, then Cathy had been my online heckler. Alan had to have decided she was in the way and enticed her to come to the store for a different kind of Black Friday special. Then, after killing her, he pretended to be her via email, to make it look like she was a victim of the unnamed corporate killer?

2. No.

Then Alan, who coincidentally started advertising at about the same time as CC appeared, had posed as CC all along, heckling and writing from various emails, while Cathy Carter was a random innocent person who happened to share the initials of my online stalker? And happened to change her mind about going to Bargain Barn at the last moment...?

3. Maybe?

Alan had to be CC or was tracking CC.

In any case, why did Cathy end up at the store when she wasn't planning to go?

Furthermore, how did Alan know who she was or what she looked like when she got there?

The front doors to the precinct opened behind Anastasia, and Aunt Louise and John Carter emerged with Louise's husband and the other male relative.

All were still dressed for the memorial service in dark suits.

"First a funeral, and then having to spend the afternoon answering questions at the police station," Anastasia said as they made their way over. "I can't imagine what a difficult day this has been for your family."

"Unbearable." Aunt Louise shook her head. "Can you believe Mr. Bader was planning to head to my nephew's house and keep him company when they arrested him?"

"Truly shocking," Anastasia said, quickly pointing her microphone at John Carter. "Mr. Carter, I'm so sorry for your loss."

"Thank you," he croaked in a gravelly, anguished voice, and looking like he'd rather be anywhere than on camera.

"You have to be relieved the police made such short work of such a terrible situation."

"Very," he managed.

"How do you feel knowing Mr. Bader was heading to your house at the time of his arrest?"

"I just can't believe the deception." Tears now welled in his eyes. "He put himself out there as a comfort and a true friend."

"Devastating insult to injury," Anastasia said.

"I just want my wife back." John began to sob.

"If you'll excuse us, we really need to get him home," the younger of the two men said, putting an arm around John Carter.

As Anastasia attempted to summarize the story with some sort of *justice served despite it all* spin I watched, once again, as a slump-shouldered John Carter slipped into the limo Alan had rented for them and headed off toward a future of loneliness, sadness, and the certainty of uncertainty.

I was outraged by the idea that Alan Bader could have blind-sided both of us with what could only be sheer cold-hearted cruelty. I also couldn't help but feel that if it weren't for me and my discount shopping call to arms, the Frugarmy wouldn't be short one nice, kind, bland member.

Considering I hadn't had a chance to pay my sympathies to the widower like Anastasia had, I decided it was high time to try and counterbalance the damage done by placing a condolence call of my own.

I was turning away from the TV to begin wading my way through the online White Pages for people named John Carter in the Denver metro area when Anastasia added, "This story has apparently touched the hearts of viewers at home, many of whom have asked where they can send their condolences. Donations in Cathy Carter's name should be made to the Mile High Pet Adoption Society…"

And then she added a footnote that gave me an even better idea.

"If you would like to send a card to Mr. Carter directly, the address is at the bottom of your screen."

———

Grabbing one of the oversized wicker baskets I'd picked up during a buy-one-get-one-for-a-penny sale at the craft store, I put together a condolence basket [32] filled with a variety of snacks and easy-to-prepare food items. Seeing as there was no reception or wake to speak of, John Carter would have little or nothing in the way of casseroles or baked goods to keep him nourished while he adjusted to life without a wife and hot dinner waiting for him.

I arranged the basket of goodies, wrapped it in plastic,[33] tied some raffia around the top, and made my way up the stairs.

While I'd rather have left a note saying I was off to do a few errands, there was no avoiding the boys. As they'd been all weekend, they were stationed in front of the family room TV, in view of the basement stairs.

"Where are you going?" FJ asked without looking up from the post-apocalyptic disaster scenario playing out on screen.

"Just headed out for a quick errand," I said, making a mental note to pay a bit more attention to what was actually going on in those games they were so into.

---

32. The time to shop for significant life cycle events is not when they happen. Birthdays and anniversaries happen every year, so be prepared and buy everything from toys to clothing on sale in anticipation of that gift you'll need to give in a matter of months. Other than fresh flowers or perishable food, which obviously can't be bought and stored, you'll save big.
33. Purchased, once again, on clearance and in bulk at the craft store.

"With a giant gift basket?" Trent asked with the hint of an eyebrow raise.

"It's for Cathy Carter's husband," I said.

"You're going over to his house?" FJ asked, actually glancing up.

"Considering his wife was a member of my Frugarmy, I can't help but feel somewhat responsible."

"You think what happened is your fault?" Trent asked.

"Not exactly," I said. "But either Alan was posing as my stalker CC and Cathy Carter died as a result, or he was stalking her and now she's dead."

"Which still doesn't make it your fault," FJ said.

"I suppose not," I said. "But the least I can do is bring Mr. Carter some food to help him through the next few difficult days and let him know how sorry I am about everything that's happened."

"Whoa!" Trent said, as something exploded on screen.

"Sounds like a good idea, Mom," FJ added, and they disappeared back into their game.

———

Seeing as I'd rushed over to the Carter home without a thought as to whether John Carter might not want further sympathy, support, or visitors of any kind, I figured I should probably leave my gift basket and sympathy card on the front stoop—along with the growing pile of gifts and assorted flowers—and then disappear.

And I might have done just that, had the front door not opened before my finger reached the bell. And there I was, standing face to face with John Carter.

"Hi, Mr. Carter, I'm Maddie Michaels," I said. "Mrs. Frugalicious."

"Of course," he said. His jacket was off and his tie was loosened, but he was otherwise still dressed in his suit, as though he hadn't even thought about changing into something more comfortable.

"I thought you might be able to use this," I said, handing him the basket.

"Thank you." He offered the saddest of smiles in return. "You're very kind."

"With all the awful surprises that have come to light this morning, I figured …"

"Please come in," he said, looking every bit as beaten-down and sad as he'd looked in the church and on TV. "And call me John."

"John," I said. "I really don't want to impose."

"Not at all," he said. "I'm glad you're here."

The sweat that had broken out at the base of my neck began to cool as he motioned me to follow him inside.

Somehow I'd pictured sweet, innocent Cathy Carter living in a typical suburban two-story or split-level decorated with country flair and wall accents to match. (Picky, disapproving CC, on the other hand, might well have lived in a similar house, but her decorating style would have been more contemporary and uncluttered.)

I'd also expected Cathy to live in the middle of a long block of nearly identical homes, differentiated by the right or left placement of the garage, roof slope and/or slight variation of beige trim. Instead, the Carter home was an older, single-story ranch on a quiet street of ten or so homes separated by mature trees and sizeable yards. The décor, eclectic to say the least, was cluttered with furniture and accessories, especially for a couple with no children, and who'd only lived there a few years.

"My wife was a huge fan of yours," he said, putting the gift basket down on the coffee table beside a series of framed photos of Cathy from the glamour shot session Channel Three had been broadcasting all weekend long. "Would you believe she decorated this entire living room without buying a single thing that wasn't at least half price?"

"That's fantastic," I said, even if the lavender suede five-piece seating group and the family of chartreuse ceramic geese crossing the mantel definitely weren't.[34] In fact, the house appeared to be an homage to buying anything and everything that came with a RE-DUCED sticker.

"I can't believe you're standing in our living room. If Cathy were here, she'd insist on giving you a tour of all the great deals she's gotten thanks to your website, but I just can't bear ..." A tear began to roll down his sallow, grief-aged face. "She'd have given anything to have met you in person."

"But I did meet her!"

"Really?" A trace of hope tinged his voice. "You did?"

"We met that night," I said, not adding the *just before* ... "We even took a picture together," I said, but I realized as I said it that the photo had been taken with a camera phone that had likely suffered the same fate as Cathy herself.

He must have thought the same thing at the same time, since neither of us said anything for a few awkward seconds.

---

34. It's always fun to score a great deal, but an ugly accessory doesn't grow much prettier just because of a beautiful price.

He glanced over at the flowers and gift baskets. "If only I had been beside her, I'm sure I'd have seen the pallet slip."

"John, there was no way of anticipating something like that was about to happen."

"I know I'd have been able to get her out of the way before..."

"Believe me, I understand," I said, "I keep going over every interaction I ever had with Alan Bader, wondering what I should have picked up on, or if there was any suspicious behavior on his part that could have tipped me off that he'd been planning something like this."

"He seemed like the best of folk, didn't he?"

"That he did."

"Which somehow makes it all that much harder." John grabbed a tissue from the box beside him and began to sob silently.

Unsure whether to offer another insufficient *I'm so sorry* or a very awkward hug, I stood beside him, helpless to do anything more than look at the overabundance of kitschy knick-knacks covering the tabletops and lining the shelves.

"Why her?" he said through his tears. "Why did it have to be her?"

I was asking myself the same question.

"How long have you been married?" he finally asked.

"Sixteen years," I said, not deducting the last three months from the equation.

"We'd just hit seven." He sighed. "I always figured I'd be single until I saw her."

"How did you meet?"

"She was into antiques and collectables before she got into bargain hunting," he said. "I spotted her at a vintage transportation toys tent at a car show. She was helping an elderly friend liquidate his collection."

Given her tastes, at least where home décor was concerned, and the fact she really did seem as sweet, kind, and too-nice-to-be-truly-believable as everyone said, Cathy Carter simply couldn't have been Contrary Claire. Which had to mean her death was either entirely random, or she'd been singled out for a reason that had yet to make any sense to me.

"John, may I ask you a question?"

"Of course."

"Your Aunt Louise said you had Thanksgiving at her house and planned to go straight home afterwards."

He nodded. "If only we had..."

"I hate to ask, but how did you end up at Bargain Barn instead?" My eyes were drawn to the picture of Cathy, her expression somehow searching, as if she were awaiting his answer too.

"She mentioned a few of the deals for Frugarmy members as we were driving by on our way home." Pure pain filled his face. "When I realized we had a good shot at getting a TV or one of the other big-ticket items if we parked and got right in line, I insisted we go for it."

I patted his shoulder.

"Even though she was a little tired, I knew it would be worth it if she got to meet you in person."

The divorce butterflies, having taken up a new cause, began to flutter wildly in my guts.

"And Alan," he added. "She wanted to meet Awesome Alan, too."

"Did she get the chance?" I had to ask.

He nodded. "As soon as we came in the front door."

My cell phone rang. "I should check to see who this is," I said, glad for the momentary distraction of fumbling in my purse. "In case it's one of my kids."

The blood began to pulse in my ears when I located the phone and read the caller ID: *South Metro Police.*

"I'm afraid I'll need to take this."

"Of course," John said.

"McClarkey here," the detective said with my hello.

"Yes," I said trying to modulate any particular emotion from my voice. "What is it?"

"Can you get down to the station?"

"When?"

"Preferably now."

"I mean, I—"

"Alan Bader is insisting he talk to you."

"Me?"

"And Detective Reed thinks we should let him."

"I ... isn't this a bit unusual?" I asked turning away from John Carter and stepping toward the front door so as not to upset him any further. I lowered my voice to a whisper. "Shouldn't he be meeting with his lawyer or something first?"

"Already has," Detective McClarkey said. "And now he wants, *insists*, that he speak with you."

"Why?" I asked.

"That's what we want to know."

TWENTY-TWO

"I only met her for a second at the door to the store," Alan said. "I didn't even catch her name."

Needless to say, the orange jumpsuit, handcuffs, crazy hair, and frantic look in his eyes didn't do anything to help his credibility. Nor did the stark surroundings of the interrogation room where we met.

"I certainly didn't kill Cathy Carter."

"The police seem to think otherwise," I said, noting the guard at the door.

"I'm innocent," he said. "I shouldn't be here."

"Neither should I," I said, although Detective McClarkey hadn't exactly asked so much as told me to get down to the station.

"Thank you for coming." His angry edge seemed to soften.

"To be clear, I didn't come because I think you're innocent," I said, not mentioning the *be natural and say what you're going to say* briefing I'd just had with McClarkey and Ross. "Mostly, I wanted to be able to look into your eyes and judge for myself if you could have really..."

"I didn't," he said emphatically.

"I was with John Carter when the police called to tell me you wanted to talk to me."

"At his house?"

I felt awful rushing off, not to mention lying to him by saying that one of my kids needed me. But I had promised I'd come back to check in on him after my Monday-morning segment with Anastasia. "I couldn't bear the thought that he was there alone. Not only having lost his wife, but—"

"Betrayed for sport by the most cold-hearted psychopath alive?"

Despite his protestations of innocence, I still found myself waiting for that creepy moment I'd watched play out on countless crime dramas. That moment when the psycho killer couldn't help but smile wryly at a gory job well done.

"I can't tell you how glad I am you were there for him," he said instead, his voice cracking with what seemed to be relief. "Almost worse than getting falsely arrested was seeing John look into the police car and know he had to think I was some kind of sick, sadistic killer with a fetish for comforting my victim's family."

Was I being played or was Alan really as sincere as he sounded?

"You did foot the funeral bill," I finally said, "which you have to admit is more than a little unusual."

"He's between jobs and his wife was crushed by a pallet in my store." He paused. "What would you have done?"

I hadn't doubted his kindness and honesty for a second until I doubted everything about him, but with his question, I found myself doubting my doubts. "Alan, I'd like to believe you. I want to believe you, but the evidence is stacking up against you."

"It's circumstantial evidence and it only appears to point to me."

"Be that as it may—"

"If I were a killer, why not do in my money-grubbing ex instead of an innocent customer and the business I've loved since I was a child?" He shook his head. "To this day I don't know why I was compelled to do right by that woman and marry her knowing she loved pretty, shiny things above all else …"

"They don't think you wanted to kill the business," I said, trying not to think about the similarities between his ex and mine—or would Frank now be my ex-ex? "Just depress profits temporarily."

"As though that's possible after someone is *accidentally* crushed in your store," he said. "If you hadn't been there to help keep Bargain Barn open, I'd be boarding the place up now." He paused. "If I weren't here, that is."

"But you had no way of knowing Frank and I were going to do that."

"I'm very thankful you did, though."

"Then why did you shut yourself away in your office with Cathy Carter's husband and leave the fate of the store in the care of an assistant manager?"

"I was in no condition to be out on the sales floor." Anguish filled his face. "I'm sure you've heard how my first wife died?"

I managed a nod.

"Thank God our son is deployed out of the country right now. The real killer has to be found before he hears I'm being accused of …" Tears brimmed in his eyes. "How anyone could think I would ever harm anyone, much less his mother. I loved her more than anything."

As he put his head in his hands and began to sob, I found myself running through the list I'd made of Alan's incriminating behavior.

Despite feeling slightly indelicate about cross-examining a man who was openly sobbing over his long-deceased first wife and proclaiming his absolute innocence, the situation called for a desperate times/desperate measures approach.

I also knew Detectives McClarkey and Reed were on the other side of the two-way mirror listening.

If Alan was guilty, I could only hope they were hearing what they were looking for.

If not, at least I was giving the man an opportunity to make his case.

"Alan?" I asked, after giving him a minute to cry it out and collect himself. "Why did you contact my website in the first place?"

"Demographics. We're a local discount retailer and MrsFrugalicious.com is a locally based bargain hunting site. It was an ideal advertising investment," he said, wiping his nose. "For one thing."

"And for another?"

"Honestly?"

"I think the situation calls for honesty."

"I heard you were getting a divorce too and figured that since we were both in the same boat ..." He shook his head. "But given how things are working out at the moment, I guess I miscalculated."

Despite it all, I felt myself blush. It had been years since any man but Frank had openly expressed an interest in me. "I ..."

"I have to admit, I was a little taken aback when I saw you and Frank were back together."

"It's been a weekend full of the unexpected," I heard myself say, before awkwardly trying to get back on track with another question. "I assume it was your plan to do a Black Friday promotion involving the Frugarmy all along?"

"From the moment I found your website."

"Which was when?"

"The same day I called you, three months ago," he said. "The whole campaign was going well, as you know, and should have been an all around win-win, particularly with a news crew on hand."

"Why did you try to stay off camera?"

"I don't like the way I look without the makeup and hair people that get me ready for my commercials."

After three days of seeing myself on TV, I had to admit I understood that particular excuse.

"You did pre-plan exactly where the Frugarmy would line up, though."

"Until Anastasia Chastain switched things around so they could get better tape."

A fact I'd been there to confirm.

"Where were you when the pallet fell?"

"In the executive washroom."

"Another spot where the store security tape wasn't properly date and time stamped?"

"We don't have cameras inside the bathrooms, employee or public, for obvious reasons," he said. "And I'm not sure why the tape I provided wasn't properly date and time stamped. It should have been, but whoever's looking at it just needs to hone in on the products on the shelves. There has to be a serial or model number that can be used to confirm production dates."

"I'm told it was too blurry to figure out who was even climbing the shelves."

"Dear Lord, I need something to break in my direction." He put his head in his hands. "If only I could have found tape of the perpetrator climbing up, or something to prove—"

"I'm afraid it's going to take more than video to support your corporate assassin theory, which, while compelling—"

"Was wrong," Alan said, finishing my sentence.

"What?" I asked, my voice going up an octave.

"My lawyer told me that the company I was most suspicious of, who's known for some serious dirty dealing, are after a small chain of discount stores in the Southwest and not Bargain Barn at all."

"Meaning you don't think there was any sort of corporate conspiracy?"

"No." Color crept up his neck and into his cheeks. "I feel silly for having been so convinced."

Not as silly as I felt for believing him. "If you didn't kill Cathy, and there was no hit man or anything like that, who *do* you think killed her, then?"

"That's what we have to figure out."

"We?"

"Mostly you, I'm afraid. At least until they set bail and my soon-to-be-ex gets me out of here."

"Your ex is bailing you out?"

"She doesn't get anything if I end up in prison," he said. "Making her one of the few people I don't suspect at this point."

My head was spinning. "Who *do* you suspect?"

He took a deep breath, presumably to recover from all of my rapid-fire questions. "All I know for sure is it's far too coincidental to believe that Cathy Carter just happened to share the same initials as your stalker."

"So you definitely think Cathy Carter was CC?"

"Had to be."

"If so, she was the nicest, kindest heckler on the face of the planet."

"Maybe she was Dr. Jekyll in person but Mr. Hyde at her keyboard."

"It's possible, but that would mean whoever killed her left threatening messages pretending to be her after the fact," I said.

"Seemingly threatening messages."

"Seemingly?"

"I really think the killer would have targeted you at Bargain Barn if that's what he or she was really intending," he said.

"Then why the warning on my car?"

"I believe the note was just supposed to scare you off from investigating any further," Alan said. His expression was honest, genuine, and concerned but tinged orange from the reflection of his jail jumpsuit.

"It's working," I said.

"You can't let it," he whispered, clearly aware or at least suspicious we were being listened in on. "Because I also think Cathy Carter may have been killed because of, or on behalf of, Mrs. Frugalicious."

"What do you mean? Why?"

"I'm not sure—maybe to ruin you on your big night?"

My stomach felt like a concrete mixer. "Alan, that's basically the same theory you had about Bargain Barn, now applied to Mrs. Frugalicious."

"Whoever killed her could also have done it to protect you from your crazy stalker, or, worse, maybe even frame you."

"Twice in three months?" I asked, just like Detective McClarkey was probably saying from behind the glass. "Come on, Alan."

"All I know is you show up at Bargain Barn with news cameras in tow and a pallet crushes your number-one naysayer," Alan said. "I may have misapplied the facts to Bargain Barn at first, but I think we can both agree that there has to be a connection to you."

My pulse, already racing, went into hyper drive. "Why?"

"Figure that out and we have the real killer."

———

"You heard Alan swear he's innocent." I said to Detective McClarkey as he escorted me across the parking lot.

"Yup." He nodded. "Our prison system is overcrowded with innocent men and women."

"So you're saying you don't believe anything he said?"

"I'm saying I'll reserve judgment until we've checked everything out."

"But you're going to? Check it out?"

"I don't expect to find anything but more evidence against him."

"But what if Alan's right and there's a killer still on the loose?"

"We'll be on it," Detective McClarkey stopped at my car and eyed the back seat before opening the driver's side door for me to slip inside. "In the meantime, how about you lay low this time and let us do the investigating?"

"No problem," I said.

"It'll only be a problem if you don't," he said, closing the door.

TWENTY-THREE

WAS ALAN BADER GUILTY and trying to deflect the focus from himself, or was he innocent, falsely-imprisoned, and correct that whoever had killed Cathy Carter, AKA Contrary Claire, AKA CC, was on some sort of twisted Mrs. Frugalicious mission the whole time?

As I drove home, I felt certain only that I was being followed, despite a lack of suspicious nondescript vehicles hovering two to three cars back. Alan's new theory, or deflection or whatever it was, was definitely worrying me.

If he was right, the killer had to have known Cathy Carter was my cyber stalker CC.

Which still meant Alan remained the primary suspect.

But if he was right, it also meant someone else could have killed Cathy—either in some kind of misguided attempt to protect Mrs. Frugalicious, to frame me, to ruin my business, or for some other reason I was racking my brain to imagine.

Someone with a motive Alan Bader seemed to lack.

By the time I made my way into the house and managed to duck into my office for a few minutes before dinner, I already had a growing and increasingly distressing suspect list in mind.

I opened the spreadsheet entitled *Alan Bader Guilty As Charged* and removed the *Alan Bader* so the title became *Guilty As Charged*.

Leaving Alan's name in the number one slot, I began to list everyone else I could think of who knew about my online stalker and was at Bargain Barn at the time of the accident.

Anastasia Chastain

Anastasia qualified as a suspect because she was at Bargain Barn, had definitely rerouted the Frugarmy line before the incident, and had left me with the cameraman for a supposed visit to the little girl's room just before the pallet fell.

And, of course, there was her keen and ever-present interest in boosting ratings.

Death always boosted ratings, right?

Somehow though, I couldn't see her taping our segment, rushing across the store, shimmying unnoticed across the upper storage shelves, killing Cathy Carter, and rejoining me to film the aftermath.

Not in the stilettos she was wearing that night, anyway.

The Piggledys

The Piggledys were at the store and knew about the existence of CC, but given that Mrs. Piggledy was injured as a result of the falling pallet and Mr. Piggledy was far too heavy to have climbed to the upper shelves, much less scrambled back down to his wife's side in time, they were both innocent.

I put a line through their names.

L'Raine

L'Raine was certainly at the store shopping, and might well have known of the existence of CC, since she followed my blog, but given she was in the Frugarmy line at the time the pallet fell, she couldn't be guilty. She'd also put one of the first calls into Griff, who was not only a cop, but her apparent love interest.

I put a line through her name as well.

Wendy Killian

Wendy from *Here's the Deal* magazine was at Bargain Barn and likely knew about CC before Cathy Carter was killed since she also followed my blog, but what possible motive could she have to kill her then take on her identity? Besides, she was in the TV line at the time the pallet fell—a fact I could easily substantiate.

Which is where the real problem came in.

The one person I could most easily ask was also a suspect. He also happened to share a last name with the rest of the names I needed to add to my *Guilty As Charged* spreadsheet. Michaels. As in:

Craig Michaels

Craig—who knew about CC and just happened to volunteer to come along to Bargain Barn Thursday night—was purportedly in the TV line, but was then detained in the back of the store along with Wendy Killian right after the accident.

Frank Michaels

Where was Frank at the crucial moment?

Joyce Michaels

Hadn't she asked Frank to meet up with her right beforehand?

Gerald Michaels

Despite not being all there, he had to have been somewhere when the pallet was pushed.

Barb Michaels

She was supposedly with Joyce, Frank, Gerald, and (I felt downright nauseous to add to my list) …

Eloise Michaels

As their random voices and general noise echoed through the house, the room felt like it was starting to spin.

Alan Bader had to be guilty because if he wasn't, the Michaels' family Thanksgiving convergence was starting to feel a lot less like an oddly fortuitous coming together and a lot more like part of a bigger, increasingly disturbing plan.

Before I dabbed the sweat that had broken out across my forehead, or allowed myself to consider what that plan could possibly be, I picked up the phone and started to dial Anastasia.

I hung up before I finished pressing the numbers.

Since she was technically a suspect, I decided to wait to call her to ask about any possible (and possibly far-fetched) suspicions, at least until I'd confirmed Craig's whereabouts at the time of the murder. He should have been with Wendy.

I didn't dial Wendy but instead sent her what I hoped sounded like a friendly, non-urgent text with a *please get back to me as soon as it's convenient* addendum.

Once she confirmed that she'd seen Craig at the time of the accident, I planned to ask Craig the same question. That would hopefully eliminate two names on my lengthy suspect list.

There was only one other person left that I could think of in the meantime who could shed some light on what was or wasn't going on—if only in the form of police station chatter.

Griff.

"If it isn't the South Metro PD's newest interrogator," he said by way of hello.

I was counting on the fact he'd not only heard about my visit, but all the latest station scuttlebutt in the aftermath of my meeting with Alan. "So, you heard I was there today?"

"And that you did a better job than a few of the seasoned pros around the station."

"Really?"

"So good, you may get a call next time there's an opening on the force."

"But not good enough to get a confession out of Alan Bader," I said as a pizza delivery truck pulled into the driveway. "He swears he's innocent."

"If I've learned one thing since I was hired," Griff said, "it's that they all swear they're innocent."

"You're sounding more and more like Detective McClarkey."

"He's a smart guy."

"But not always right," I said.

"Are you saying you've been convinced that we've got the wrong guy?"

The doorbell rang and Frank and what sounded like Barb both called, "Got it!"

"Everything I've heard so far links Alan to the crime," I whispered, as they passed the closed glass-paned doors to my office, "but the evidence seems too circumstantial, at least to me, to say for sure.

"I can—"

"Griff," I said. "Please don't say you can neither confirm nor deny."

"I was going to say I can't hear you very well," he said. "But they wouldn't have made an arrest unless there was some sort of solid evidence."

"Which is?"

"All I know is they've sent that surveillance tape to a tech expert downtown to see about further enhancements."

"That's good," I said. "The thing is, if it turns out it wasn't Alan …"

"Who else could it logically be?" Griff asked.

I was weighing whether I should share my concerns and how much when I spotted a piece of paper wadded up in a temporarily empty planter that looked like, but wasn't, a trash can.

"I'm not sure," I said un-crinkling what appeared to be a reservation for a Mr. and Mrs. Gerald Michaels.

A reservation that originated in Los Angeles and ended not in Ft. Lauderdale with a connection in Denver, but flew nonstop from L.A. to Denver only.

"Hey, everyone!" Frank's voice echoed through the house. "Last supper is served!"

TWENTY-FOUR

"This pizza is to die for," Joyce said, offering me a piece of Canadian bacon and pineapple.

Since I couldn't be sure whether she meant figuratively or literally, I accepted the slice, set it down, and pushed the antipasto salad around on my plate instead.

Once again, I couldn't quite fill Griff in on my worst suspicions. I trusted him implicitly, but if I were to tell him I feared my husband and maybe his family might well be involved in yet another *situation,* didn't he, as an officer of the law, have the obligation to report my concerns to Detectives McClarkey and Ross?

And then what?

No. Alan had to be guilty. Simple as that.

But as I forced myself to try and eat a bite or two of salad, I couldn't help but connect a few dots where the events of the weekend were concerned.

First, Craig begged his way into what was supposed to be our last Thanksgiving under one roof. Then, lo and behold, the cruise Gerald, Joyce, Barb, and her kids were supposed to take was cancelled, *stranding* them in Denver for the weekend.

A cruise they were never planning to take in the first place.

While it wasn't exactly suspicious that Anastasia contacted me soon after to do a Black Friday weekend special for Channel Three, Frank's unexpected eagerness to lend a hand definitely was. So was the enthusiasm of the Michaels clan, none of whom had shown any particular interest in Mrs. Frugalicious in the months since my alter ego came to light.

Why were they suddenly so eager to accompany me to Bargain Barn for my evening in the spotlight? An evening that included the murder of a person with the initials CC…

"Everything okay, Maddie?" Frank asked, wiping grease from the meat lover's delight pizza off his chin.

No! I wanted to scream. *I'm completely, utterly freaking out that Alan Bader could be innocent and you're all guilty of…*

The question was what?

Having been married to Frank for sixteen years, I knew the Michaelses were capable—individually, and as a group—of all sorts of shenanigans along the lines of a Thanksgiving *coming together* that was anything but an unexpected twist of fate. In the context of our marital woes, it even made some sense. Considering how much making up there was to be done on his part, I'd have called in reinforcements to help make my case if I were Frank, too.

You have Frank over a barrel. Joyce's words rang through my head. *No time for divorce.*

"I'm fine," I managed. "I think I'm just a little worn out after everything that's happened today."

"How could you not be?" Barb asked. "I mean, a memorial service, a TV appearance, and an unexpected arrest all in one day?"

"Not to mention that above-and-beyond condolence call to the Carter home," Joyce added.

"I feel so badly for him," I said, not mentioning I'd actually spent most of the afternoon down at the police station interrogating Alan Bader.

"How's he doing?" FJ asked.

Alan? I almost said, but managed to mumble something about John Carter's sad, shocked state instead.

"He's gotta be a lot better now that his wife's killer's off the streets," Trent said.

As heads bobbed in agreement, I still couldn't completely shake the feeling that I was somehow in a scene from a horror movie where everyone nodded and smiled like zombies, pretending they weren't involved in all manner of mayhem.

The fact was, every person at the table knew about CC—Frank and the kids knew for months. Frank had (with Anastasia) rearranged the path of the Frugarmy line inside Bargain Barn before everyone scattered to different points around the store just before the pallet fell.

Craig had begged off toward the TV line with plenty of time to find a remote corner of the store and weave his way over to the kitchen electronics section before the police conveniently kept him from joining us.

Instead of excusing myself to my room and barricading myself inside until I could figure out what was or wasn't going on, I smiled and prayed no one but me could hear the thump of my heartbeat over the benign plinks, clinks, and chewing noises of the attractive, dark-haired, blue-eyed but suddenly more sinister than innocent Michaels family.

"Craig couldn't join us for dinner tonight?" I asked.

"He's out on another date with a woman he met at Bargain Barn," Barb said.

My resident stomach butterflies began to take flight. "What's her name?"

"I can't remember," Joyce said. "But he did say he was taking her out for the third night in a row."

"L'Raine?"

"Sounds familiar," Barb said.

"That blond, buxom gal Craig was chatting up right after they took Mrs. Piggledy to the hospital?" Frank asked.

"That's Uncle Craig for you," Trent said.

Everyone laughed but me.

If L'Raine was stepping out with Craig, didn't I have the obligation as a friend to report my findings to Griff?

"I still can't believe he was trolling for dates in the middle of everything," Eloise said.

"But wouldn't it be something if he finds love again as a result of all this craziness?" Joyce asked.

"We'd be batting a thousand," Gerald muttered between bites.

A meaningful, split-second glance passed from Joyce to her daughter.

"What he meant," Barb quickly added, "was that with Frank and Maddie working things out and Craig meeting someone, there's been a silver lining to the dark clouds that have hovered over this weekend."

"Speaking of silver linings," Frank said. "Anastasia offered to do a little subliminal real estate marketing for us and get a few interior and exterior shots of the house as long as they're taping the Cyber Monday segment here."

"Good idea," Joyce said.

Gerald and Barb smiled in agreement like satisfied cats with bellies full of canary.

"Trent and I were thinking maybe we could be on camera shopping tomorrow," FJ suggested.

"What?" I asked, trying to calm my monkey mind and focus on the conversation at hand.

"I mean, everyone else in the family has been on TV this weekend but us," Trent said.

"The boys make a good point," Frank said.

"And Eloise has been on twice," FJ added.

"We could be on computers in the background pretending to buy stuff while you talk or whatever," Trent said.

"I do have to figure out an angle for tomorrow," I said, rubbing a knot in my shoulder.

"So that's a yes?" FJ asked.

"That's an, I don't know yet," I said. "I'll have to see how having you on camera fits in once I finish my Cyber Monday research on what I'm actually going to talk about."

"Which is what?"

"I plan to figure that out as soon as Dad and Eloise take off for the airport."

"I sure wish our beautiful Eloise didn't have to leave us to go back to school tonight," Joyce said, reaching across the table to grasp Eloise's hand.

Her elbow grazed the pizza boxes perched between her and Barb.

Two of the three slid off the table and hit the ground with an oddly familiar, jarring thunk.

"Oops," Joyce said.

Frank jumped up from his seat to pick up the boxes while Barb reached for the slices of meat lover's pizza that had catapulted across the floor.

"I've got seltzer right here," Joyce said, grabbing her drink glass and kneeling to drizzle water onto the oily tomato sauce that was already oozing into the beige Berber carpeting. "Should take the stains right up."

Barb and I dabbed at what looked like blood spatter until all traces of the accident had disappeared.

"Phew," Joyce said, as we all returned to our seats to finish what was left of dinner. "What a terrible mess that could have been."

"You know what I always say," Gerald said, lifting the lid from the pizza box that had remained closed and helped himself to an overturned, but no worse for wear, slice of Canadian bacon and pineapple. "All's well that ends well."

———

All's well that ends well?

As in *push* had just *come to shove?*

Almost worse than hearing Gerald actually utter those words was the pointed pretending by everyone at the table that he'd said nothing more noteworthy than *pass the salt*. Not to mention Frank's sudden insistence that Eloise grab her stuff and they get rolling to the airport.

"Have a wonderful rest of your semester," I said, trying to sound calm after Eloise collected her bags and we hugged goodbye in the front hall.

"Thanks, Maddie," Eloise said.

I took a deep but silent breath as the scenario seemed to come together:

Gerald, Joyce, and Barb had walked to my car behind, not in front of, Eloise after the Piggledy's commitment ceremony. There was no way any of them could have placed the note on my car before she got there.

Someone had to have stolen away during the reception.

Or, worse, given the note to Eloise to plant on the windshield, pretend to find, and then summon me … ???

"I'm so glad you got to spend time with the family," I barely managed.

"It was great," she said.

"Craziest of weekends, though."

"That's the understatement of forever," Eloise said.

"At least things can get back to normal now," I croaked. "Seeing as Alan Bader's in custody."

Eloise shrugged. "I guess."

I could barely breathe. "What do you mean by that?"

"Nothing really." Eloise took a deep breath. "It's just that—"

"Eloise," Frank's voice boomed down the hall. "Time to move it or you're going to miss your plane."

Eloise smiled—and not her usual toothy, posed sorority girl smile—but earnestly, like she used to when I agreed to read her that extra bedtime story or let her play an extra five minutes before lights out. "You're a great stepmom," she said. "And an awesome person too."

"Oh," I said, trying, not entirely successfully, to swallow back my surprise. "Thank you, sweetie."

"Even if Dad sometimes isn't."

"What are you trying to—"

"Eloise!" Frank appeared in the hallway. "Honey, we have to leave now."

"The main thing is you're back together," Eloise said, giving me a final hug. "Right?"

TWENTY-FIVE

Was Eloise's last comment in reference to her father's misdeeds of the past, or something of a much more recent variety?

Seeing as she would be in the car with him for the better part of the next hour, I couldn't exactly call her for clarification. I scrolled through my recent messages for her name thinking I'd text her instead, but I was stopped by our last set of back-and-forths—from Thursday night at Bargain Barn:

Omg! Where are you? Eloise had written.

At layaway. Looking for you, I'd responded.

We were coming to find you when it happened.

Who is we?

Everyone but Daddy and Uncle Craig.

Unless she'd been lying that night and had continued to lie for the rest of the weekend without a hint of remorse, Eloise had an alibi for when the pallet fell.

An alibi that also accounted for Barb, Joyce, and Gerald.

And Craig was theoretically in the TV line.

But what about Frank?

I decided to wait to send Eloise a text until I was sure she was through airport security and safely away from Frank peering at her text messages. Instead, I closed myself back in my office and opened my *Guilty As Charged* spreadsheet.

Everyone had an alibi of some sort at the time the pallets were pushed off the shelf. Everyone but Frank.

A band of sweat dampened the nape of my neck.

Frank, who was so supportive of my TV appearance, he actually did my on-camera makeup. Frank, who helped shift the direction of the line so it snaked through the toaster aisle. Frank, who reappeared after the pallet fell to help with the rescue effort of both Cathy Carter and Bargain Barn itself. Frank, who'd known CC—AKA Contrary Claire, AKA Cathy Carter—had been heckling Mrs. Frugalicious…

Was he, not Alan Bader, CC all along?

Worse, was CC also a combination of people like Alan suggested?

Frank was on the air doing his weekend financial report when CC—someone other than Cathy Carter—left that note on my car during the Piggledy commitment ceremony.

Meaning someone else had to be involved.

Someone with a penchant for cliché.

Gerald?

My heart began to pound.

No. Frank's dad moved far too slowly to have shuffled across the mall and back unnoticed. And Joyce, even in sensible heels, wasn't much faster.

Barb, on the other hand, was nothing if not a middle-aged hard body…

Running down the spreadsheet, I began to add to the information I'd already listed beside each member of the Michaels family.

Craig Michaels

Casually flirting with Griff's girlfriend after the incident he'd somehow been involved in implementing?

Frank Michaels

Unaccounted for at the time the pallet fell?

Coincidentally there to save the day in the aftermath of the accident, the note on my car, and the arrest of Alan Bader?

Joyce Michaels

Had a cooler of leftovers on hand after the fact, as if she knew it would be a long night at Bargain Barn?

Was at the base of the stairs listening when I told the boys about my initial visit to the police station and could have known I was suspicious about the accident.

Gerald Michaels:

Author and cliché provider of the messages and notes (masterminded by Frank or even Joyce) to keep me from investigating?

Barb Michaels:

Note courier? All around-enabler?

Thankfully, when I got to Eloise, the only thing I had to add beside her name was a question mark.

Eloise was pampered, emotional, and opinionated, but she'd always seemed to know right from wrong. My gut told me there was no way she'd have agreed to plant a threatening, anonymous note supposedly from CC any more than she'd have agreed to sit back quietly and allow Alan Bader to rot in jail if she knew he was innocent.

But she definitely knew something.

About her father?

About her grandparents and aunt and uncle aiding and abetting?

I texted Frank: DID ELOISE GET OFF OKAY?

With his return confirmation that her flight was on time and he'd left her at curbside check-in, I fired off another quick text to my loving stepdaughter.

YOU'D TELL ME IF THERE WAS SOMETHING I NEEDED TO KNOW, RIGHT?

My head began to pound along with my heart as I awaited a response.

In the meantime, I tried to digest the hard-to-swallow possibility that my soon-to-be-ex, his family, and even his business associate Anastasia Chastain may have conspired to kill Cathy Carter.

The big question was why.

I thought of Alan and his certainty that a big corporation was out to destroy Bargain Barn. Was it possible Frank had been pretending to be supportive since he'd found out I was Mrs. Frugalicious but was secretly consumed with jealousy and out to ruin *my* business instead?

Could he have killed my online heckler to frame me, Mrs. Frugalicious?

Or, maybe he'd planned the whole thing to look like an accident to scare advertisers and the Frugarmy away.

Was it my investigating that prompted the post-mortem messages from CC to get me to stop?

I powered down my computer, rushed upstairs, and locked the door to my bedroom.

I drew a hot bath, added a mixture of aromatherapy oils all bearing the word *calming,* and soaked until my skin was wrinkled to the point of calm and the wrinkles in my brain smoothed enough for rational thought.

As the water cooled down, so did some of my panic about the supposed guilt of the Michaels family. Things looked dicey, but there were definite holes in the scenario. Namely, even though Frank was missing at the time the pallet fell, he was back and helping the emergency personnel almost as quickly as I was. Even though Frank and the others knew about the existence of CC, how would he or anyone else have known who Cathy Carter was among the throng of Frugarmy members? For that matter, how could any of them have known she was planning to show up at Bargain Barn that night at all?

And then my text alert pinged.

Expecting a response from Eloise, I quickly got out of the tub, dried off, and grabbed the phone.

The message was from Wendy Killian: I THINK I KNOW WHAT YOUR QUESTION IS ABOUT.

She did?

YOU DO?

Not wanting to outright ask her whether Craig was in the line with her via text, I wrote back, How about I call you now so we can discuss it?

Now's not a good time.

When's good?

I'd prefer to talk in person.

Okay ...

How about tomorrow a.m.?

I have a TV segment to tape in the morning.

What time?

Ten.

I'll be at Starbucks by the mall at eight ...?

Before I could type back with a Yes, No, or It's really just a simple question, there was a knock on my bedroom door.

A knock I had no intention of answering.

For one thing, I was only wearing a towel. For another, it just didn't seem judicious to let in a potential murderer and/or accomplice, at least until Wendy filled me in on what she knew I wanted to know.

How could she have known what I wanted to talk to her about?

"Mom?" Trent, judging by the slightly deeper timbre of his voice, jiggled the knob.

"I'm just getting out of the bath," I said, thankful it was him, and more thankful that neither of my boys had gone to Bargain Barn on Thursday night and were thus free of the cloud of suspicion hovering over everyone else.

"Okay," he said, but he didn't say he was leaving or would come back later.

"Be there in a second," I finally said, setting the phone on the vanity and grabbing my robe from the hook.

I opened the door, reminding myself that whatever it was Wendy wanted to talk to me about, the most likely suspect (despite his protestations of innocence) was already in custody.

"Do you think Alan Bader really did it?" Trent asked, stepping into my room.

"Why are you asking me that?"

"I mean, you locked your door."

"Because I was taking a bath," I mumbled unconvincingly.

"You could have just locked the bathroom door."

"True," I said, not elaborating any further. "Is that why you came in here—to talk about Alan Bader?"

"Well, the whole thing is kind of freaky."

"That it is," I said. So was Trent and FJ's seeming ability to key into whatever was weighing most heavily on my mind at any given moment. "But there wouldn't have been an arrest unless the police had good reason to believe he's behind Cathy's death."

"True that," Trent said.

Neither of us said anything for a moment.

"So FJ and I were online, and we discovered that people under twenty-five make up a huge percentage of online shoppers."

"You guys really have been doing research," I said, relieved he hadn't actually come into my room to talk about Alan Bader but just thought about it when he discovered the door was locked.

"So maybe we can be in the background shopping while you talk about the best deals on the top online purchases for people around our age."

"Interesting."

He brushed a light brown curl out of his eyes. "I mean, we thought it was a good idea."

"It's definitely a good idea."

"So, yes?"

"I don't see why not," I said. "Unless Anastasia has some kind of a problem with it."

"Cool," Trent said, but he didn't make a move to leave—I presumed because he was waiting for me to offer to email or call her, which I wasn't about to do until I had the clarity I needed.

"I'll mention it to her in the morning," I said.

"Great," he said.

"Everything okay?" I asked, when he continued to stick around.

"Fine," he said, glancing through the blinds and out the window that faced the street, as though checking to make sure no one lurked outside. "So do the police think Alan killed Cathy because she was CC, or do they think he was CC all along and had some crazy scheme planned?"

"I'm not sure they've figured that out yet," I said, trying not to look as uptight as I suddenly felt. "Why?"

"Well, FJ and I figured Cathy Carter was CC and Alan killed her because she was threatening his business by bothering yours."

"It makes a certain amount of sense," I said, noncommittally.

"But then FJ figured out CC wasn't just heckling Mrs. Frugalicious."

A jolt of ice cold ran up my spine. "What?"

"While we were researching deals, he found some interesting comments on some other bargain hunting sites."

"From CC?"

He nodded.

"For sure?"

"They were critical, cranky, and signed CC," he said. "All from different web addresses too."

"So CC wasn't just heckling me?"

"Nope."

"And the comments stopped as soon as Alan was arrested?" I managed.

"Yep," he said. "But there were definitely some from after Cathy Carter died."

My breath came in short bursts. "On what websites?"

"There were a bunch—Deals Galore, Saver's Station, I Love a Bargain…"

"Any others? I asked, rushing into the bathroom, where I retrieved my phone and reread my recent interchange with Wendy Killian.

I THINK I KNOW WHAT YOUR QUESTION IS ABOUT.

"FJ would know if there are more," he said.

"Where is he?"

"Downstairs figuring out a movie to watch with Joyce, Grandpa, and Dad."

"Dad's home?"

"He just rolled in a couple of minutes ago," Trent said. "Want me to yell down to FJ that you need to talk before they start?"

"That's alright!" I said, a bit too emphatically.

Trent shrugged. "Whatevs."

I looked down at my phone again. I'D PREFER TO TALK IN PERSON.

"Does *Here's the Deal* magazine happen to ring a bell?"

"Didn't I say that one?" he asked. "CC was heckling on that site as much or more as he or she was on yours."

TWENTY-SIX

I WALKED DOWN A long hallway and peered into a slightly open door. The room, dimly lit and filled with filmy cigar smoke, contained a round table, chairs, and a dilapidated couch.

"Dealer's choice," Joyce said, handing out playing cards.

FJ and Trent had their backs to me, but I could see their oversized cards as they picked them up off the table.

Cathy Carter was the Queen.

Frank, the King.

I was the Joker.

Anastasia, seated to FJ's left, looked at her hand. "A deal's a deal."

"She's the real deal," Craig said from the couch, where he was too busy groping Griff's busty girlfriend L'Raine to join the game.

"You're all double-dealing," Alan shouted from a cage in the corner with a padlock affixed to the front. "All of you!"

"Don't make such a big deal out of it," Barb said.

"Exactly," Frank said, a cigar hanging from his mouth. "No big deal."

"It's a good deal," Eloise said, playing her hand. "Right?"

"More like a done deal," Gerald said, folding.

"Ladies and gentlemen!" A voice, Wendy Killian's, filtered through the hallway from a loudspeaker system. "Here's the deal…"

———

Despite waking up surprised I'd actually dozed off for long enough to have a nightmare, I found myself pulling into the parking lot of my local Starbucks wondering what I was doing stepping willingly into a new one.

I'd promised Detective McClarkey I'd lay low, but even though last night's revelations pointed away from Frank and the family and directly at Wendy Killian, I still wasn't entirely sure I was any safer in my house than a Starbucks filled with people nursing their turkey and family hangovers with Monday morning venti espressos.

Never mind I was there to meet the one person who not only had the method and the opportunity, but possibly the most solid motive for murder.

Was Wendy Killian, publisher of *Here's the Deal*, so angry about the threat CC posed to her business that she decided to get rid of her? Given CC was heckling *Here's the Deal* and Mrs. Frugalicious— admittedly her biggest competitor—had she decided to kill two birds with one stone, as it were, and destroy both of us with a staged "accident" during my live Black Friday broadcast?

I had to admit, it would be something of a brilliant plan.

A plan that could easily evolve into a Plan B to frame me for wanting *our* heckler out of *my* business, if necessary.

Had Wendy then quickly resorted to a Plan C after I told her Alan was suspicious about the accident and pretended Cathy Carter was an innocent victim and CC was still alive, well, and penning nasty comments and notes?

The scenario brought me both relief and a newfound sense of horror.

Not to mention fear.

Did she want to meet to admit what she'd done, or was I about to be subjected to some sort of Plan D?

I scanned the people in line and the tables around the store for a slim, murderous, dishwater blonde with her hair pulled back in a tight, no-nonsense ponytail.

Ordering a skim latte, I located a table in full view of the front counter—a spot close enough so no one could miss my shouts for help, but far enough away from the next table that extraneous chatter wouldn't drown out my conversation with Wendy.

A conversation I planned to record.

I no longer had my Eavesdropper, since the handy listening device became police evidence after my last run-in with a murderer. Thankfully, my trusty smartphone, which I had at the ready to dial 911, also had the ability to record.

I picked up my drink, took my place at the table, and sat down to wait. Despite what was turning into chronic sleep deprivation, I was so keyed up, I was afraid to do much more than lick the foam and cinnamon from the top of my pumpkin spice latte.

A few more minutes passed.

At 8:11, I decided I'd give her four more minutes.

At 8:14, just as I was deciding whether I should give Wendy another five minutes to square her shoulders and unburden her heavy soul, she sauntered in.

Smiling.

Maniacally?

Her hair, always pulled back, hung loose around her shoulders. While I'd never thought of her as beautiful exactly, she walked in with a glow I'd never seen before.

The crazy-eyed glow of a murderess?

As she waved and signaled she was going up to the counter to get a beverage, I checked the phone in my jacket pocket on the bench beside me to make sure the mic was pointing at what would soon be her seat.

"Wow, Maddie, you look fantastic," she said, arriving at the table, coffee in hand.

"I'm dressed for TV," I said, not able to say she looked great too. Wendy, who was usually casual but always put together, was wearing a short, rumpled skirt and a slouchy, metallic, off-the-shoulder top. In fact, she looked a lot more up-since-last-night than Monday-morning confession.

Then again, what *did* one wear to admit to killing someone?

"Thank you so much for fitting me into your busy morning schedule."

"No problem," I said, trying not to sound as nervous as I felt.

If she did confess she'd been up all night consumed with guilt over whatever she'd done, and I got it on tape, then managed to call 911, what was I going to do about it while I waited for the authorities?

Grab her by the wrist and hold on tight? Announce to the store there was a killer in our midst and to bolt the doors?

What if she had a weapon, for God's sake?

"Sorry I'm a little late," she said, definitely emitting the stale base notes of last night's perfume as she sat down across from me. "My night kind of blended into morning, if you know what I mean ..."

Sweat broke out at my temples. "My whole weekend's kind of been that way."

"I can't imagine what a terrible shock it was to see Alan Bader led away in handcuffs yesterday."

"It definitely was," I said, waiting for her to blurt something along the lines of, *I spent the whole day battling between right and wrong but ultimately couldn't live with myself so I called you, hoping it would make my difficult confession that much easier ...*

She sighed. "I feel like such an awful person ..."

As I forced myself not to check and see if my phone was recording, she spotted something across the room.

Suddenly, she was standing.

"Sorry, but I've been waiting for the little girls' room to open up since I walked in! Can you excuse me for a moment?"

Before I could answer, she was scampering over to beat out anyone else who might have had the same idea.

Or at least I hoped that was what she was doing.

With the click of the bathroom door, I was on the phone with Griff just in case.

"Where are you?" he asked, after my breathless hello.

"At Starbucks—having coffee with the person I think might actually be Cathy Carter's killer."

"Aren't you supposed to be laying low?"

"I thought I was, but—"

"But you decided to have coffee with … ?"

"Wendy Killian," I whispered even though she was well out of hearing range. "She's the publisher of *Here's the Deal* magazine. She has the perfect motive because the boys discovered that CC was heckling her online even more than she was Mrs. Frugalicious. She was at Bargain Barn on Thursday night, supposedly in the back of the store right before the pallet was pushed. I'm here with her because she asked to meet with me and I'd agreed before I found out CC was pestering her too. You may want to send someone down here. I think she's going to—"

"Enjoy your coffee, Miss Marple. Cathy's killer is already in custody where he—"

"Confess!" I interrupted. "I was about to say I really think she's about to confess!"

"Not to murder," he said.

"How do you know?"

"They were able to clean up the tape enough to determine a few things."

"Meaning what?"

"Meaning we know the perp was dark-haired, of medium height and build, and wearing what looked to be a black polo."

Wendy was about five-seven, but neither dark-haired nor of medium build. She'd also been wearing a floral blouse at Bargain Barn. "So, not Wendy?"

"Not unless she had an accomplice that was both male and Alan Bader."

I took a breath akin to, but not exactly of, relief. "So it *was* Alan?"

"That's the general consensus."

"Does Alan know you've enhanced the tape?"

"Yup," he said.

"What's he saying?"

"Apparently his lawyer's doing most of the talking now."

"I can't believe this," I said, feeling more than a little foolish. "Not only was I taken in by him, he actually had me believing I needed to be looking everywhere *but* at him."

"The smarter they are, the more convincing they can be, I'm afraid."

"I still feel like such a dummy."

"Don't beat yourself up. This Wendy Killian sounds like she might have made an otherwise logical suspect."

Little did he know how illogical my suspicions had really been. "I suppose."

There was rustling noise on his end of the line.

"Can you hang on for a second," he said then seemed to move the phone away from his mouth. "Be there in a second, Lare," he said in a muffled whisper. "I promise."

Lare, as in L'Raine?

"Sorry about that," he said, returning to our call.

As I took a breath to steel myself against how sorry he was going to be once I forced myself to fill him on my concerns about his *Lare,* the bathroom door swung open.

"Griff, can I call you back a little later?"

"Sure," he said.

I tossed the phone back into my jacket just as Wendy, giddy and smiling, made her way back to the table.

"Phew! I didn't mean to jump up mid-sentence, but it was kind of an emergency."

"I understand," I said, infinitely relieved that I wasn't sitting across the table from a murderer.

She slid back down into her chair. "Where were we?"

"I think you were saying something about feeling badly," I said, a lot less worried but somehow all the more curious as to why we were meeting.

"Awful. As in I'm an awful person." She shook her head. "All I could think about after I heard Alan was arrested was what was going to happen to the six-month advertising campaign we'd almost finalized in *Here's the Deal*."

"Advertising campaign…" I repeated.

She took a long, slow sip of coffee. "I wish I were a bigger person, but I feel badly that it might not happen now."

"That doesn't make you a bad person," I said. "I'm in the same boat, actually."

"I figured you might be," she said.

Was that what she'd assumed my *quick question* was about?

"Bargain Barn is my biggest advertiser and our contract expires next month. With Alan in jail, there's no knowing what's going to happen to either of our accounts."

"Isn't this just crazy?" she asked.

"Completely."

"I guess we should just be relieved he's off the streets," she said.

"Definitely," I said.

As we both took long, slow sips of coffee, I had to wonder why she felt we needed to meet in person to talk about our up-in-the-air advertising with Bargain Barn.

"I can't honestly say I'm surprised he killed her, though," she finally said.

"What?" I sat up straighter in my chair.

"I mean, I know it's wrong to speak ill of the dead and everything, but she was heckling you and she was certainly heckling me enough to think about wanting her to go away." Wendy shook her head. "She must have been heckling Alan, too."

"How did you know she was heckling me?" I asked. "Or that Cathy Carter was CC?"

"That's what I wanted to talk to you about," she said.

My cell began to ring in my jacket pocket.

"Do you need to get that?" she asked.

"No," I said. "Not important."

"Here's what is …" She smiled that crazy-eyed smile that had me sure she was guilty of something. "Craig."

"Craig?"

She nodded.

"As in, Frank's brother Craig?"

Her smile grew bigger.

"He told you CC was heckling me?"

"No, I knew that from your website," she said. "But he told me Cathy Carter was CC."

"How did he know?" I asked.

"Frank told him," she said.

Besides me, the boys were the only ones who should have had an idea that Cathy and CC could be one in the same, and I'd sworn them to both to secrecy, claiming it could hinder the full police investigation.

"And I think Anastasia Chastain had told him," she said.

"Anastasia?" Anastasia had told Frank, who told Craig, who told Wendy? "But—"

"Craig and I are seeing each other."

My brother-in-law—an enthusiastic chubby chaser, whom I was certain had been wining, dining, and generally trying to lure curvy L'Raine away from Griff Watson—was really seeing sinewy, formerly severe Wendy Killian?

"Craig?" I asked again, this time more incredulously.

Her cheeks blushed crimson. "We met on Thursday night and have been all but inseparable ever since."

"So that's what you wanted to tell me?"

"I know we're competitors and everything, but we're also friends." She patted my hand. "With all the turmoil you've had over the last few months in your relationship, I thought I should get your blessing to pursue mine."

"My blessing?"

"I haven't felt this way about anyone since I got divorced," she said. "Maybe even ever."

My head was spinning.

I'd come to coffee sure Wendy was going to confess to murder, not to have an awkward but otherwise innocuous conversation between two friends who were now involved with brothers.

"So you say you've been seeing each other all weekend?"

"Friday night we had cocktails and talked for hours," she said wistfully. "Saturday night it was dinner and dancing. Then, last night—"

"That's fantastic," I said before she gave what was threatening to be way too much information.

"Better than fantastic."

True though it seemed to be, I was having a hard time believing that Craig, who I'd never seen look at a woman any less than twenty pounds heavier than athletic Wendy, had fallen as hard for her as she had for him.

"That dark curly hair and those blue eyes … I can't believe I didn't spot him while I was in the TV line."

"You didn't?" I asked, lamely addressing the question I'd originally thought I'd come to ask.

"We met right after the pallet fell. He came out of the men's room and asked me what was going on. I told him everything I knew, and …" She paused. "Maddie, I really think he's The One."

With that, her cell rang.

She grinned like a lovesick teenager, turning the phone so I could see his name in the display. "I just can't believe it took someone dying for my life to come alive like this."

———

With a quick hug and the legitimate excuse that I needed to get home to prepare for Channel Three to arrive, I left Wendy to flirt and coo with my brother-in-law.

I got into the car, put my nearly full coffee into the cup holder, and plugged my phone (which had a five-minute recording limit and the sense to shut off long before I'd been smart enough to realize I wasn't going to be hearing anything of note) back into the charger. It was then I noticed that the call, which had come in during Wendy's *confession,* was from an unfamiliar number.

I turned on the engine and listened to the message:

Maddie,

This is Joe, the acting store manager here at Bargain Barn. I just got off the phone with Mr. Bader down at the jail. His voice cracked. *And, um, he insisted I call to fill you in on a few things.*

First off, he told me to tell you that he'd have to be a complete fool to have given the police surveillance video of himself climbing down from the upper shelves.

Second, the video showed the person from behind so they couldn't positively ID the face.

Third, that face was not Alan's and he asked me to reiterate that he didn't kill anybody.

Ever.

Joe paused to take a breath, and exhale.

Listen, he continued. *I just want you to know I wouldn't have delivered this message if I didn't believe Mr. Bader was absolutely, positively innocent. I've worked at Bargain Barn for over ten years and the man is top shelf.*

Pardon the analogy.

The main reason I'm calling is that we've discovered some new evidence down at the store. When I called Alan to fill him in, he insisted I have you come down to Bargain Barn and take a look before the police get here.

At this point, you're the only one he trusts …

TWENTY-SEVEN

I HAD NO IDEA whether my trip to Bargain Barn was really a mission of mercy, or if I was falling for Alan Bader's nonsense yet again, but seeing as it was 8:30 and I needed to be home by 9:30 so I was camera ready by 10:00, I had a less than an hour to find out.

Before I did, I texted Griff back with one question:

HOW DID THEY ID ALAN'S FACE?

I wiled away the seconds that felt like hours, thankful my unfounded suspicions hadn't ruined Griff's relationship. Craig and Wendy seemed almost as unlikely as Griff and L'Raine, but, as my father-in-law would certainly say, love is blind.

WASN'T PRIVY TO THAT INFO, SO NOT SURE finally popped up as a return message. WILL FIND OUT AND GET BACK.

With his equivocal response, I backed out of my space. My coffee was sloshing out of the lid and into my cup holder as he followed up with another text I couldn't return while driving.

WHY?

"Thank you for agreeing to come."

Joe, the former assistant and now acting store manager, greeted me at Bargain Barn's Customer Service desk. He not only looked like he'd aged ten years since Thursday night, but like he'd grown a permanent furrow between his sandy brows.

"I only have a few minutes," I said, a convenient truth in case this was some kind of weird ploy or trap. "Anastasia Chastain and the Channel Three news cameras are expecting me at my house to film a Cyber Monday segment in less than an hour."

"This won't take long," he said. "And you've been great on TV all weekend, by the way."

"Thanks," I said, following him inside. We started toward the back of the store.

"As I said, I've worked with Mr. Bader for almost ten years and he's never been anything but generous and honest," Joe said, cutting through the hardware aisle.

"Were you working here when his wife died?" I asked.

"I started just after," he said. "He put up a tough front, but the man was grieving until he met The Floozy."

"The Floozy?"

"That awful new wife he's finally getting rid of."

"But you don't think he had anything to do with getting rid of the first one?"

"I was starting to worry that I had no choice but rethink everything I believed about him and his values." He led me back into to the restroom area, stopped at the employee breakroom, and opened the door. "Thankfully, I don't have to."

A very tall, husky, African-American man of about twenty stood beside a bank of lockers.

"This is Eli. Eli, this is Maddie Michaels, better known as Mrs. Frugalicious."

"Nice to meet you," he said, extending his hand and offering a meaty handshake.

"Eli is in college here in town, but his family lives in Chicago."

"That's nice," I said.

"I'm telling you this because we require all of our employees to be on the clock during the Black Friday weekend," Joe said. "All except for Eli."

"Mr. Bader knows I'm putting myself through college and don't get the chance to see my family very often. He gave me the whole weekend off to be with them."

"That was very generous," I said, my mind wandering to Eloise, who'd gone back to school without responding to my text message.

Because she had nothing to say, or nothing she was willing to say?

"Today was my first day back on the schedule." Eli clicked open a locker marked with his name. "I found this inside."

A black polo shirt lay rumpled in the corner.

"For liability reasons, employees can't leave anything in their lockers when they clock out," Joe added. "In fact, they even provide their own padlocks, which they take back and forth with them."

"So you couldn't have accidentally left it inside your locker?"

"I own two work shirts. The one I'm wearing and the one in my laundry basket at home."

"Cathy Carter's murderer was wearing that shirt," Joe said. "He climbed down from the upper shelves, came in here, pulled it off, and threw it in the locker."

My pulse began to race. "You're sure of that because … ?"

"For one thing, I'm a size 2XL," said Eli, who had to be six-five and at least 300 pounds "That polo is a medium and says Smith on the label."

"Have you talked to this Smith person?" I asked. "Maybe he accidentally tossed it in the wrong locker."

"Charlie Smith quit two weeks ago," Eli said.

"Was he disgruntled or anything like that?" I asked.

"Not at all," Joe said. "He moved to Colorado Springs and got into management at a store down there thanks to Mr. Bader's referral."

"Did he have dark hair?"

"Smithy's a ginger." Joe crossed his arms over his chest. "And Cathy Carter's killer may have been wearing a Bargain Barn shirt, but he wasn't an employee."

That low feeling of dread I thought I had at bay began to rise again like flood waters. "How do you know?"

"Follow me."

The next thing I knew we were standing in Alan's office.

Joe turned on a monitor and dimmed the lights.

"You found more video?" I asked, expecting to see someone scrambling up into the rafters from some remote spot in the store.

"The police took everything they thought was important," Joe said as a pair of vending machines and a up-close view of the first row or two of the employee lockers filled the screen.

"But no one thought anything about the breakroom camera since it's really only there to keep employees from tampering with the snack machine."

Joe pressed play and we watched as what seemed to be a disembodied arm open Eli's locker, toss a black polo inside, shut the door, and disappear.

"This was recorded exactly one minute and fifty-four seconds after the pallet fell, when no one was on break because every other Bargain Barn team member was required to be on the sales floor."

"But you can't see a body," I said. "Much less a face."

"No, but you can tell that the person who threw the shirt is using his right hand because you can also see the left." He played the tape again, stopped at the three-second mark and pointed at the lower part of the screen. "Right here."

"Which proves what?" I asked.

"Mr. Bader can't be the killer."

"Why's that?"

"He wears a gold medical alert bracelet on his right wrist."

Whoever threw the shirt into the locker was wearing what seemed to be a clear surgical or food service glove, but there was no sign of Alan Bader's heavy gold jewelry.

"He could have taken it off," I said. "Right?"

"Wrong," Joe said. "It's so valuable, he actually had that bracelet soldered on his wrist so it won't ever fall off."

"Oh," I said, my resident butterflies taking wing and beginning to flutter frantically throughout my body.

"Exactly."

"And you've called the police to let them know?"

"Right before I called Mr. Bader," Joe said, nodding. "They're supposed to be sending someone out, but I got the distinct feeling they weren't in any particular hurry to examine a shirt in an employee locker."

I, however, was suddenly frantic for answers.

If Alan was innocent and Joe was right that all store employees were out on the sales floor, didn't that once again narrow my suspect list down to two dark-haired men of medium height and build that still weren't accounted for at the time the pallet was pushed?

Namely, Frank and Craig.

Frank was the most likely suspect, except that he was helping with the rescue effort within a couple of minutes of the pallet falling. Wouldn't he have been held with the rest of the people in the back of the store if he'd climbed down and tossed the shirt into the locker?

And then there was Frank's likely accomplice—his brother Craig.

I can't believe I didn't spot him while I was in the TV line. Wendy's words rattled in my head. *He came out of the men's room and asked me what was going on ...*

Craig said he was in the TV line when the pallet fell. But seeing as we were let into the store first, shouldn't he have been up at the very front? Mr. Piggledy came back to the middle of the Frugarmy line with a voucher of some sort. Why hadn't Craig gotten his TV when he met up with us, nearly a half-hour later?

Maybe because he hadn't been in that particular line at all, but had instead gone to some predetermined site somewhere in the store, climbed up, pushed the pallet, and scrambled back to be caught from behind on a grainy, older surveillance camera?

Craig, who'd thrown the black shirt into a random locker then run into Wendy on his way out of the employee locker room and taken up with her thinking it would give him an alibi?

"You said the police took all the important surveillance tape," I said to Joe. "Would that include footage taken of anyone going in or out of the restroom area?"

"The camera in that area records right outside the entrances to the bathrooms themselves, but it doesn't cover the length of the hallway."

"Were there cameras on the various lines throughout the store?"

"Depends on the line."

"What about the flat-screen TVs?"

"The surveillance is mainly in the parts of the store with easy-to-steal items. In the big-ticket areas, there's really no need because no one can really march out of the store with a television under their jacket."

"Makes sense, I suppose."

"But that particular line started near Sporting and Camping and eventually wove past Automotive," Joe continued. "So it's possible there were some images captured on the Zone C and maybe even the Zone D cameras."

"Which the police have?"

"Not sure," he said turning to the computer, presumably to take a look. "What are you looking for?"

Before I could figure out a way to tell him I needed to confirm the whereabouts of my own brother-in-law in such a way that he wouldn't suspect I was suspicious of not only him, but my entire extended family including my husband, the store intercom beeped.

"This is Joe," he said, pressing the speaker button.

"This is Courtney at Customer Service. Detectives Reed and Mc-Clarkey are here to see you."

"Be right there," he said.

As the furrow between his brows seemed to ease, I could feel a huge one forming between mine. There was no way my presence at Bargain Barn could ever be considered *laying low*.

"Will you join me?" he asked.

"Under normal circumstances, I definitely would," I lied. "But Anastasia's going to be at my house any second and I really do need to rush home or I'll never make it on time."

"Of course," he said, leading the way out of Alan's office. "I'll walk you out."

"I'm pretty sure I parked right near the employee entrance," I said. "Mind if I head out that way, instead?"

"No problem," Joe said, cracking open the door to the executive offices. "But—"

"But those two detectives have pretty big egos. For Alan's sake, it's probably best if you don't mention I was here before they were," I said, checking to make sure the detectives weren't looking in our direction so I could slip away down a side aisle and out the employee doors. "Or, better yet, not at all."

TWENTY-EIGHT

I SLUMPED DOWN IN the driver's seat of my parked car.

Laying low—as it were.

Very low.

It was 9:07 and I had just enough time to get home, freshen up, and be ready when Anastasia and crew arrived—except that I couldn't get myself to put the key into the ignition.

Not with the utterly distressing scenario coming together in my head:

There was now no question in my mind about the onslaught of Michaels family members appearing for Thanksgiving. There was never a delayed cruise, no unexpected layover in Denver.

Frank's family had come for a purpose.

While I still believed that purpose was to support their brother/ uncle/son clean up the terrible mess he'd made of his marriage and his life, the murkiness of the plan seemed to be growing clearer and clearer.

Frank, who didn't want a divorce in the first place, had to have been monitoring my budding business and website from the moment he learned I was Mrs. Frugalicious. He knew about CC and was aware of my concerns about her potentially negative impact on my happy, growing Frugarmy. A nagging issue he filed away for future reference until he found out I was going to live-blog at Bargain Barn and seized the opportunity to get rid of the scourge known as Contrary Claire.

First, he'd mobilized his suddenly sweet, solicitous family to help implement his solution, then looped in Anastasia, for what I had to believe was a preplanned, on-camera shopping expedition complete with Black Friday *incident*.

While I couldn't be sure how he'd known CC was Cathy Carter, everything else seemed to line up like dominoes:

1. Frank's family, including Craig, *volunteered* to come along with me to shop on camera.

2. Anastasia met us there to document the big night for Channel Three, complete with a cameraman and a *big scoop* gleam in her eyes.

3. Everyone in the Michaels clan disappeared moments before the pallet was pushed off the upper shelf, but reappeared on camera almost immediately afterward to help with the rescue effort.

4. All but Craig, who'd already created an excuse to be in the back of the store by claiming he was headed to the flat-screen TV line. Craig had been assigned the dirty work of pushing the pallet.

5. A task he'd accomplished, as planned.

Or had he?

Had they really intended to kill her, or just scare her off?

And why?

I found it hard to believe Frank would intentionally kill anyone. It was even harder to believe that Anastasia, whose fiancé was in law enforcement, would knowingly conspire to harm anyone—even for guaranteed huge ratings. I also didn't believe Frank was trying to sabotage Mrs. Frugalicious or frame me, as Alan had postulated. However, given my husband's enormous ego, the embarrassing blow it had suffered these last few months, and the fact that he'd called his whole family in to talk me into staying with him, I had to think the whole idea had been to stage a scare so Frank could come riding in on his horse (or leased black Mercedes, as it were) to redeem himself in both my eyes and those of his formerly adoring public.

In light of this theory, Frank's on-camera appearances throughout the evening at Bargain Barn seemed entirely intentional:

Assisting in the rescue effort.

Comforting his estranged wife, Mrs. Frugalicious, his family, and shocked shoppers in the aftermath of Cathy Carter's death.

Mounting a brave and valiant campaign to save the store from closing with the help of his family.

In retrospect, there was nothing that had simply just *happened*—not the producers suddenly wanting to run a weekend's worth of Mrs. Frugalicious bargain hunting segments, not Joyce's suggestion of a grocery-shopping expedition, not Anastasia's appearance to film a Friday segment there. And hadn't the mysterious Frugarmy member who'd suggested we all band together for Small Business Saturday been named Barbara M.?

As in Barb Michaels, who only used her given name for official purposes?

Frank had to have masterminded this entire scenario. And while he might not have intended for Cathy to die, her death was a problem that might not have been a problem at all had Alan Bader and I left well enough alone.

Upsetting as the unexpected deadly turn of events must have been, they had still worked to Frank's advantage, allowing him to show up when I needed comforting after CC left a note on my car or just before Alan was seemingly about to abduct me.

My guts churned as I sat waiting for Detectives McClarkey and Reed to emerge from the store, weighing whether I should come clean with my suspicions or simply call Griff and have him verify that Craig had never gone to TV line—that he'd somehow found a spot out of the camera or anyone else's watchful eye just before the store opened, climbed into the upper shelves, and waited for the right moment to push the pallet off the shelf.

All at the behest of my ex-ex, soon-to-be-ex-again-husband, Frank.

Who'd been aided and abetted by his mother, sister, father, and possibly even his daughter—my stepdaughter, Eloise.

I couldn't very well put the key in the ignition and head home to the murderous Michaels clan and complicit Anastasia Chastain and pretend nothing was wrong. Maybe I was decent in an interview format, but I was no actress.

I also couldn't drag the entire Michaels family through the mud once again on a hunch, even a strong one, until I knew for sure they were behind Cathy's death—intentionally or otherwise.

I sat, unable to move, until the sound of a delivery truck door rolling closed gave me an a idea of one thing I could do in the hopes of finding out.

Mr. Piggledy had returned to Mrs. Piggledy and the Frugarmy right before the accident with a voucher for a 42-inch flat-screen TV he was having delivered—meaning he'd been one of the first twenty people in the TV line.

I dialed his number.

And was greeted by voicemail.

With the beep, I left a concise but pointed message:

Hi Mr. Piggledy, it's Maddie Michaels. I'm hoping you might remember seeing a man with dark curly hair and blue eyes who looked a lot like my husband at the front of the TV line before the pallet fell on Thursday night? I know it was chaotic, especially for you, that evening, but anything you can recall would be of great help. Can you please let me know as soon as you get this? It could be really important.

Oh, and my best to Mrs. Piggledy, I added. *I'm thankful her injuries weren't much worse.*

Which gave me another idea …

TWENTY-NINE

"I'M ON MY WAY," I said, talking into my hands-free device as I headed north on I-25, way north of home. "Almost."

"What do you mean by *almost*?" Anastasia asked.

"I'll meet you at the house, but if I'm a few minutes late, the boys can kick things off for me."

"As in, your boys?"

"They did all the research for what I'm planning to discuss this morning, anyway."

"Which is?"

"The top Cyber Monday deals for people under twenty-five," I said. "And how to get them at the very best prices."

"Hmmm," she said. "Very interesting."

"I thought so," I said.

"And more than a little surprising," she said. "Here I thought Frank was the one with all the big ideas in your family..."

"I need you to go into my office and log on to my computer," I said to FJ, trying not to read any more than I had to into what Anastasia meant by Frank's *big ideas*.

"Okay…" FJ said.

I exited the highway and headed west. "My password is—"

"Frugaliciousbargain1," he said. "Already logged on."

I made a mental note to change my password to something completely random next time. "There should be a Word file called *Cyber Monday Talking Points* on my desktop."

"Got it," he said.

"Please print it out."

"Done," he said, over the whir of the printer in the background.

"I should be home in time to go on the air," I said, pulling into an older, tree-lined neighborhood. "But if I'm running a little late—"

"I should give this to Anastasia?"

"Or you and Trent use it for reference."

"Us?" he asked incredulously.

"You wanted to be on TV today, right?"

"Yeah—in the background, pretending to buy stuff online while you do your thing."

"Which you will be unless I'm caught in traffic or something." I pulled up to the curb beside John Carter's house and killed the engine. "In which case, you have the talking points."

"You're saying you want Anastasia to interview us?"

"Only if I'm not back in time."

"Is everything okay, Mom?"

"I just need to check on something before I head home."

"Must be important," he said.

"That's what I'm trying to find out." I'd promised John I'd visit him again at some point on Monday. John had insisted he and Cathy go to Bargain Barn so he could be one of the first twenty people in the flat-screen-TV line.

If he confirmed that he'd seen Craig ahead of him, I would still need to contact Griff and somehow clue him in on my suspicions so the police could look into things further.

If he couldn't confirm Craig had been there, though, I'd be heading straight home to confront Frank in the relative safety of my news crew–filled home.

"Mom," FJ asked. "Does this have to do with the CC comments I found last night on all those other websites?"

"In part," I said.

"What's the other part?"

I sighed. How exactly did I tell him I suspected his entire family of a drawn-out conspiracy?

The front door of the Carter home swung open.

"I promise to fill you in when I get there," I said as John appeared on his front stoop. "Gotta run."

"Mom, do you need me to—"

"What I need is—"

A smile lit up John's otherwise sad face.

"—for you and Trent to just go ahead and take the mic today."

"You can't be serious," he said. "What's Anastasia going to say about that?"

"My guess?" I paused for the briefest of seconds. "The show must go on."

———

"So many well-wishers," I said, trying my best to make pleasant conversation as John led me into his front hall, now much more crowded with flower arrangements, gift baskets, and even boxes.

"The packages were ordered by Cathy before…" He shook his head as if trying to shake away his thoughts. "I guess I need to dig through and figure out what to do with it all, but I don't even know where to start."

"Maybe I can help," I said.

"Really?" His face seemed to brighten.

"Whatever I can do."

"I'd really appreciate it," John said. "But aren't you supposed to be on the news soon?"

"I have a few minutes," I said. "The boys had an idea for this morning's segment so I'm letting them run with it until I get there."

"Interesting," he said.

"I hope so," I said. "May I ask you a question?"

"Of course."

I took a deep breath. "It's about Thursday night."

"Okay…" he said, like he wasn't entirely sure it was.

"The thing is, there've been some developments."

"As in?"

"Well." I took another breath. "The police are sure they have their man, but—"

"But you're not?"

"Not entirely," I said. "When I was here yesterday, you mentioned that you'd decided to go to Bargain Barn mainly for the flat-screen TV."

With his nod, a teapot began to whistle in the kitchen.

"Sorry," John said. "Can you excuse me for a moment?"

"No problem," I said.

He had already ducked into the kitchen.

"You'll have some tea, right?" John asked a few seconds later.

"Sure," I said, mainly to be polite but also because my mouth was parched from stress.

"Cathy kept a drawer full of pretty much every type there is," John said. "What do you want?"

Mostly, I wanted to be living in a reality where I wasn't about to have to admit to a grieving widower that my extended family belonged on the FBI's Most Wanted list, nor to have to rush home and confront them all about what I planned to do about it. "Whatever you're having is fine by me."

"Ginger Peach something-or-another is on top."

"Sounds perfect," I said, setting my purse on the front hall table and venturing into the dining room/coupon command post.

"So why the interest in the line for the flat-screen TVs?" he asked from the kitchen.

"I have reason to believe the killer said he was there at the time of the incident."

"As an alibi?"

"Something like that."

"Hmm," he said. "Definitely couldn't have been Alan, then."

"No," I said.

"But wasn't he already identified on that security tape?"

"A man that closely matched Alan's description was ID'd on the tape."

"And it wasn't him?"

"Alan's maintained his innocence all along," I said, "Which has been harder and harder to buy, except that I was just at Bargain

Barn and the employees found surveillance tape of someone tossing a black shirt into a locker right after the pallet was pushed."

"Seriously?" John asked over the clank of silverware dropping into the sink.

"The tape didn't show as much as the other video, but there was a clear shot of the right hand of a man who wasn't wearing a soldered-on gold medical alert bracelet," I said. "Which Alan does."

"I see," he said. "What do the police have to say about all this?"

"They're over at Bargain Barn checking into it right now, but I'm afraid it's just going to be considered more circumstantial evidence," I said. "I was hoping that by coming to talk to you, I might be able to help figure out who else could have been behind this."

He reappeared beside me looking as pale as I felt.

"Thanks," I said as he handed me a mug.

"Thank you for filling me in," he said. "I hope I can be of help."

"Did you happen to see a man ahead of you in the line with dark hair that maybe fit the description of Alan?" I took a sip tea to somehow gird myself with the bitter sweetness but was still unable to quite get myself to utter the name *Craig*. "Or my husband?"

"Your husband?"

"*Like* my husband." I nodded. "Generally."

"And you think this person was really the one responsible for my wife's—"

"If he was in line, no." I sighed. "If he wasn't, then it's possible."

"I see," he said again.

We sipped our tea together in silence.

While I awaited his response, I distracted myself by looking at the neat stations Cathy had set up on the dining room table for collating, organizing, and clipping what was an admittedly impressive pile of Sunday circulars, printed online coupons, in-store flyers, and mailers.

"Cathy was a really adept couponer," I finally said.

"That she was," he said, then shook his head. "Maddie, I'm afraid that evening is still mostly a blur."

"And I'm so sorry to ask you to try and recall anything about it," I said. "But if he was there, he'd have been at the very front, or close to—"

"I was toward the back of the line," he uttered, and again there was silence punctuated by the sounds of sipping. "Do you think I could show you something while I'm trying to remember who was ahead of me?"

I needed to get back soon, but the poor man had been through too much for me to dump my story in his lap and simply take off, leaving him alone to try and process it all. "Sure."

"Thank you," he said, tears choking his voice as he stepped across the room to the hall and opened a door leading to the basement. "Cathy would have given anything for you to see this."

I glanced surreptitiously at the wall clock again before I followed him downstairs. 9:27. I figured I had fifteen minutes to admire what was surely going to be her stockpile room and ooh and ahh enough to hopefully jar his memory before I absolutely had to leave.

As I made my way down the steps behind him, I was the one who was jarred.

The basement, typical in its mid-century layout, consisted of a rec room and a hallway that contained a guest bedroom, bathroom, and what looked to be a utility room.

That was where the similarities to all other ranch-style basements ended.

The main room had essentially been transformed into a warehouse—complete with merchandise-filled, floor-to-ceiling shelves lining all four walls. Inside the open guest bedroom was the equivalent of a small, overstuffed clothing store, complete with multiple racks and rounders.

"Oh my gosh!" I said, even before I reached the bottom step and attempted to maneuver around the various lamps, end tables, and still-tagged furniture filling the room like a bargain showroom.

"Everything was bought on close-out, final sale, or using multiple discounts," John said.

"This is incredible."

"You know what they say," he said. "One man's trash..."

Maybe it was just claustrophobia from the sheer volume of stuff crowding the relatively small space, but I suddenly felt light-headed.

John made his way over to a computer in the corner and jiggled the mouse. "She coded everything by where she got it, retail price, and what she actually paid for it all," he said. "Average savings of over seventy percent."

"That's amazing," I said.

"I'm glad you think so, because she followed your advice religiously."

"She accumulated all of this merchandise by following Mrs. Frugalicious?"

"She followed a lot of other websites, too," he said pointedly. "A lot of them."

"Like?"

"Let me see," John said, checking the browser history. "Deals Galore. Saver's Station. I Love a Bargain ... Oh, and she talked about *Here's the Deal* quite a bit.

I was definitely dizzy.

"But Mrs. Frugalicious was her far and away favorite."

Clearly, pleasingly plump Cathy with her sweet, heart-shaped face, bobbed hair, and neon pink sneakers, was as big a fan as she proclaimed. One look around the basement and it was also clear she had a major bargain-shopping addiction.

The warning signs rattled my brain like an alarm:

Compulsive bargain shoppers head for the sales and clearance racks when they feel angry or down.

And/or wrote online complaints on bargain-hunting sites when the shopping didn't turn out quite as planned?

"Did she ever, by any chance, have any particular criticisms about Mrs. Frugalicious or any of the other sites?" I asked.

"Cathy?" He seemed incredulous. "Never."

Compulsive bargain shoppers see sales as opportunities that can't be passed up.

"This really is incredible," I said, trying not to sound as weird and off-balance as I was feeling. "What did she plan to do with all this merchandise?"

"I think she had it in her mind that she would open some sort of store of her own." His voice sounded somehow tighter. "But she couldn't seem to part with anything."

Compulsive bargain shoppers routinely forget what they've purchased and find unused things in their closets.

"Everything seems very organized," I heard myself say, like I was somehow trying to talk my way out of believing what I was seeing.

"By make, model, and size," he said. "It's even color-coded."

Compulsive bargain shoppers spend so much time tracking down deals that they compromise time with family and friends.

"I can't imagine how much time she spent down here," I said, now feeling as tingly in my arms and legs as I was dizzy.

"Way too much," John said. "Not to mention money."

Compulsive bargain shoppers spend more than they can afford.

"You know." My throat felt tight. "Since everything is all catalogued, it would be easy to put anything you don't want up on Ebay or one of the auction sites."

"Do you think I might recoup my costs on some of this?"

"I'd expect you would and then some," I said.

"I need to," he said. "Her little hobby has 'saved' us right into bankruptcy."

Why hadn't I noticed before that the faraway look in his eyes, which I'd assumed was profound sadness, also contained more than a hint of desperation?

My text message alert pinged from inside my purse, upstairs in the front hallway.

"I should probably get going," I said.

"You sure?" He smiled "You ain't seen nothin' yet."

Suddenly, I felt sick. And so tired.

"How about I come back another time to see the rest?" I walked through what felt like marshmallow fluff, around a cherry red leather loveseat with an 80%-off tag hanging off the side.

"I don't believe I answered your question about the dark-haired man ahead of me in line yet," he said.

"That's okay," I said, fearing his answer.

"Now that I think about it, I don't believe there was a man of that description in the line," he added.

"Great," I said, starting up the first and then the second step. "I'm really not feeling very well."

"That's because your tea was sweetened with Cathy's sleeping and anxiety pills." The desk chair creaked as he stood. "All that shopping gave her terrible insomnia."

My legs, instead of responding to what I'd hoped would be an adrenaline rush that would enable me to bolt up the stairs and out the front door, went leaden instead.

"You poisoned me?"

"Of course not," he said. "I gave you something to help you relax."

My knees buckled. The next thing I knew, I was falling.

John caught me in his arms.

"Why?" I asked, trying in vain to escape his firm grasp.

"Why did you have to keep looking into the circumstances of my wife's accident?"

Half-awake and trapped in a real-life nightmare, all the pieces started to fall into place.

"You …" I managed. "It was you all along."

"What choice did I have?" he asked. "I tried to be nice and nip things in the bud by warning you and all your fellow bargain bloggers that this money-saving, coupon-clipping rage had a dark, downside…"

Sure, some stores offer a free frozen turkey with $50 minimum purchase, but what they don't tell you is they're so deep frozen you could miss Thanksgiving waiting for the bird to thaw…

There's nothing gained by buying off-brands. The kids don't like them, they scare off the parents, and chances are the treats will just end up in the trash…

"By heckling on our websites?"

"I was hoping to poison your Frugarmy and advertisers with doubt."

I, for one, plan to take a pass on tonight ... The sound system is the only special addition that seems all that special. To be honest, this whole event smells of a scheme cooked up by you, your TV reporter husband, and Bargain Barn to line pockets with kickback dollars. Namely yours ... Everyone knows the deals are way better online these days, anyway.

"Too bad no one took CC or any of the problems *she* raised about your dangerous advice seriously. Worse, when I gave Cathy an ultimatum—me or the bargain shopping—she cut back but still couldn't stop herself from the had-to-have deals she kept finding online." He shook his head. "I finally realized I had no choice but take action."

"Let me go," I punched, scratched, and wondered how I could have been so stupid not to have thought about the fact that John was also of average height, build, and had dark hair.

Or that Cathy Carter had known everything about me, but CC hadn't even known Frank and I were separated.

Or that the spouse was always the initial suspect.

But not *my* spouse.

Particularly not with the help of my in-laws in a scenario too far-fetched even for a movie of the week, much less the plot of a campy crime drama. A plot centering around the bad guy standing or not standing in a flat-screen TV line.

Pathetic.

I grabbed a handful of John's brown hair and pulled as hard as I could.

He grabbed my wrists and forced me down the hallway.

"Where are you taking me?"

"You haven't seen Cathy's grocery stockpile yet," he said. "You, of all people, will love it."

"Please let me go," I begged as he dragged me into the utility room like the sack of potatoes I was quickly becoming.

He kicked the door closed behind us.

"You're just like her," he said, letting go of me with one hand and reaching for the yellow utility rope from the workbench beside him. "You just won't stop."

"I'm sorry," I said. "All I ever wanted to do was help—"

"If you wanted to help me, you should have stayed out of the middle of it all." He wrapped the rope around my waist. "I had everything planned so perfectly."

As he looped the rope around the leg of the heavy workbench, I glanced at the small, single, barred window and tried, through my growing brain fog, to plan an escape.

"You don't have to do this," I pleaded, wondering if he'd leave a tool that would enable me to get the bars off after he left me there. Would I even be able to squeeze my smaller-than-usual hips through the tiny, code-violating egress window?

"You did this to yourself." He chuckled. "Really, so did Cathy when she insisted, on your advice, that we *pre-shop* for a few must-haves at Bargain Barn three days before the sale." He tightened the rope, tied it, and stepped across the room toward a shelf filled with various brands of laundry soap, stain remover, cleaning supplies, and utility items like sponges. "I ended up doing a little advance work of my own."

"Like finding a spot where you could climb up to the upper shelves without being seen?"

"That was the easy part," he said fumbling around until he found what turned out to be a key. "Did you know they only keep their cameras trained on the easy-shoplifting aisles?"

"And you were caught on one of them," I said, starting to slur. "Coming down."

"From the back, and wearing a Bargain Barn polo like any other employee authorized to be on the upper shelves." He chuckled. "Like Alan."

"How did you get the employee shirt?"

"I saw it on a hook in the breakroom on my way to the bathroom. No one was around, so I snatched it and took it out to my car." He shook his head. "While Cathy spent the next half-hour caught up in scoping out Black Friday pricing, I learned the layout of the store and where the various lines would be on Thursday night. All I really had to do after that was drive by Bargain Barn on our way home from Thanksgiving dinner, mention it might be nice to have the new TV and sound system she couldn't get early, and she practically jumped out of the car before I'd parked."

"And then you lurked in the rafters until you had the perfect opportunity to push a double pallet on her?"

"Kind of ironic she met her end under a mountain of reduced-price toasters, don't you think?" He put the key into a padlock beside the shelf, twisted, and pulled open what appeared to be part of the concrete wall but was really a door. "Gotta love these Cold War–era houses."

"A bomb shelter?" My voice was starting to sound gurgly even to me.

"Cathy called it her stockpiling Eden," John said stepping inside and pulling on an overhead light to reveal a windowless room twice the size of my stockpile room. It was filled from floor to ceiling.

"I can't believe—"

"You know, I never realized just how out of control things really were until I went to Bargain Barn and saw how much the place resembled my basement."

"So you had to kill her?"

"What was I supposed to do? Divorce her and split the debt?"

"And sell your half of the merchandise to recoup some of the losses."

"First thing I looked into," he said. "But the transaction costs of getting divorced outweighed any possible gains—at least according to Sandy."

"Sandy?" My head felt like it had rope around it too.

"The woman who spoke at the memorial."

"Cathy's telecommuting co-worker?"

"In a manner of speaking. She makes a living buying and selling on those auction websites you mentioned. They'd met because Cathy was buying from her. I went in to cut off Cathy's account, began to chat with her a little, and the rest, as they say..."

"You've been having an affair with Sandy?"

"Unconsummated until Cathy was gone. I'm not a cheater," he said defensively.

Just a murderer.

"Sandy is a minimalist," he said dreamily. "She believes in saving money by not spending."

My eyelids felt like they were holding tiny barbells. "So you planned this together?"

"What *I* planned was to get rid of my wife in an unfortunate shopping accident, collect the insurance money, and take Sandy, who had nothing to do with this, down to Ecuador or somewhere with fuzzy extradition laws and a low cost of living. I was going to enjoy the rest of my days sipping tropical drinks and living a modest, minimalist lifestyle—which, if you'll excuse me, is what I have to do now, way ahead of schedule."

"What about me?" I asked, panicked but too drugged to feel.

"You, the constant thorn in my side?" He began to untie me from the leg of the workbench. "Who kept nosing around despite the warnings I had to go to the trouble to create on new and different email addresses? Who kept me from being able to sue on top of collecting insurance money by trying to help free the perfect scapegoat and perpetrator of bargaining madness, Alan Bader? Who's so relentless that you came over here and catapulted yourself right into the lion's den?" He grabbed the ends of the rope and began to drag me across the room. "I have the perfect plan for you."

"Are you going to kill me?"

"I don't need to," he said, lifting me up by the rope still around my waist. "You're going to do it to yourself."

"What the hell are you doing to me?"

"I'm banishing you to an eternity of canned and processed food bought using your very best couponing techniques," he said strongarming me into the stockpile room/bomb shelter. "Or at least until you get past the expiration dates."

"You're not going to get away with this."

"I already am," he said. "You'll be out cold in a minute."

The last thing I heard was the click of the door, the whoosh of a deadbolt, and the scraping sound of a shelf full of cleaning supplies being pushed in front of the already concealed entrance to the Carters' bomb shelter.

THIRTY

I woke up with a pounding headache, a furry mouth, and an overwhelming feeling of utter despair.

I opened my eyes to complete darkness and remembered exactly why.

My first instinct was to cry, which I did for what felt like days, or at least hours. There was no knowing how long without the watch I'd given up as pointless in the age of cell phones.

My second instinct—which kicked in as soon as I realized crying wasn't going to change anything and that I might have forever to do just that—was to stand, adjust to balancing on my wobbly legs, and feel my way to what seemed to be the middle of the room. I put one foot in front of the other and walked slowly with one arm ahead of me and one arm raised in search of the overhead light cord.

Days or hours or minutes passed as I collided lightly (and sometimes not so lightly) with the shelves lining the walls—their mere existence the only thing keeping me from believing I wasn't trapped in a terrible hallucination.

I knew I was definitely living a nightmare that began with John Carter drugging me and admitting he'd killed Cathy, and ended with me locked in a basement bomb shelter.

Alone.

Surrounded by darkness.

My finger finally grazed cold metal.

The cord swung away into the blackness only to hit the back of my hand.

Twice.

I'd never felt so relieved as when I finally grasped the short string of tiny, cool, conjoined metal beads and pulled.

The room lit with blessed florescent light.

I began to cry again when I saw the shelves and realized that the stockpile was three times as extensive as I had imagined.

While the bottles of cooking oil, condiments, pasta, rice, and jars of pre-made sauce weren't going to do me much good, there were shelves filled with cereal, granola bars, peanut butter, applesauce, crackers, fruit snacks, pudding cups, and what looked to be an infinite supply of canned corned beef, ravioli, peaches, pears, soup, and the like—many with metal pulls.

Everything was dusted, labeled, and organized both alphabetically and by expiration date.

From looks of things I could survive a solid two years before...

I tried not to think about the passage of time, instead choosing to focus on the mountain of sports beverages, enhanced water, soda, and plain old water bottles amassed against the back wall.

John's plan for me was clear.

I was going to be a prisoner, living on processed food until I died from old age or overconsumption of artificial colors, food additives, and products containing corn syrup as their primary ingredient.

On the plus side, there were mass quantities of deodorant, feminine products, over-the-counter medications, antacids, shampoo, and body wash. More than I could ever use, particularly in the rusty but blessedly functional half-bath.

And paper towels.

I said a prayer aloud to Cathy for the lifetime supply of toilet paper.

———

And a lifetime it so quickly became.

Luckily I found the pen and notepad Cathy kept in the room to track supply levels. To prepare for what I prayed would be my quick rescue, the first thing I did was recount John's entire confession before I forgot a single clichéd *you ain't seen nothin' yet* statement.

Had I actually believed that my father-in-law, Gerald, could have penned those notes?

To stop from beating myself up about being so incredibly, fatally stupid that I'd walked right into my own prison, I also listed the reasons why I would surely be found any second:

My Cell Phone—Once I was reported missing, the police would surely track my most recent whereabouts using cell phone towers and would soon figure out I'd stopped at or near the Carter house.

My Car—Someone had to have seen my vehicle parked in front of the house and reported it to the authorities.

Frank, Griff, Detectives McClarkey and Ross, Anastasia, and even Alan—All of them had to be looking for me. Someone was sure to put the pieces of my sudden disappearance together and connect it to John Carter. Somehow.

John Carter Himself—At some point, someone besides me would have reason to contact him, discover he'd fled the country, and track him down in Ecuador or wherever it was he'd gone.

I was going to be rescued any time because I simply had to be.

I didn't allow myself to write down the one compelling reason I might never be found:

I was locked in a hidden concrete bunker concealed from view behind a shelf filled with household supplies.

———

I started every day, or what I perceived to be a day (the time defined by careful conservation of my precious florescent light, toilet paper rolls, fruit roll-up wrappers, and empty cans and bottles) by doing push-ups and sit-ups, dusting the stockpile with Cathy's feather duster, appreciating something simple like the fresh and/or fruity scents of the health and beauty products, figuring out alternate uses for the growing wrappers, and penning Mrs. Frugalicious blog posts.

Posts I was saving up for later.

When I was free …

Posts that were necessarily shaped by my intimate experience with stockpiling and the tragic circumstances that led to said knowledge. But I also wrote them as hopeful and open-ended, in the hopes of someday interacting again with my Frugarmy.

Dearest Frugarmy,

We all know that while couponing saves us money and helps manufacturers and stores rid themselves of overstocked and feature products, extreme couponing can sometimes raise ethical questions. For instance, is it okay use a coupon specified for a certain size item on a smaller size to get a bigger discount?

Even though the grocery store computer may scan the discount because it's in the same product family, with a similar UPC, does that make it right?

I say it's both unethical and illegal to break the rules, even if the store accepts the coupon.

What do you think?

———

Dearest Frugarmy:

Many of us store our goods, goodies, and deals in stockpiles generally in our basements or garages. While most couponers have a good grasp on how much to store to feed their families for a specific period of time, sometimes the high of scoring deals can cloud our better judgment.

If you feel you don't quite know when to stop or notice your stockpile is creeping out of your designated area and migrating to spots like your family room, your children's bedroom, or in closets alongside clothing, it may be time to set limits.

If you already have enough stockpiled deodorants to last a year, you don't need more just because you can get another 15 free with your coupons. If you have to buy them, don't keep them— donate to your local food banks. Do good with your couponing while keeping your stockpile from overtaking your home.

And your life.

———

Dearest Frugarmy,

Are you spending 30–60 hours a week clipping coupons and shopping? If so, are you really saving your family enough to justify the time, or has bargain hunting become a serious fixation?

If you have any doubt about the answer, you may want to consider getting some professional help. Remember that having healthy finances isn't just about scrounging for opportunities to save money. Especially when those savings come at the expense of spending time with loved ones.

Obsessions can have serious effects on your marriage and family happiness. Don't let the thrill of scoring bargains turn into an addiction.

———

And then there was the post I wrote not so much from the heart, but straight from my gut.

Dearest Frugarmy,

Are you putting your family's health at risk as a result of your couponing habits? While it feels fantastic to score a very big deal at precious little cost, how will it feel to your body? Even if it's free, does it make any sense health wise to stock the pantry with sugary soda, junk food, and cans of prepared food like chili that can contain 1000mg of salt per serving? Fresh produce may cost more but is money in the bank for your health. If coupons aren't available for fresh fruits and veggies, try frozen (particularly flash frozen, which retains more nutrients) instead of canned goods, which often contain preservatives and have lower nutritional value.

As they say, an apple a day.

What I would have given for an apple…

———

As the granola bar wrappers, potato chip bags, and empty cans began to pile up, most recent expiration dates first, my blog titles began to reflect my growing despair.

Are You a Bargain Shopping Addict? Take This Quiz and See.
Surviving Coupon Hell
When Frugality Kills

And my lists simply morphed into page upon page of questions:

Why didn't I give more information to Griff, or Joe at Bargain Barn, or even FJ, so they'd have more to go on about where I might have gone?

How could I have been so stupid as to not suspect John Carter before it was too late?

When the label says cheese food, *doesn't that mean it's not really cheese, which has to mean it's not really food, either?*

Thanksgiving—will I ever get to enjoy the smell of roasting turkey or have Thanksgiving with the Michaels family, or anyone, again?

Will I ever see my kids again?

I penned messages of love and guidance to them, just in case:

Dear Eloise,

You have turned into a beautiful young woman, but you will always be my darling little girl. I hope you are taking good care of your dad and brothers and finding your path as an adult. With your appreciation for the finer things in life, you'll need to find a way to sustain the lifestyle you were, and would once again like to be, accustomed to. Some advice? Find a career you love and make it work for you. A good man will come along, but then you'll always be confident in what you yourself were able to create in the meantime.

I love you,
Maddie

———

Dear Trent:

I know you will get a football scholarship and maybe even go on to the NFL. I am proud of how tough and strong you are. With all your physical abilities, please don't forget to exercise your mind just as hard in college and beyond. And keep your room clean.

I love you,
Mom

P.S. Marry a nice girl—and by nice, I don't just mean nice-looking.

————

Dear FJ,

You are such a special soul—good at everything from football to theater to your knack for the computer. I only wish I had shared my suspicions with you, off as they were, about Cathy Carter's murderer. I know you'd have sent me in the right direction. I also know you will soar in college and beyond, no matter what career path you decide upon. I suspect there may be more than one—even simultaneously. Even though your father sometimes projects his own expectations onto you, we both know they don't always suit who you really are. You, of all people, must follow your heart, both professionally and personally, no matter what anyone else wants or expects.

I love you,
Mom

I saved the last page of the notepad to compose my note to Frank:

Dear Frank,

Even though I technically agreed to try and reconcile, I wasn't at all sure it was the right thing to do. Not for me, anyway.

I was still so suspicious of you, and your motives, and I got myself into this mess trying to get to the bottom of it all.

Which I did. The rock bottom.

If I've learned anything, it's that life is way too short and precious.

I forgive you.

Love,
Maddie

With no more notepad on which to write, I clicked off the light, rested my head on my makeshift toilet-paper-package pillow, and covered myself in long strips of paper towel to sleep away a few more endless hours.

THIRTY-ONE

I woke up to a sound.

The first sound I'd heard since John Carter had snapped closed the padlock and hidden the bomb shelter behind the utility room shelving.

Footsteps?

Above me?

My first thought was that I was enveloped in concrete and had to be imagining things.

My second was to ignore my first thought and throw cans at the ceiling, or better yet (to avoid destroying what might one day be precious remaining food), bang the handle of the feather duster repeatedly until someone realized I was trapped below.

My third thought was that maybe it was John Carter, not yet gone from the house and walking around in a room he didn't usually go into.

If it was him, it wouldn't be any surprise that I wanted out.

I decided to bang as hard as I could, shouting a few times as though anyone could hear through the cement.

The sound stopped as abruptly as it started.

Brutal, unbearable silence filled the room once more.

I picked up the project I was working on—a makeshift blanket of snack bar wrappers, braided together like I'd learned to do with gum wrappers as a girl. While I worked, I tried not to think about whether I'd imagined the noise, or worse, that whoever was above hadn't heard my desperate banging from below.

Days or hours or minutes went by.

And then I thought I heard another noise.

This time in the utility room.

With the scritch of movement across the concrete floor on the other side of where I was hidden away, I grabbed two pull tab can lids, flipped off the light, and got into position beside a shelf of cake and muffin mixes.

If John Carter thought he'd come down to finish the job, he had another thing coming…

My heart pounded in my chest while I waited for the sound of the key in the lock. As soon as he opened the door, I would strike him quickly with the razor-sharp can edges and rush past him even faster.

What I heard instead was the sound of a saw cutting through the padlock.

I put my weapon down.

Tears were streaming down my face when the door finally opened and I was greeted by what looked like half the South Metro Police force.

Standing in the very front were Detective Reed and broad-shouldered, squared-jawed Detective McClarkey.

"Maddie," he said, reaching out his hands. "When I told you to lay low, this was absolutely not what I meant."

THIRTY-TWO

"KEEP YOUR EYES CLOSED," Detective McClarkey said, helping me up the basement stairs. "The paramedics have sunglasses for you upstairs."

"Did you get him?" I asked, my eyes watery despite keeping them squeezed shut. "Did you get John?"

"Oh, we definitely got him."

"In Ecuador?"

"Argentina, actually. He made it as far as the airport, where he was greeted by the authorities. They were only too glad to coax a confession while they waited for us to get someone down there to take him right back."

"I'm so glad he confessed," I said, as he led me across what I assumed was the living room and helped me to sit on what had to be the lavender sectional. "And that he told you where I was."

"From what I hear, it wasn't the most pleasant experience for him." Detective McClarkey let out a little chuckle. "Apparently the

Federales, or whatever it is they're called down there, don't follow the same interrogation protocol as we do."

Someone slid a pair of sunglasses onto my face and I opened my eyes to the unspeakably happy sight of not only him, but a houseful of police activity.

"How long was I in there?" I asked as two paramedics began to check my vitals.

"A week," he said. "And some change."

I began to choke up. "Forever."

"For all of us," Detective McClarkey said. "There's been a massive police search, not to mention the civilian effort spearheaded by Alan Bader."

"Alan?"

"Alan turned Bargain Barn into a search headquarters and started distributing flyers the second he made bail."

"Try and keep still, Mrs. Michaels," one of the paramedics said, putting a stethoscope to my chest.

"So the case against him wasn't dropped?" I asked as soon as I finished breathing in and out.

"Not immediately."

"I was hoping the video Joe from Bargain Barn found would exonerate him."

"It was definitely compelling but still circumstantial. It wasn't until your family reported you missing that we knew for sure we had the wrong man." Detective McClarkey ran a hand through his graying crew cut. "The big problem was figuring out who we were actually looking for."

"Don't I know it," I said, as a paramedic put a blood pressure cuff around my arm. "Isn't the husband always supposed to be the first suspect?"

"Everything seemed to point to Alan."

"Except for the truth."

"Which we only started to uncover after Joe told us you'd been in Bargain Barn that morning and filled us in on everything he showed you and what you'd asked in response. We were already looking for whatever tape we could find of the flat-screen TV line when Mr. Piggledy confirmed that you'd asked him who he'd seen standing there that night. Then your son FJ reported that you'd said you were going to check on something."

"But since John Carter was never in the line ..."

"We had little to go on."

One of the paramedics hooked me up to a machine of some sort.

"I knew you'd eventually track me here. I mean, my car was parked out front and my phone was inside," I said, glancing at the empty table where I'd left my purse. "At least it was a week ago."

"We didn't need to. John called in to the police department to tell us you'd come by asking him questions, and that when he couldn't answer them, you seemed to have some sort of epiphany and rushed off."

"Never to be heard from again."

"We did send some officers out to the house to check things out in response and that weasel not only welcomed them in, but even showed them around."

I swallowed back tears with the thought of the police in the house, totally unaware that I was trapped on the other side of a hidden door.

"Weren't they suspicious of the bargain cache that is the entire basement?"

"Believe me, it isn't any weirder than a lot of things we see," he said. "Especially given his wife was a confirmed fan of your website, and the fact that your car turned up abandoned in the *Here's the Deal* building parking lot."

"Seriously?"

"The morning after you were reported missing."

"He had to be trying to frame Wendy Killian for my disappearance," I said. "John was angry at all the bargain hunting websites for encouraging his wife's addiction."

McClarkey snorted in disgust. "I thought I'd heard every rationalization in the book."

"You know, there was a part of me that felt badly for him at first, a victim of his wife's addictions…"

The paramedic pulled over an oxygen tank, put a tube around my head, and affixed it under my nose.

"I have to admit, I'm kinda over that now."

"You know…" Detective McClarkey raised a bushy eyebrow. "You're really something else."

"I feel like something the cat dragged in," I said. "Only worse."

"We'll get you all fixed up." He smiled kindly. "I just wish you'd have told someone where you were going last Monday morning."

"I'd planned to." The choking shame that had kept me both awake and sleeping those endless days suddenly burbled in my throat. "But given my suspicions…"

"Which were?

"At first I went back and forth between believing and not believing Alan, and narrowing down other possible suspects along the way. But after I saw the surveillance tape with Joe at Bargain Barn, I knew it couldn't be him." I took a deep breath. "I'm embarrassed to admit this, but I'd narrowed things down to the point where I was left with my husband and his family as the primary suspects."

"You weren't the only one."

"I wasn't?"

"We'd come to about the same conclusion and were investigating the connection between your interest in the TV line and the Michaels family."

"I was trying to see if my brother-in-law was in the line."

"He was," Detective McClarkey. "And that's what we figured out, particularly after we accessed your computer and found your various spreadsheets related to the case."

"You found my suspect list?"

"Your boys gave it to us."

"Oh, no," I said. "So everyone in the family knows I was suspicious of them? That I thought Frank had masterminded—"

"Speak of the devil," he said pointing out the window.

Frank was barreling up the front walk toward the front door.

"Maddie!" Tears ran down his face as he rushed into the house, spotted me and, ignoring the continuing ministrations of the paramedics and the various tubes they'd connected to me, rushed over and scooped me up in his arms. "Thank God you're okay! Thank God!" He looked me up and down. "Are you okay?"

Tears once again filled my eyes. "I've been better, and I definitely need something fresh to eat and a real shower, but—"

"But your blood pressure is high and your some of your vitals are bit shaky," the paramedic said as a stretcher appeared through the open front door.

"I don't want to go to the hospital," I said.

"Just for observation."

"But I—"

"Nonnegotiable," Detective McClarkey said. "But is there anything I can do for you before they transport you?"

I watched Detective Reed come up from the basement with an evidence bag.

"My notepad," I said. "There was a notepad I left down in there. And my blanket."

"I didn't see a blanket."

"It wasn't really a blanket. It looks more like a sheet of woven wrappers."

"I'll see what I can do," he said, heading downstairs.

"Frank," I said as the stretcher approached. "I'm so sorry. I can't begin to imagine what I've put everyone through. I—"

"It's okay, sweetheart," he said. "Everything's okay now."

"I'm sorry that my unfounded suspicions—"

"No apologies," he said, his arms still around me. "The thought of not knowing if you were alive or … All that matters is you've been found. Safe."

"Your family. They must hate me."

"Hate you? Not a chance. Maddie, they love you." He pulled me closer. "I love you."

"Got 'em," Detective McClarkey said, re-emerging from my hell with the two items that kept me from plummeting into total insanity. "This blanket, or whatever it is, is pretty slick."

"Thank you, Detective McClarkey."

"My pleasure," he said.

"I don't know how to thank you for saving my wife's life," Frank said.

"I wish I could take all the credit." Detective McClarkey looked suddenly sheepish. "To be honest, it was actually Officer Watson who finally put the crucial pieces together."

"Griff?"

He nodded.

I looked around. "Is Griff here?"

"He's just a rookie so he's on traffic duty today," McClarkey said. "But that young man definitely has a big future ahead of him. He was the one who thought to make the call to Bargain Barn for the names of the twenty people who received TV vouchers. John Carter, who stated on the record that he was in line for a TV when the pallet was pushed, wasn't on the list."

Before he could elaborate any further, the cell phone at his hip began to chirp the *Hawaii Five-0* theme song.

"McClarkey," he answered, listened for a second, and glanced out the bay window at the Channel Three news van that had pulled up. The crew filed out and began to set up on the grass. "No surprises there."

"I didn't call them," Frank said, as he hung up.

The detective gave him the eyebrow raise.

"I would never do that," Frank said emphatically. "Ever."

"I'm sure," Detective McClarkey said, with less conviction than he could have. "But would you mind calling them off?"

Frank was already on his way out the door.

As he dispatched his compatriots with a vehemence that told me he was telling the truth, McClarkey reached into his chest pocket and handed me a business card.

"Maddie, we'll talk more later." His eyes, a pale blue, held a softness I hadn't noticed before. "In the meantime, if you need anything at all, just know I'm a phone call away."

THIRTY-THREE

Frank remained by my side while I was poked, prodded, analyzed, and finally admitted overnight for observation. He stayed in the room while I had the longest, hottest, most divine shower of my entire life.

When I emerged from the bathroom, he'd been joined by a huge, fragrant bouquet of flowers.

Complete with a card:

Dearest Maddie,

Words can't express my joy in knowing that you are safe and sound. I am forever indebted to you for your faith and belief in me throughout this awful ordeal. I have no idea how I will ever repay you for your friendship and sacrifice, but rest assured, I will figure out a way …

Love and appreciation,
Alan Bader

I smiled and got settled into bed just in time for an even bigger arrival.

"Mom!" Tears streamed out of both FJ's and Trent's swollen eyes as they bounded into the room and hugged me in unison.

Joyce, Gerald, Barb, my own sister, and her assortment of kids filed in behind, followed by Craig and his apparent ladylove, Wendy Killian.

All of them looked equal parts elated to see me and as utterly exhausted as I was from the past week's events.

My kids, who were reticent to let go of me, finally allowed everyone to hug me, one by one, in an oddly silent receiving line.

"I brought a bag of fresh vegetables," Joyce finally said, pulling a gallon-size freezer bag filled with carrot and celery sticks, cherry tomatoes, and sliced peppers from her purse.

"How did you know?" I asked, reaching inside for a ring of green pepper and the most beautiful orange piece of carrot I felt like I'd ever seen. Or tasted.

With that, the silence was broken and everyone began to talk at once.

"We also brought you clothes for tomorrow," Barb said. "And a proper nightgown."

"But you look fabulous," my sister said. "Considering…"

"Incredible." The nieces nodded in agreement.

"I just can't believe that awful man would blame you—blame us—for his wife's addiction," Wendy said.

Gerald shook his head. "Too much of a good thing…"

"Not when it comes to prison time," Craig said. "He deserves to rot forever."

"Speaking of time," Frank said. "Eloise wanted so badly to come back home and be part of the search, but we didn't know how long..."

"We changed our tickets to stay for the long haul," Joyce said.

Barb nodded. "And I sent the kids back home to stay with their father so I wouldn't have anything to distract from the search to find you."

"I can't imagine surviving in there like you did for a day," another of the nieces said, "much less..."

"Did you really have enough food to last ten years?" Trent asked.

"You're really okay and everything, aren't you, Mom?" FJ asked.

The room went silent.

"I'm a lot better now that everyone's here," I said.

And I was.

"But are you okay that we're all talking about what happened?" my sister asked.

"I'm fine," I said. "To be honest, I'd rather hear about what I missed, though."

Everyone began to talk simultaneously once again.

"We put posters of you all over Denver," one of my sister's sons said. "Fort Collins, too."

"Everything's been on hold while we searched," Craig said, now holding Wendy's hand.

"Needless to say," Barb added.

Joyce dabbed her eyes. "To say we've been worried..."

"All of us have been camped out at Bargain Barn day and night," my sister said.

"I did try keep the boys on something of a normal schedule," Frank said. "School and practice and such."

"But it wasn't like we could focus or anything," FJ said.

"I'm just so glad they caught him." Trent began to sob. "So glad you're safe, Mom."

I pulled both boys in to me for another long hug.

We were enjoying a happy group cry when Frank's text pinged.

"It's Anastasia," he said, looking at his phone. "She says to give you a huge hug and to let you know she's on the air tonight, but she's planning to celebrate with you soon."

"Which reminds me," I said giving the boys an extra squeeze. "How did you do on TV without me?"

Trent lifted his head. "Pretty well."

"By pretty well, he means terrific," Frank said.

"We did okay." FJ pulled a DVD from his jacket pocket. "I brought this in case you wanted to see."

Much as I was loving the hubbub of the family around me, I was delighted when FJ slid the DVD into the player connected to the hospital TV and my boys' handsome faces appeared beside Anastasia as she introduced the segment:

Cyber Monday—the Monday after Thanksgiving—has officially surpassed Black Friday as the most popular holiday shopping day of the year. Last year, according the National Retail Federation, over ninety-six million Americans shopped online during Cyber Monday, surpassing the brick-and-mortar Black Friday retailers by more than fifteen million.

With me today are two young men who belong to the demographic that comprises a large percentage of online shoppers. Coincidentally, they are also the sons of Mrs. Frugalicious and our own Frank Finance Michaels. As you might expect, they have more than a few great online shopping tips as well as some special advice for the under-twenty-five crowd…

I watched with pride as my boys—both of them smiling a lot more like seasoned professionals than teenagers pressed into last-second, ill-advised servitude on my behalf—began their spiel.

We don't like to shop, Trent said first.

But when we do, FJ added, *it's always online.*

Taking turns, they proceeded to recite the general Cyber Monday tips I'd provided them and went on to list their top 25 deals of the day on everything from gaming systems and sports equipment to makeup and fashion.

For the ladies, Trent added with a devilish grin.

FJ wrapped up the segment with a final tip they'd come up with themselves:

While you're busy saving money on all the cool stuff you've been wanting, save a little more by buying discounted gift cards at sites like plasticjungle.com, which can be used to make online purchases.

"Clever, huh?" Mrs. Piggledy said, appearing in the doorway in her wheelchair. Higgledy sat in her lap and Birdie perched on her shoulder.

"Naturals," Mr. Piggledy said from behind her. "Which came as a surprise to absolutely no one in the Denver Metro area."

"Thank you for coming," I said, as the sea of Michaels family members parted to allow them through. Higgledy leapt from Mrs. Piggledy's arms to give me a big hug. "Thank you all for so many things, I can't even begin—"

Frank's phone began to chirp the tune to "Brown Eyed Girl."

"Eloise!" he said, answering. "Yes, we're all right here with her—"

"Which I've been trying to conveniently overlook," a nurse said, trying to enter my completely stuffed room and staring pointedly at the monkey nestled against me.

"We're animal therapists." Mr. Piggledy winked in my direction. "Higgledy and Birdie here are our service pets."

"Riiight," she said, drawing out the word. "And the rest of you are?"

"Family," Joyce announced.

"The family rule is no more than four at a time, not four dozen," she said. "Besides, I need to draw some blood and take her vitals. I'm afraid this party will have to continue tomorrow after she's released."

"Are you coming home tomorrow, Mom?" Trent asked.

"If you let her get some rest," the nurse said, motioning for Frank to finish his call outside and everyone to mosey along.

I was too exhilarated to feel tired, but too exhausted to protest as everyone hugged me goodbye and began to file out.

The minute they were gone, there was a quick needle prick and the squeeze of a blood pressure cuff, and the next thing I knew my eyelids were growing heavy.

I dozed off to Frank smiling from the chair beside me.

———

When I opened my eyes, it was morning.

Frank was gone.

In his place, however, was none other than Griff Watson.

He smiled his dimply smile. "Hey there!"

"Griff?" I heard myself ask, as though there was some way I wouldn't recognize the man who'd saved me now, twice.

"Apparently Frank felt it was safe to leave you in my care while he went down the hall to make a few phone calls."

"I can't tell you how glad I am to see you." I gave him a big, long hug. "And thank you so much. Again."

"This time it was a team effort," he said, humbly.

"Detective McClarkey told me you were the one who finally figured everything out."

"He did?"

"He also mentioned that you have a big future ahead in law enforcement."

Griff looked entirely pleased. "Nice to hear."

"You seem surprised."

"I guess I didn't expect he'd mention my small part in it all."

"I'd hardly call figuring out that John Carter lied about being in the TV line a small part. My life depended on someone making that connection and finding him before he disappeared and I was locked away forever."

"There were a lot of people besides me who were committed to making sure that didn't happen."

"But you ultimately figured out John Carter was the killer."

"In the end, he was the one person who not only fit the general description, but knew exactly where his wife was that night at Bargain Barn. Really, all I had to do was check it against the interview he gave down at the station after Alan was arrested and I knew we had our man.

"You definitely have a knack," I said. "At least when it comes to saving me."

"No better than your knack for getting in outrageous trouble."

"Guilty as charged, I'm afraid."

"Next time, you think you could make it a bit easier for me?"

"How about there isn't a next time?"

"That would be ideal." He smiled. "But knowing you ..."

Maybe it was the simply the enormous affection I felt for him after saving my life twice, but if I were a few years younger and a lot more single, his innate kindness and those dimples might have had a different effect on me.

"All I know is that L'Raine is one lucky girl."

"L'Raine?" His cheeks colored. "Did she tell you that ... ?"

"She didn't have to."

He looked confused.

"You did," I said.

"I did?"

"Wasn't she at your house on Cyber Monday—when I called you from Starbucks?"

"At my house?"

"I thought I heard you say something to her about hanging on for a second because you were on the phone."

"L'Raine?"

"You called her Lare."

"Ah!" He began to laugh. "I think you must mean Larry."

I felt my own face color. I'd been reticent to introduce L'Raine to Griff because she didn't strike me as his type, but I hadn't even considered that she didn't have any chance whatsoever. "Larry?"

"Larry," he said. "As in, my cat."

"Your cat?"

"He'd climbed up on the couch and was kneading me with his paw."

I began to laugh too.

"As if I needed another sign this sleuthing business isn't for me," I finally said. "I really thought you and L'Raine were ..."

"She's a nice person and we did have dinner once," he said. "But that's as far as it went. For me, anyway."

At least my intuition was right about something. "I kind of didn't think you were a match when she begged me to introduce you two, but then she had your number ..."

"So do you," he said.

"And you were in the gym parking lot when she started her shift."

"Because I was following you."

"Me?"

"I was bugged that your heckler had the same initials as Cathy Carter, and I knew you were too, so I decided to keep an eye on you —which I did until you got that note on the windshield and Detective McClarkey pulled rank."

"And then he took it from there?"

"Officially." Griff exhaled deeply. "Unofficially, I might have been able to help you figure things out a heck of a lot sooner if you'd just been straight with me about all your suspicions when we talked on Sunday night. Or told me where you were going on Monday after you left Starbucks."

"I couldn't," I said. "Not until I confirmed for sure it wasn't—"

"Frank," Griff finished my sentence.

I nodded.

"For the record, I thought it was him at that point, too."

"You did?"

"With the combination of his recent track record and the fact he and Channel Three happened to be broadcasting from Bargain

Barn that night, it just made sense," he said. "Until you disappeared. I knew then it wasn't him."

"Because?"

"Even he wouldn't go that far."

"Oh good, you're awake!" Frank said, appearing in the doorway before Griff could elaborate. "I'll let the nurse know so we can get you breakfast and hopefully get you sprung from here ASAP."

"Speaking of which," Griff said, as Frank headed for the nurse's station. "I should probably get rolling myself."

"Griff," I said as he stood to go. "Thank you."

He hugged me. "Until next time…"

———

I was that much more thankful and indebted to Griff when I discovered he'd come by with my purse (which according to Frank had apparently been recovered along with my car) and had stowed it in the cabinet with my clothing.

Not only was everything still there—ID, credit cards, cash, lipstick, and even gum—but my cell phone had been charged.

I ate breakfast scanning hundreds of emails, voicemails, and comments on the Mrs. Frugalicious website from friends, business associates, Frugarmy members, and total strangers who wanted to let me know how happy they were about my safe return.

While I waited for the final release paperwork, I worked my way backward, reading the prayers and messages of love and concern that had come in during the never-ending week I was locked away.

As the orderly pushed my wheelchair for the obligatory roll down the corridors of the hospital to the front entrance where I was to meet Frank and the car, I forced myself to listen to the frantic, gut-wrenching *where are you* messages from my terrified family and closest friends.

Frank was opening the passenger door to the car when I finally worked my way back to a text dated a week ago Monday.

As in Cyber Monday at 9:38 a.m.

The text I'd heard ping while in the basement but was never able to read.

From Eloise:

I WASN'T SUPPOSED TO TELL YOU THIS, BUT SOMETHING IS DEFINITELY UP. NOT EXACTLY SURE WHAT IT IS, BUT DAD SAYS NO WORRIES—THE END WILL MORE THAN JUSTIFY THE MEANS.

THIRTY-FOUR

"Obviously I was way off with the Cathy Carter business and any family involvement," I said as we exited the hospital parking lot. "And for that I'm truly sorry."

Frank patted my leg. "Honey, I told you, it really is okay."

He began to whistle the tune to "Celebration" by Kool and the Gang.

"What exactly was going on, though?" I asked as we approached the freeway on-ramp.

"What do you mean?"

"Why did they show up here in the first place?"

"Why did who—"

"Your family," I said. "Why did they show up here? In Denver? At our house?"

"Because their cruise got cancelled halfway across—"

"Frank, I saw a receipt for their plane tickets. I know there was never a cruise."

"Oh," he said.

Other than the sound of passing cars, there was silence.

"You invited them for Thanksgiving weekend, correct?"

He nodded.

"I figured I needed them," he said. "I didn't think I had any chance of getting you back without their help."

"Gotcha," I said.

As he began to whistle again, I took another glance at the nine-day-old text from Eloise:

THE END WILL MORE THAN JUSTIFY THE MEANS.

And thought about Griff's comment:

Even he wouldn't go that far.

How far had Frank actually gone?

"I also know there was something more going on than just asking everyone to come for the holidays," I said. "To talk me into staying."

The whistling stopped again.

"I was just trying to make things right," he finally said.

"So you admit there was a plan?"

"More of a really good idea that evolved over the course of the weekend."

"Which was?"

"How about I explain everything when we get home?"

"How about now?"

"Hang tight." He smiled but said nothing more as we exited off the freeway and headed west toward the house.

"I don't like surprises," I added. "Not anymore, anyway."

"Completely understandable," he said. "But this one's a good one."

We stopped for a welcome back hug from Louis, the retired security guard who waved cars through our neighborhood gate between games of Sudoku.

As we rolled up to the house, I noticed the cars parked in front and across the street.

I also noticed the UNDER CONTRACT placard atop the FOR SALE sign.

"The house has an offer on it?"

"For the moment," he said as he pushed the remote and we pulled into the garage beside my car—the one I wondered if I'd ever see again.

"Meaning what?"

He killed the engine, gave me a quick kiss on the cheek, came around to the passenger side, and helped me into the house.

"Soon," he said. "I promise."

The next thing I knew, I was surrounded by family and friends, including Alan Bader, who'd underwritten the smorgasbord of cold cuts, fruit, and salad that might have otherwise been left to Joyce and Barb.

And Eloise, who'd flown home and was so overjoyed to see me safe that I didn't have the heart to question her about her last text.

As soon as I'd hugged, kissed, and cried with everyone (particularly Alan), given assurances to the others I was okay, and promised multiple people I'd never *give them a scare like that ever again*, I cornered Frank in the front hall.

"Frank, I really do want an answer about what's been going on."

"And you'll have it," he said. "I'm just waiting for Anastasia to get here."

The doorbell rang.

"Speaking of the devil?" I asked.

"More like an angel," he said, opening the door.

"Maddie!" Anastasia rushed in and embraced me in a huge but makeup- and hair-preserving bear hug. "I can't tell you how wonderful it is to see you. There's nothing like a happy ending!"

The next thing I knew, Frank had gathered everyone in the living room and she was leading me to the front of the room.

Frank cleared his throat.

"Family and friends. I would like to thank you for your outpouring of help and support during the most awful, agonizing, and now joyous week of our lives."

There were claps and cheers.

He slipped his arm around me and pulled me in close.

"I also have a confession to make."

The room fell so silent, I was afraid everyone could hear the flutter of my resident butterflies, suddenly flying Kamikaze-style through my body.

"As you all are certainly aware, things have been, shall we say, less than ideal, financially and otherwise, in the Michaels family for some time now." He looked down at his feet. "For which I'm entirely to blame."

Joyce, Barb, Gerald, and even Craig bobbed their heads in agreement.

"I've been racking my brain for a way to not only make things up to my family, but get us back on financial track." He looked back up and smiled sheepishly. "After all, that's what I do. Right?"

"You know it," Anastasia said from the other side of him.

"And then I came up with an idea." He turned to me. "Or rather, Maddie did."

"Me?"

"Black Thursday at Bargain Barn," he said. "When I realized you were planning to live blog surrounded by your Frugarmy, I got an idea and took the liberty of turning up the volume."

"Way up," Anastasia added.

"By having Anastasia interview me for the Channel Three news?"

"And get enough tape to repackage my TV show idea, *Family Finance Fixers*, so the national network folks would give us another look."

"Us?" I asked.

"Instead of Frank Finance and Anastasia Chastain, I planned to pitch a revamped show with Frank Finance and his sidekick Mrs. Frugalicious—the husband-and-wife financial-fix-it team."

"With me executive producing," Anastasia added. "And doing guest spots."

"It just makes good sense," Joyce said with an attempted wink.

Gerald smiled. "The family that plays together..."

"Channel Three liked the idea enough to authorize a weekend's worth of Mrs. Frugalicious segments to see how you handled yourself on camera," Frank said.

"It was just going to be a matter of presenting it to the national folks from there," Anastasia said.

With her satisfied smile, John Carter AKA CC's words suddenly, painfully, rushed through my head:

To be honest, this whole event smells of a scheme cooked up by you, your TV reporter husband, and Bargain Barn to line pockets...

"Why didn't you tell me that's what you were planning?" I asked.

"Your stage fright," he said. "For one thing."

"Which turned out to be a nonissue," Anastasia added. "Which, I have to say, I predicted all along."

"There was also the much bigger issue…"

"Maybe that we were getting divorced?" I asked.

"That's where we came in," Barb said.

"The last thing anyone wanted was to lose you from our family," Joyce added. "To think we almost did anyway…"

Other than the occasional crunch or some random chewing, dead silence prevailed in the crowded living room.

"I see," I finally said.

As Frank laid out his "original plan" almost verbatim from the list I'd made, but minus the murder—first, mobilizing his family to get me back on board with our marriage, then looping in Anastasia to document the big night for Channel Three, etc., etc., I realized I'd been right all along. At least partially.

As I'd suspected, little about the weekend had simply happened—not the producers suddenly wanted to run the Mrs. Frugalicious bargain hunting segments, not Joyce's suggestion of a grocery-shopping expedition, not Barbara M.'s suggestion of Saturday Cash Mob, not any of Anastasia's sudden appearances.

"But then Cathy Carter was murdered," I said.

"Which threatened to put a giant wrench in our overall plan," Anastasia said. "Initially."

"But, as I always say, folks really can't ever get enough tragedy or celebrity," Frank said. "Since we had Mrs. Frugalicious and Channel Three already on location, we just went with it and kept taping."

"We were quickly certain the network execs were going to love the footage," Anastasia said. "We had everything from Frank assisting in the rescue effort and comforting his estranged wife, Mrs. Frugalicious, to your joint campaign to save the store from closing in the aftermath of it all."

"Not to mention all the fan testimonials," Frank said with a smile.

Hi, Mrs. Frugalicious. I'm Debbie and I'm a huge fan!

Will you sign my slow-cooker box?

"I was sure the additional footage we got over the next few days from the grocery store, Small Business Saturday, and especially of the two of you reunited and mourning together at Cathy's memorial service was going to make this thing a slam dunk," Anastasia said.

"Especially after Alan was arrested," Frank added.

"Glad I could be of help," Alan said, with more than a hint of sarcasm.

"You've been an incredible help," Joyce said, patting his hand. "Wonderful."

"Fact is, your alleged *involvement* upped the whole Black Friday danger angle a hundredfold," Anastasia said, "Not wanting to let a second go by while this situation was hot, I approached the network people first thing Monday morning."

"But then Maddie went missing," Eloise, who'd obviously had her suspicions too, said from the couch.

"Yes, almost immediately after I made the call," Anastasia said.

"And all bets were off," Gerald added from the recliner in the corner.

"The only thing that mattered after that was finding you," Frank said, a tear rolling down his cheek.

The room erupted in chatter—how people had felt and reacted when they heard I was missing, their various theories as to what had happened, and what they'd specifically done as part of the rescue effort.

A small group formed around Alan, suspect-cum-hero, who'd suffered almost as much as me then gone on to help so much upon his release from jail.

"The thing is, the real killer was caught," Frank said over the din. "And our Maddie was found, safe and sound."

Everyone began to clap again.

"It gets better," Anastasia said. As soon as the room quieted, she added. "As you might have expected, with the unforeseen consequences of the past week, Mrs. Frugalicious became an instant household name across the country."

"Apparently the wife of one of the East Coast network bigwigs, bigger even than the people we'd been in contact with, has been glued to the Mrs. Frugalicious disappearance and rescue," Frank said.

"And I got a call after Maddie was rescued yesterday afternoon," Anastasia said. "THE call."

"So *Family Finance Fixers* is getting the green light?" I asked.

"Sort of," Anastasia said.

"What do you mean, sort of?

"They definitely want to do a show."

Frank beamed. "Even bigger than either of us ever imagined."

"What kind of show?" I asked.

"A reality show."

My heart, which had enough excitement for a lifetime, began to thump. "What?"

"The working title is *The Family Frugalicious*."

"Catchy, huh?" Joyce remarked.

"The network wants to have cameras following Mrs. Frugalicious, respected blogger and well-heeled housewife, living the bargain shopping life as the wife of financial guru Frank Finance Michaels."

Hoots and wolf whistles filled the room.

"Whoa," I heard myself say. Not at all sure what I thought or felt, I somehow added, "Isn't the well-heeled part a bit of a stretch?"

"Not anymore," Frank said. "The paycheck will more than allow us to keep the house, pay off the credit cards, and restart our savings."

"Of course, you'll be contractually obligated to maintain your penny-pinching lifestyle," Anastasia said.

"I can't imagine doing things any other way anymore, but Anastasia, I'm not sure I—"

"It's high time you started calling me Stasia, don't you think?"

"Stasia, I'm not sure I'm reality show material," I said.

"Frank will play prominently too, of course," Anastasia continued. "And his life on and off camera as a television financial advisor."

"So like a TV show within a TV show?" Craig asked.

"With special appearances by everyone in the family," Anastasia said. "The network brass loved all of you—Joyce, Frank, Barb, Craig, Eloise, but particularly the boys, who were a big hit on Cyber Monday before everything else went down."

"We're gonna be famous!" Trent said.

"And we already have footage for an Emmy-worthy pilot."

"I suppose you do," I said.

"Incredible, huh?"

"Everything's all lined up to get rolling ASAP, while interest in you and your family is at its peak. Initial peak, I should say," Anastasia said. "We only need one thing."

"Which is?" I asked.

She reached down, pulled a contract and a pen from the brief-case beside her, and handed them both to me.

"Your signature on the dotted line."

© Impact Images

ABOUT THE AUTHOR

Linda Joffe Hull is a graduate of UCLA. She lives in Denver, Colorado, with her husband and children. Linda is a longtime member of Rocky Mountain Fiction Writers and currently serves on the national board of Mystery Writers of America. You can visit her online at LindaJoffeHull.com.

Acknowledgments

Many thanks to Terri Bischoff, Nicole Nugent, Beth Hanson, and everyone else over at Midnight Ink for the opportunity to bring Mrs. Frugalicious to life.

Thank you to Josh Getzler and Danielle Burby at HSG for their ongoing enthusiasm, ideas, and support.

Thank you to my friends, fellow writers, and ever-supportive family who helped make this book and my career possible in a million different ways: Ben LeRoy, Cary Cazzanigi, Margie and Bob Moskowitz, Bill Joffe, Elizabeth Heller, Patricia Heller, Julie Heller, the Hulls, the Mitchell/Hendrickson/Springer/Moskowitz gang, Carleen Evanoff, the Goldsmith Family, Jennee and Bob Julius, Wendy Kelly, Keir Graff, Rocky Mountain Fiction Writers, and the Rocky Mountain chapter of Mystery Writers of America.

A special thank you to my Black Friday shopping gang: Julie Goldsmith, Claire Goldsmith, Abby Mitchell, Brooke Stevens, and Evan Hull.

The greatest thanks, as always, to Andrew, Evan, Eliza, and, especially, Brandon.

An Excerpt from the Next
Mrs. Frugalicious Shopping Mystery

ONE

THE SCENARIO WAS SUPPOSED to be straightforward—I, Maddie Michaels, AKA online blogger Mrs. Frugalicious and (most recently) matriarch of The Reality Channel's newest offering, *The Family Frugalicious*, was in beautiful coastal Mexico to tape a sun-soaked, South-of-the-Border, budget-destination-wedding episode of my show.

Considering our arrival had been delayed by a freak ice storm that left us stranded for a day in Houston, and the fact that I was there to play savings-minded matron of honor for my producer, Anastasia Chastain's, televised nuptials, I knew better than to expect a relaxing long weekend at the beach gazing out at the impossibly azure waters of the Mayan Riviera. Really, given the tumultuous events of the last year,[1] it was crazy to expect things to go smoothly at all.

---

1. Including, but not limited to, my financial newscaster husband losing all of our money in a Ponzi scheme, my transformation from well-heeled housewife into reality TV's Mrs. Frugalicious, a series of savings-related scrapes, and two murders.

"I'm not feeling so well," my husband[2] Frank said rubbing his stomach as we, the Family Frugalicious, pulled up to the grand columned portico of the Hacienda de la Fortuna a full twenty-four hours after we were due to arrive.

Before I could reach into my purse for a furry Tums, our director Geo appeared at the passenger window.

"Finally," he said, running his hands through his fashionably long hair and leaning into the resort's official SUV to hand me the day's schedule:

11:00 a.m.: Arrival of travel-weary but excited Michaels clan

11:05 a.m.: Enter hotel and comment on beauty and charm of lobby

11:07 a.m.: Introduction of hotel staff

11:15 a.m.: Appearance of Anastasia Chastain and wedding planner for "chance" greeting

"Holy moly," I said, continuing to scan the first of two single-spaced pages. "Is all of this just for today?"

"All we could do yesterday were visual shots and a few cut-ins of the bride and groom. We've gotta play catch-up today so we don't get behind," Geo said, snatching the schedule and motioning our driver to take another spin around the circle so the cameras could document our "spontaneous" arrival. "Starting now."

Luckily, the kids were so enthusiastic about their new status as reality TV personalities that oohing and ahhing for the cameras while re-arriving once or twice for our beach "vacation" was hardly a problem. Their enthusiasm made the larger problem—that Frank and I were over and done, married in name only, and solely for the sake of the show—somewhat easier to conceal. As far as they and the

---

2. So to speak—see next footnote.

network knew, we'd reconciled our various issues[3] and arisen from the ashes—new, improved, and full of valued advice for our viewers.

We'd sailed through the small amount of shooting involved in pulling together the clips from my Black Friday murder misadventure for our pilot. We'd adjusted quickly to a crew with backward baseball caps and cameras strapped to their shoulders making themselves comfortable in our house and everywhere else we decided to go.

I questioned, however, just how we were going to keep up our charade sharing a hotel suite under the watchful eye of our kids, our producer bride, and a wedding's worth of guests.

Nevertheless, we managed to kick things off with big smiles as we stepped out of the car, entered the opulent lobby of the Hacienda de la Fortuna, and stepped over to our mark in front of a second camera.

"Wow!" Frank said, looking thrilled even while rubbing his stomach. "What a place!"

"Totally cool!" our teenage son FJ said.

"Where's the pool?" asked my college-coed stepdaughter Eloise.

"The website said there are like five of them," Trent, our other son and FJ's twin, added. "Not to mention the beach!"

"I expected it to be beautiful and fun here," I agreed as I took in what felt like a football field's worth of marble, gleaming chandeliers, scrolled ironwork, dark wood, and opulent colonial plantation charm. "But I had no idea it would be this elegant!"

On cue, a Hispanic man with a slim physique and a full head of salt-and-pepper hair joined us.

---

3. Including not only personal indiscretions on his part, but his creative solution to keep me in the fold by orchestrating a television deal for us as a family whereby we pretended to be happily married to secure our children's college tab and our own financial future.

"I am Enrique Espinoza, general manager of Hacienda de la Fortuna," he said, offering a fetching smile and a handshake. "*Mi casa es su casa.*"

"*Muchas gracias,*" I said, in my best Spanish.

Enrique gestured behind me. "Allow me to introduce some of the key staff assigned to making sure your stay is an exceptional one."

I turned to find a line of employees clad in the same peach, white, and chocolate color scheme of the lobby.

"You've already met Felipe," he said, as our chatty grandfatherly driver rushed in from outside and joined the group.

"Is all that Mayan sacrifice stuff he told us about on the way from the airport really true?" Trent asked.

"No one knows more about local history than Felipe," Enrique said with a nod, before moving on to the gentleman to Felipe's right. "Next we have Javier, our concierge. Beside him is Maria, housekeeping manager for the floor where you'll be staying, and Benito, our head chef, who is putting the finishing touches on a special menu for a private dinner we've arranged for your family on Sunday night."

"Sounds wonderful."

"It will be," Benito said, with no trace of humility. "I assume you're all open to local—"

"Maddie! Frank! Kids!!" Anastasia Chastain—blond beauty, bride-to-be, and all-around savvy type-A producer—came rushing across the lobby trailed by three women who looked too much like her not to be her sisters. She enveloped me in a huge hug. "I'm SO relieved you're finally here! I've bitten my nails down to the quick worrying about the safe arrival of my favorite family. Wondering when, if, you'd actually—"

"I told you everything would work out just fine," one of the sisters said, if a bit snippily.

"Mother Nature was giving you the gift of the inevitable wedding glitch early, before things really got underway," an attractive woman in official garb said, joining the group.

"This is Elena, the hotel wedding planner," Anastasia said, as though anyone that self-assured, attractive-if-severe-looking, and bearing such a firm handshake could be anyone else. "And these are my sisters, Susan, Sara, and Sally."

I gave each sister a hello hug despite Anastasia's previous warning they'd likely be slow to warm up because of their personalities in general and their irritation over her choice of me as maid of honor. It was a decision she'd made not only because her wedding was key to this episode's story line, but to keep from having to pick one sister over the others.

"I'm sorry our delay threw things off schedule," I said. "What can I do to help make sure the wedding goes off without any more unintended hitches?"

"We've got everything under control," either Susan or Sara said, with enough ice in her tone to remind me that my maid of honor slot was sheerly ceremonial.

"Just be at the rehearsal at five sharp," Elena said.

"Cut!" Geo said. "Nice job everyone."

"Good, because I think I'm about to die," Frank said, rushing off for a nearby *baño* while Elena, Anastasia, and most of the staff scattered in various directions.

"I didn't think that was supposed to happen until you were down here for a day or two," Trent remarked. "Must have been that breakfast burrito he ate at the airport."

"This is not good," Geo said, head in hands. "We're so behind schedule as it is."

"I'm sure Frank will be back in a few minutes," I said. "He was fine until we drove up."

"I guess I'll have you do a pre-cap[4] while we wait to do a second take," Geo said, reaching into a nearby folder and handing me a piece of paper. "The Hacienda de la Fortuna has a few things for you to say."

"Okay," I said, looking over a list of "candid" talking points penned not by me, but a *Family Frugalicious* staff writer. "But, I don't even have time to memorize—"

"We have cue cards."

"Do I at least have a few seconds to freshen up and do my makeup?" I asked, glad I was learning to expect the unexpected enough to leave Houston in a sundress (albeit beneath my down coat), but wondering just how peaked I looked after a mostly sleepless night, the flight, Customs, an hour drive to the resort, and the shock to my hair and skin of the bona fide humidity we lacked back home in Denver.

"You have a wardrobe change in fifteen minutes," one of the assistants said.

"Into bathing suits, I hope?" Eloise asked. "Please say you plan to tape us spending the afternoon hanging by the pool and ordering smoothies or something."

"Or something," a young man said, appearing beside her. "At least for you and your brothers."

"Meet Ivan Matteo," Enrique, the hotel manager, said. "Head of activities and recreation."

"Hi," said Ivan, boyishly cute despite the shaggy hair, beard, and nose ring. "Nice to meet all of you."

---

4. An interview of a reality show participant before or early into a major event that captures the excitement and anticipatory giddiness.

"Oh," Eloise said, not unkindly. "You too."

"You don't have an accent," FJ said.

"I'm from California," Ivan said with a broad smile. "But my heart is here, in Mexico."

"This does seem like a pretty chill place," Trent said.

"There's definitely a lot to see and do," Ivan said. "Like spending this afternoon at one of the nearby Cenotes."

"Cenotes?" Trent asked.

"Beautiful, clear, freshwater sinkholes where we can swim, snorkel, and explore underground caverns."

"Sounds cool," FJ said.

I waited for the inevitable sniff and brush-off from the typically high-maintenance Eloise.

"We have a picnic lunch already packed for you and your brothers." Ivan said, flashing a winning smiling at Eloise.

Instead of a disinterested snort, Eloise smiled back. "Sounds like a plan."

The next thing I knew, one camera was trailing the kids out the front door of the hotel and I was sitting on a barstool in front of another, pretending I wasn't reading off the aforementioned cue cards:

"We're here at the beautiful Hacienda de la Fortuna for my producer Anastasia Chastain's wedding! I was thrilled when Stasia asked me to be her matron of honor and Frank to be the best man. Being the frugal shopper I am, though, I have to admit I had a few second thoughts about the cost of travelling and staying at an all-inclusive resort..."

Geo signaled for me to smile.

"Boy, was I surprised to find out just how wrong I was! By following a few simple tips, here we are enjoying affordable paradise—all five of us!"

Anastasia gave me a thumbs up.

Considering her wedding and our entire trip had been comped by the hotel, I felt a stab of consternation, wondering what "tips" I could possibly be about to give. Luckily, as I began to recite them, they all seemed to be pretty much Budget Conscious Travel 101:

1. Instead of going on two different family getaways this year, make the wedding part of an extended family vacation or your own second honeymoon—you'll save on everything from airfare to hassle!

2. Set a price alert as soon as the bride sets her date and book your flights when a sale pops up.

3. Most resorts offer great block rates for bridal parties. Here at the Hacienda de la Fortuna, for example, rooms booked for special events are up to 50% off!

4. All-inclusive means that your meals, beverages (including cocktails), and many activities are included in the price. Plan sightseeing trips off the resort property between meal times when you can, or order box meals from the hotel so there will be few additional costs.

Nothing the show's writers had come up with served to promote the resort in any unexpected way. Not until the next tip, that was…

5. One way to get the most value out of your next resort style vacation is to sign up for the vacation ownership presentation. Here at the Hacienda de la Fortuna, for example, they offer incentives like upgraded rooms simply for agreeing to give them ninety, no-obligation minutes of your time!

I was prompted to smile once again.

"Starting with lunch!"

"Cut," Geo said. "Nice job, Maddie!"

"We're pushing the resort's time share presentation?"

"Not pushing, providing promotional consideration."

"Like an infomercial?"

"Like a reality show about bargain hunting that, to add to its overall appeal, is helping viewers navigate the ins and outs of vacation ownership."

"Okay …" I said, already distracted by the appearance of a man who could only be described as tall, dark, and *muy guapo*.

The next thing I knew, he was standing beside me in the bar/makeshift set area and the camera was rolling again.

"I'm Alejandro," he said, looking that much more chiseled, broad, and altogether attractive up close. Even his peach hotel-issue polo shirt and tan khakis looked somehow suave. "And I've been looking forward to spending the afternoon with the famous Mrs. Frugalicious."